THE
HAUNTED TRAIL

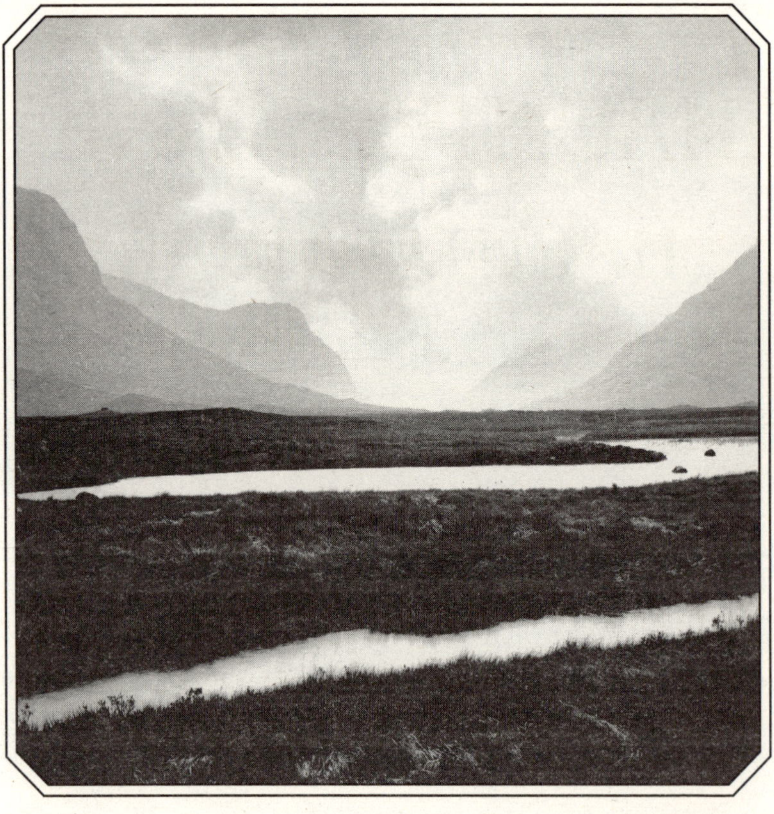

THE
HAUNTED TRAIL

*Classic Tales of
the Rambling Weird*

Edited by
WEIRD WALK

BRITISH LIBRARY

This collection first published in 2024 by
The British Library
96 Euston Road
London NW1 2DB

Selection, introduction and notes © 2024 Weird Walk
Volume copyright © 2024 The British Library Board

"Gibbet Lane" © 1935 The Estate of Anthony Gittins.
Reproduced by permission of United Agents Ltd.

"Curious Adventure of Mr Bond" © 1939 Nugent Barker.

"The Trains" reproduced by permission of Artellus
Ltd. Copyright © 1951 Robert Aickman.

Every effort has been made to trace copyright holders and to obtain their
permission for the use of copyright material. The publisher apologises
for any errors or omissions and would be pleased to be notified of any
corrections to be incorporated in reprints or future editions.

Cataloguing in Publication Data
A catalogue record for this publication is available from the British Library

ISBN 978 0 7123 5581 0
e ISBN 978 0 7123 6818 6

Photographs by Fay Godwin on pages 2 and 288 © The British Library Board
Cover design by Mauricio Villamayor with illustration by Sandra Gómez
Text design and typesetting by Tetragon, London
Printed in England by CPI Group (UK) Ltd, Croydon, CR0 4YY

CONTENTS

| INTRODUCTION | 7 |
| A NOTE FROM THE PUBLISHER | 11 |

'I dreaded walking where there was no path' JOHN CLARE	13
Sandy the Tinker CHARLOTTE RIDDELL	15
Carleton Barker, First and Second JOHN KENDRICK BANGS	33
Crowdy Marsh SABINE BARING-GOULD	57
The Hill R. ELLIS ROBERTS	71
The Garden that Was Desolate ULRIC DAUBENY	91
The Mystic Tune MARIE CORELLI	105
The Wind in the Woods BESSIE KYFFIN-TAYLOR	113
Brickett Bottom AMYAS NORTHCOTE	145
Wailing Well M. R. JAMES	161
Gibbet Lane ANTHONY GITTINS	177
Curious Adventure of Mr Bond NUGENT BARKER	189
Between Sunset and Moonrise R. H. MALDEN	219
The Trains ROBERT AICKMAN	235

INTRODUCTION

"There are powers of darkness which walk abroad in waste places: and that man is happy who has never had to face them."
R. H. MALDEN, 'BETWEEN SUNSET AND MOONRISE'

It is perhaps no surprise that journeys on foot feature in so many uncanny tales. Walking has always presented the possibility of encounters both pleasant and strange, and spectres have haunted our paths and trails since time immemorial. In the remarkable ghost stories collected over 600 years ago at Yorkshire's Byland Abbey, and now held in the British Library, such phantoms put the literal fear of God into those unlucky enough to bump into them on a lonely rural road. The Byland ghosts are strange, folkloric things that are often rooted in the landscape—a spectre haunts a field after stealing several silver spoons; a pale, shapeshifting horse appears at a crossroads; another spirit throws a man over a hedge after following him for miles.

Weirdness and walking go hand in hand in a place as storied as Britain, and, like those travellers in medieval Yorkshire, the ramblers of this collection all find their journeys taking an unusual turn. It is perhaps that combination of accumulated history, legend and folklore, alongside the incredibly varied landscape of our countryside that makes rural Britain a perfect setting for the eerie. Amid the stone circles, ancient woods and windswept moors, it is easy to imagine early hikers, stirred to action by the likes of Wordsworth and Coleridge, tripping across unseen boundaries, and coming into contact with something completely other.

INTRODUCTION

By the late nineteenth century, there was already an established tradition of exploring Britain on foot for leisure. And it wasn't just Romantic poets and the landed gentry who were finding inspiration and rejuvenation in such yomping. Victorian walking clubs had sprung up in industrial towns, steadfastly dedicated to the twin benefits of fresh air and fellowship. Such organisations catered for a myriad of persuasions, from church-led hikes to divert the congregation's attention from booze, to avowedly secular groups who rambled on Sundays to dodge ecclesiastical influence.

However, it was still much easier to head off for a wander in the period that most of these stories were written if you were (as many of our protagonists are) a person of a certain position. In R. Ellis Roberts' strange, satanic tale 'The Hill', it is with the idea of trespass that an acolyte tries to dissuade investigation of his rite. The intrepid Mr O'Brien shrugs off the suggestion as only a gentleman could: "It's so jolly to be in a country where trespassing doesn't do any harm. It's why I like Dorset, and these great grazing fields." For some, however, it was the very real fear of trespass and its potential consequences that halted their exploration of the countryside more than any supernatural dread—a sentiment best expressed by John Clare, who knew only too well how the rural poor could be treated by those in power.

Scotland has long had a more accessible landscape for ramblers of all backgrounds. Charlotte Riddell's creation, Sandy the Tinker, would have been fairly free to roam the hills of Dendeldy parish; but with the success of the Kinder Trespass in 1932, and increasing acknowledgement of the benefits of the great outdoors, the tide began to turn south of the border too. Indeed, if the interwar period is often regarded as one of the high water marks of the British weird tale, then it was also a boom time for hiking. An active engagement

INTRODUCTION

with the landscape was, for many, a very necessary antidote to the death and destruction of the First World War, and a variety of outdoor movements were striding out towards the hills. When the Third World Scout Jamboree was held near Birkenhead in 1929, over 30,000 Scouts and Guides attended, and it is this wholesome enthusiasm that M. R. James playfully inverts through the character of Stanley Judkins in 'Wailing Well', a tale of two halves if ever there was one.

More esoteric groups were also exploring the countryside between the wars—the Kindred of the Kibbo Kift presented a hermetic form of Scouting centred on world peace, while the Old Straight Track Club was founded to pursue Alfred Watkins' theory of ley lines out in the field. Today, access may have improved for ramblers, Scouts and ley hunters alike, but, as the Right to Roam campaign acknowledges, the situation in England is still pretty dire, with over 90 per cent of the countryside off limits to the public. A little of Clare's dread still lingers.

Even though many of these stories were first set down more than a century ago, they continue to resonate with us. They provide not only dark humour, pleasing chills and unsettling impressions, but also a demonstration of the rich imaginational power of our rural landscape. It is a place that belongs to all of us, and we hope that the tales in this volume inspire you to ramble somewhere new. And if you do find yourself on a quiet twilit path, a little way from the nearest inn, be sure to cast a glance behind you. There are strange things out there still.

WEIRDWALK.CO.UK

INTRODUCTION

FURTHER READING

Nick Hayes, *The Book of Trespass: Crossing the Lines that Divide Us* (London: Bloomsbury Publishing, 2021).

Sinclair McKay, *Ramble On: The Story of Our Love for Walking Britain* (London: Fourth Estate, 2012).

R. B. Russell, Rosalie Parker and Mark Valentine (eds), *Literary Hauntings: A Gazetteer of Literary Ghost Stories from Britain and Ireland* (Leyburn: Tartarus Press, 2023).

Weird Walk, *Weird Walk: Wanderings and Wonderings through the British Ritual Year* (London: Watkins, 2023).

A NOTE FROM THE PUBLISHER

The original short stories reprinted in the British Library Tales of the Weird series were written and published in a period ranging across the nineteenth and twentieth centuries. There are many elements of these stories which continue to entertain modern readers; however, in some cases there are also uses of language, instances of stereotyping and some attitudes expressed by narrators or characters which may not be endorsed by the publishing standards of today. We acknowledge therefore that some elements in the stories selected for reprinting may continue to make uncomfortable reading for some of our audience. With this series British Library Publishing aims to offer a new readership a chance to read some of the rare material of the British Library's collections in an affordable paperback format, to enjoy their merits and to look back into the worlds of the past two centuries as portrayed by their writers. It is not possible to separate these stories from the history of their writing and therefore the following stories are presented as they were originally published with minor edits only, made for consistency of style and sense. We welcome feedback from our readers, which can be sent to the following address:

> British Library Publishing
> The British Library
> 96 Euston Road
> London, NW1 2DB

1832

'I DREADED WALKING WHERE THERE WAS NO PATH'

John Clare

I dreaded walking where there was no path
And pressed with cautious tread the meadow swath
And always turned to look with wary eye
And always feared the owner coming by;
Yet everything about where I had gone
Appeared so beautiful I ventured on
And when I gained the road where all are free
I fancied every stranger frowned at me
And every kinder look appeared to say
You've been on trespass in your walk today.
I've often thought the day appeared so fine,
How beautiful if such a place were mine;
But having nought I never feel alone
And cannot use another's as my own.

1882

SANDY THE TINKER

Charlotte Riddell

Charlotte Riddell (1832–1906) was born in Carrickfergus on the northern shores of Belfast Lough, the daughter of the High Sheriff of County Antrim. She enjoyed a comfortable childhood in Ireland, reading widely and frequently composing stories, but moved to London in the bitter winter of 1855 after the death of her father. It was in London, with Charlotte and her mother facing financial hardship, that she began to write in earnest, gaining a reputation for popular novels set in the capital's financial world. Today, however, she is best known for her supernatural stories, several of which were published in her 1882 collection *Weird Stories*.

"Sandy the Tinker" starts gently enough, with the telling of a tale within a rural manse, or minister's house. A bedraggled group have arrived at the clergyman's door having been beaten by the Scottish weather, and, while they warm themselves by the fire, their host begins to recount the strange events of some thirty years ago. What follows is one of Riddell's more troubling and morally ambiguous stories, where wandering the landscape, both in reality and dreams, can have sinister consequences.

The story's setting of Dendeldy is fictional, but is suggestive of the area around the town of Dunkeld in Perth and Kinross. Here, the River Tay doubles as Riddell's Deldy, wooded peaks are abundant, and rocky crags tower above the settlement's famous cathedral. It is an area rich in treasures, not least the Birnam Oak, said to be the lone survivor of *Macbeth*'s Birnam Wood. A fine place, perhaps, for the Devil to walk.

*

PUBLISHER'S NOTE: The text for this tale has been sourced from *Weird Stories* (1882). To address some errors found in the original typesetting and hopefully improve the reading experience, the story has been reformatted slightly, with the minister's nested narrative more clearly separated and the first narrator's comments appearing in brackets.

"Before commencing my story, I wish to state it is perfectly true in every particular."

"We quite understand that," said the sceptic of our party, who was wont, in the security of friendly intercourse, to characterise all such prefaces as mere introductions to some tremendous "blank," "blank," "blank," which trio the reader can fill up at his own pleasure and leisure.

On the occasion in question, however, we had donned our best behaviour, a garment which did not sit ungracefully on some of us; and our host, who was about to draw out from the stores of memory one narrative for our entertainment, was scarcely the person before whom even Jack Hill would have cared to express his cynical and unbelieving views.

We were seated, an incongruous company of ten persons, in the best room of an old manse among the Scottish hills. Accident had thrown us together, and accident had driven us under the minister's hospitable roof. Cold, wet, and hungry, drenched with rain, sorely beaten by the wind, we had crowded through the door opened by a friendly hand, and now, wet no longer, the pangs of hunger assuaged with smoking rashers of ham, poached eggs, and steaming potatoes, we sat around a blazing fire, drinking toddy out of tumblers, whilst the two ladies who graced the assemblage partook of a modicum of the same beverage from wine glasses. Everything was eminently comfortable, but conducted upon the most correct principles. Jack could no more have taken it upon him to shock the minister's ear with some of the opinions he aired in Fleet Street, than he could have asked for more whisky with his water.

"Yes, it is perfectly true," continued the minister, looking thoughtfully at the fire. "I can't explain it, I cannot even try to explain it. I will tell you the story exactly as it occurred, however, and leave you to draw your own deductions from it."

None of us answered. We fell into listening attitudes instantly, and eighteen eyes fixed themselves by one accord upon our host.

He was an old man, but hale. The weight of eighty winters had whitened his head, but not bowed it. He seemed young as any of us—younger than Jack Hill, who was a reviewer and a newspaper hack, and whose way through life had not been altogether on easy lines.

Thirty years ago, upon a certain Friday morning in August (began the minister), I was sitting at breakfast in the room on the other side of the passage, where you ate your supper, when the servant girl came in with a letter, she said a laddie, all out of breath, had brought over from Dendeldy Manse. "He was bidden rin a' the way," she went on, "and he's fairly beaten."

I told her to make the messenger sit down, and put food before him; and then, when she went to do my bidding, proceeded, I must confess with some curiosity, to break the seal of a missive forwarded in such hot haste.

It was from the minister at Dendeldy, who had been newly chosen to occupy the pulpit his deceased father occupied for a quarter of a century and more.

The call from the congregation originated rather out of respect to the father's memory than any extraordinary liking for the son. He had been reared for the most part in England, and was somewhat distant and formal in his manners; and, though full of Greek and Latin and Hebrew, wanted the true Scotch accent, that goes straight to the heart of those accustomed to the broad, honest, tender Scottish tongue.

His people were proud of him, but they did not just like all his ways. They could remember him a lad running about the whole country side, and they could not understand, and did not approve of, his holding them at arm's length, and shutting himself up among his books and refusing their hospitality, and sending out word he was busy when maybe some very decent man wanted speech of him. I had taken upon myself to point out that I thought he was wrong, and that he would alienate his flock from him. Perhaps it was for this very reason, because I was blunt and plain, he took to me kindly, and never got on his high horse, no matter what I said to him.

Well, to return to the letter. It was written in the wildest haste, and entreated me not to lose a moment in coming to him, as he was in the very *greatest distress* and *anxiety*. "Let *nothing* delay you," he proceeded. "If I cannot speak to you soon I believe I shall go out of my senses."

"What could be the matter?" I thought. "What in all the wide earth could have happened?"

I had seen him but a few days before, and he was in good health and spirits, getting on better with his people, feeling hopeful of so altering his style of preaching as to touch their hearts more sensibly.

"I must lay aside Southern ideas as well as accent, if I can," he went on, smiling. "Men who live such lives of hardship and privation, who cast their seed into the ground under such rigorous skies, and cut their corn in fear and trembling at the end of late uncertain summers, who take the sheep out of the snow-drifts and carry the lambs into shelter beside their own humble hearths, must want a different sort of sermon from those who sleep softly and walk delicately."

I had implied something of all this myself, and it amused me to find my own thoughts come back clothed in different fashion and presented to me quite as strangers. Still, all I wanted was his good, and I felt glad he showed such aptitude to learn.

What could have happened, however, puzzled me sorely. As I made my hurried preparations for setting out I fairly perplexed myself with speculation. I went into the kitchen, where his messenger was eating some breakfast, and asked him if Mr Cawley was ill.

"I dinna ken," he answered. "He mad' no complaint, but he luiked awfu' bad, just awfu'."

"In what way?" I inquired.

"As if he had seen a ghaist," was the reply.

This made me very uneasy, and I jumped to the conclusion the trouble was connected with money matters. Young men will be young men; (and here the minister looked significantly at the callow bird of our company, a youth who had never owed a sixpence in his life or given away a cent; while Jack Hill—no chicken, by the way—was over head and ears in debt, and could not keep a sovereign in his pocket, though spending or bestowing it, involved going dinnerless the next day.)

Young men will be young men (repeated the minister, in his best pulpit manner ("Just as though any one expected them to be young women!" grumbled Jack to me afterwards)), and I feared that now he was settled and comfortably off, some old creditor he had been paying as best he could, might have become pressing. I knew nothing of his liabilities, or, beyond the amount of the stipend paid him, the state of his pecuniary affairs; but, having once in my own life made myself responsible for a debt, I was aware of all the trouble putting your arm out further than you can draw it back involves, and I considered that most probably money, which is the root of all evil ("and all good," Jack's eyes suggested to me), was the cause of my young friend's agony of mind. Blessed with a large family—every one of whom is now alive and doing well, I thank God, out in the world—you may imagine I had not much opportunity for laying by; still, I had put aside a little for a rainy day, and that little I placed in my pocket-book, hoping even a small sum might prove of use in case of emergency.

("Come, you *are* a trump," I saw written plainly on Jack Hill's face; and he settled himself to listen to the remainder of the minister's story in a manner which could not be considered other than complimentary.

Duly and truly I knew quite well he had already devoted the first five-guinea cheque he received to the poor of that minister's parish.)

By the road (proceeded our host), Dendeldy is distant from here ten long miles, but by a short cut across the hills it can be reached in something under six. For me it was nothing of walk, and accordingly I arrived at the manse ere noon.

(He paused, and, though thirty years had elapsed, drew a handkerchief across his forehead ere he continued his narrative.)

I had to climb a steep brae to reach the front door, but ere I could breast it my friend met me.

"Thank God you are come," he said, pressing my hand in his. "Oh, I am grateful."

He was trembling with excitement. His face was of a ghastly pallor. His voice was that of a person suffering from some terrible shock, labouring under some awful fear.

"What *has* happened, Edward?" I asked. I had known him when he was a little boy. "I am distressed to see you in such a state. Rouse yourself; be a man; whatever may have gone wrong can possibly be righted. I have come over to do all that lies in my power for you. If it is a matter of money—"

"No, no; it is not money," he interrupted; "would that it were!" and he began to tremble again so violently that really he communicated some part of his nervousness to me, and put me into a state of perfect terror.

"Whatever it is, Cawley, out with it," I said; "have you murdered anybody?"

"No, it is worse than that," he answered.

"But that's just nonsense," I declared. "Are you in your right mind, do you think?"

"I wish I were not," he returned. "I'd like to know I was stark staring mad; it would be happier for me—far, far happier."

"If you don't tell me this minute what is the matter, I shall turn on my heel and tramp my way home again," I said, half in a passion, for what I thought his folly angered me.

"Come into the house," he entreated, "and try to have patience with me; for indeed, Mr Morison, I am sorely troubled. I have been through my deep waters, and they have gone clean over my head."

We went into his little study and sat down. For a while he remained silent, his head resting upon his hand, struggling with some strong emotion; but after about five minutes he asked, in a low subdued voice,

"Do you believe in dreams?"

"What has my belief to do with the matter in hand?" I inquired.

"It is a dream, an awful dream, that is troubling me."

I rose from my chair.

"Do you mean to say," I asked, "you have brought me from my business and my parish to tell me you have had a bad dream?"

"That is just what I do mean to say," he answered. "At least, it was not a dream—it was a vision; no, I don't mean a vision—I can't tell you what it was; but nothing I ever went through in actual life was half so real, and I have bound myself to go through it all again. There is no hope for me, Mr Morison. I sit before you a lost creature, the most miserable man on the face of the whole earth."

"What did you dream?" I inquired.

A dreadful fit of trembling again seized him; but at last he managed to say,

"I have been like this ever since, and I shall be like this for evermore, till—till—the end comes."

"When did you have your bad dream?" I asked.

"Last night, or rather this morning," he answered. "I'll tell you all about it in a minute;" and he covered his face with his hands again.

"I was as well when I went to bed about eleven o'clock as ever I was in my life," he began, putting a great restraint upon himself, as I could see by the nervous way he kept knotting and unknotting his fingers. "I had been considering my sermon, and felt satisfied I should be able to deliver a good one next Sunday morning. I had taken nothing after my tea, and I lay down in my bed feeling at peace with all mankind, satisfied with my lot, thankful for the many blessings vouchsafed to me. How long I slept, or what I dreamt about at first, if I dreamt at all, I don't know; but after a time the mists seemed to clear from before my eyes, to roll away like clouds from a mountain summit, and I found myself walking on a beautiful summer's evening beside the river Deldy."

He paused for a moment, and an irrepressible shudder shook his frame.

"Go on," I said, for I felt afraid of his breaking down again.

He looked at me pitifully, with a hungry entreaty in his weary eyes, and continued,

"It was a lovely evening. I had never thought the earth so beautiful before: a gentle breeze just touched my cheek; the water flowed on clear and bright; the mountains in the distance looked bright and glowing, covered with purple heather. I walked on and on, till I came to that point where, as you may perhaps remember, the path, growing very narrow, winds round the base of a great crag, and leads the wayfarer suddenly into a little green amphitheatre, bounded on one side by the river, and on the other by rocks, that rise in places sheer to a height of a hundred feet and more."

"I remember it," I said; "a little farther on three streams meet and fall with a tremendous roar into the Witches' Caldron. A fine sight in the winter-time, only that there is scarce any reaching it from below, as the path you mention and the little green oasis are mostly covered with water."

"I had not been there before since I was a child," he went on, mournfully, "but I recollected it as one of the most solitary spots possible; and my astonishment was great, to see a man standing in the pathway, with a drawn sword in his hand. He did not stir as I drew near, so I stepped aside on the grass. Instantly he barred my way.

"'You can't pass here,' he said.

"'Why not?' I asked.

"'Because I say so,' he answered.

"'And who are you that say so?' I inquired, looking full at him.

"He was like a god. Majesty and power were written on every feature, were expressed in every gesture; but O, the awful scorn of his smile, the contempt with which he regarded me! The beams of the setting sun fell full upon him, and seemed to bring out, as in letters of fire, the wickedness and hate and sin, that underlay the glorious and terrible beauty of his face.

"I felt afraid; but I managed to say—

"'Stand out of my way; the river-brink is as free to me as to you.'

"'Not this part of it,' he answered; 'this place belongs to me.'

"'Very well,' I agreed, for I did not want to stand there bandying words with him, and a sudden darkness seemed to be falling around. 'It is getting late, and so I'll e'en turn back.'

"He gave a laugh, the like of which never fell on human ear before, and made reply,

"'You can't turn back; of your own free will you have come on my ground, and from it there is no return.'

"I did not speak; I only just turned round, and made as fast as I could for the path at the foot of the crag. He did not pass me, yet before I could reach the point I desired he stood barring my progress, with the scornful smile still on his lips, and his gigantic form assuming tremendous proportions in the narrow way.

"'Let me pass,' I entreated, 'and I will never come here again, never trespass more on your ground.'

"'No, you shall not pass.'

"'Who are you that takes such power on yourself?' I asked.

"'Come closer, and I will tell you,' he said.

"I drew a step nearer, and he spoke one word. I had never heard it before, but, by some extraordinary intuition, I knew what it meant. He was the Evil One; the name seemed to be taken up by the echoes, and repeated from rock to rock and crag to crag; the whole air seemed full of that one word; and then a great horror of darkness came about us, only the place where we stood remained light. We occupied a small circle walled round with the thick blackness of night.

"'You must come with me,' he said.

"I refused; and then he threatened me. I implored and entreated and wept; but at last I agreed to do what he wanted if he would promise to let me return. Again he laughed, and said, Yes, I should return; and the rocks and trees and mountains, ay, and the very rivers, seemed to take up the answer, and bear it in sobbing whispers away into the darkness."

He stopped, and lay back in his chair, shivering like one in an ague fit.

"Go on," I repeated again; "'twas but a dream, you know."

"Was it?" he murmured, mournfully. "Ah, you have not heard the end of it yet."

"Let me hear it, then," I said. "What happened afterwards?"

"The darkness seemed in part to clear away, and we walked side by side across the sward in the tender twilight, straight up to the bare black wall of rock. With the hilt of his sword he struck a heavy blow, and the solid rock opened as though it were a door. We passed through, and it closed behind us with a tremendous clang; yes, it closed behind us;" and at that point he fairly broke down, crying and sobbing as I had never seen a man even in the most frightful grief cry and sob before.

The minister paused in his narrative. At that moment there came a most tremendous blast of wind, which shook the windows of the manse, and burst open the hall-door, and caused the candles to flicker and the fire to go roaring up the chimney. It is not too much to say that, what with the uncanny story, and what with the howling storm, we every one felt that creeping sort of uneasiness which so often seems like the touch of something from another world—a hand stretched across the boundary-line of time and eternity, the coldness and mystery of which make the stoutest heart tremble.

*

I am telling you this tale (said Mr Morison, resuming his seat after a brief absence to see that the fastenings of the house were properly attended to), exactly as I heard it. I am not adding a word or comment of my own, nor, so far as I know, am I omitting any incident, however trivial. You must draw your own deductions from the facts I put before you. I have no explanation to give or theory to propound. Part of that great and terrible region in which he found himself, my friend went on to tell me, he penetrated, compelled by a power he could not resist to see the most awful sights, the most frightful sufferings. There was no form of vice that had not there its representative. As they moved along his companion told him the special sin for which such horrible punishment was being inflicted. Shuddering, and in mortal agony, he was yet unable to withdraw his eyes from the dreadful spectacle; the atmosphere grew more unendurable, the sights more and more terrible; the cries, groans, blasphemies, more awful and heart rending.

"I can bear no more," he gasped at last; "let me go!"

With a mocking laugh, the Presence beside him answered this appeal; a laugh which was taken up, even by the lost and anguished spirits around.

"There is no return," said the pitiless voice.

"But you promised," he cried; "you promised me faithfully."

"What are promises here?" and the words were as the sound of doom.

Still he prayed and entreated; he fell on his knees, and in his agony, spoke words that seemed to cause the purpose of the Evil One to falter.

"You shall go," he said, "on one condition: that you agree to return to me on Wednesday next, or send a substitute."

"I could not do that," said my friend. "I could not send any fellow-creature here. Better stop myself than do that."

"Then stop," said Satan, with the bitterest contempt; and he was turning away, when the poor distracted soul asked for a minute more ere he made his choice.

He was in an awful strait: on the one hand, how could he remain himself? on the other, how doom another to such fearful torments? Who could he send? Who would come? And then suddenly there flashed through his mind the thought of an old man to whom it could not signify much whether he took up his abode in this place a few days sooner or a few days later. He was travelling to it as fast as he knew how; he was the reprobate of the parish; the sinner without hope successive ministers had striven in vain to reclaim from the error of his ways; a man marked and doomed—Sandy the Tinker; Sandy, who was mostly drunk, and always godless; Sandy, who, it was said, believed in nothing, and gloried in his infidelity; Sandy, whose soul really did not signify much. He would send him. Lifting his eyes, he saw those of his tormentor surveying him scornfully.

"Well, have you made your choice?" he asked.

"Yes; I think I can send a substitute," was the hesitating answer.

"See you do, then," was the reply; "for if you do not, and fail to return yourself, *I shall come for you*. Wednesday, remember, before midnight;" and with these words ringing in his ears he was flung violently through the rock, and found himself in the middle of his bedroom floor, as if he had just been kicked there.

"That is not the end of the story, is it?" asked one of our party, as the minister came to a full stop, and looked earnestly at the fire.

"No," he answered, "it is not the end; but before proceeding I must ask you to bear carefully in mind the circumstances already recounted. Specially remember the date mentioned—*Wednesday next, before midnight.*"

Whatever I thought, and you may think, about my friend's dream (continued the minister), it made the most remarkable impression upon *his* mind. He could not shake off its influence; he passed from one state of nervousness to another. It was in vain I entreated him to exert his common sense, and call all his strength of mind to his assistance. I might as well have spoken to the wind. He implored me not to leave him, and I agreed to remain; indeed, to leave him in his then frame of mind would have been an act of the greatest cruelty. He wanted me also to preach in his place on the Sunday ensuing; but this I flatly refused.

"If you do not make an effort now," I said, "you will never make it. Rouse yourself, get on with your sermon, and if you buckle to work you will soon forget all about that foolish dream."

Well, to cut a long story short, the sermon was somehow composed and Sunday came, and my friend, a little better and getting over his fret, walked up into the pulpit to preach. He looked dreadfully ill; but I thought the worst was now over, and that he would go on mending.

Vain hope! He gave out the text and then looked over the congregation: the first person on whom his eyes lighted was Sandy the Tinker—Sandy, who had never before been known to enter a place of worship of any sort; Sandy, whom he had mentally chosen as his substitute, and who was *due on the following Wednesday*—sitting just below him, quite sober, and comparatively clean, waiting with a great show of attention for the opening words of the sermon.

With a terrible cry, my friend caught the front of the pulpit, then swayed back and fell down in a fainting fit. He was carried home and a doctor sent for. I said a few words, addressed apparently to the congregation, but really to Sandy, for my heart, somehow, came into my mouth at sight of him; and then, after I had dismissed the people, I paced slowly back to the manse, almost afraid of what might meet me there.

Mr Cawley was not dead; but he was in the most dreadful state of physical exhaustion and mental agitation. It was dreadful to hear him. How could he go himself? How could he send Sandy?—poor old Sandy, whose soul, in the sight of God, was just as precious as his own.

His whole cry was for us to deliver him from the Evil One; to save him from committing a sin which would render him a wretched man for life. He counted the hours and the minutes before he must return to that horrible place.

"I can't send Sandy," he would moan. "I cannot, O, I cannot save myself at such a price!"

And then he would cover his face with the bedclothes, only to start up and wildly entreat me not to leave him; to stand between the enemy and himself, to save him, or, if that were impossible, to give him courage to do what was right.

"If this continues," said the doctor, "Wednesday will find him either dead or a raving lunatic."

We talked the matter over, the doctor and I, in the gloaming, as we walked to and fro in the meadow behind the manse; and we decided, having to make our choice of two evils, to risk giving him such an opiate as should carry him over the dreaded interval. We knew it was a perilous thing to do with one in his condition, but, as I said before, we could only take the least of two evils.

What we dreaded most was his awaking before the time expired; so I kept watch beside him. He lay like one dead through the whole of Tuesday night and Wednesday, and Wednesday evening. Eight, nine, ten, eleven o'clock came and passed; twelve. "God be thanked!" I said, as I stooped over him and heard he was breathing quietly.

"He will do now, I hope," said the doctor, who had come in just before midnight; "you will stay with him till he wakes?"

I promised that I would, and in the beautiful dawn of a summer's morning he opened his eyes and smiled. He had no recollection then of what had occurred; he was as weak as an infant, and when I bade him try to go to sleep again, turned on his pillow and sank to rest once more.

Worn out with watching, I stepped softly from the room and passed into the fresh sweet air. I strolled down to the garden-gate, and stood looking at the great mountains and the fair country, and the Deldy wandering like a silver thread through the green fields below.

All at once my attention was attracted by a group of people coming slowly along the road leading from the hills. I could not at first see that in their midst something was being borne on men's shoulders; but when at last I made this out, I hurried to meet them and learn what was the matter.

"Has there been an accident?" I asked, as I drew near.

They stopped, and one man came towards me.

"Ay," he said, "the warst accident that could befa' him, puir fella'. He's deid."

"Who is it?" I asked, pressing forward; and lifting the cloth they had flung over his face, I saw *Sandy the Tinker!*

"He had been fou' coming home, I tak' it," remarked one who stood by; "puir Sandy, and gaed over the cliff afore he could save himsel'. We found him just on this side of the Witches' Caldron, where there's a bonny strip of green turf, and his cuddy was feeding on the hill-top with the bit cart behind her."

*

There was silence for a minute; then one of the ladies said softly, "Poor Sandy!"

"And what became of Mr Cawley?" asked the other.

"He gave up his parish and went abroad as a missionary. He is still living."

"What a most extraordinary story!" I remarked.

"Yes, *I* think so," said the minister. "If you like to go round by Dendeldy tomorrow, my son, who now occupies the manse, would show you the scene of the occurrence."

The next day we all stood looking at the "bonny strip of green," at the frowning cliffs, and at the Deldy, swollen by recent rains, rushing on its way.

The youngest of the party went up to the rock, and knocked upon it loudly with his cane.

"O, don't do that, pray!" cried both the ladies, nervously; the spirit of the weird story still brooded over us.

"What do you think of the coincidence, Jack?" I inquired of my friend, as we talked apart from the others.

"Ask me when we get back to Fleet Street," he answered.

1898

CARLETON BARKER, FIRST AND SECOND

John Kendrick Bangs

The American author and satirist John Kendrick Bangs (1862–1922) wrote prolifically, while also finding time for lecture tours, politics (he ran for mayor of Yonkers, New York in 1894) and spells as editor of *Harper's Weekly* and *Puck*. He gave his name to the subgenre of Bangsian fantasy, which uses the afterlife as a setting and allows historical figures to interact in the narrative, a device he utilised several times. Although primarily a humorist, Bangs wrote many ghost stories, often imbuing the supernatural with a darkly comedic touch. "Carleton Barker, First and Second" was first collected in *Ghosts I Have Met and Some Others* (1898).

The story's initial Lake District setting will be familiar rambling territory for many—the disturbing character of Carleton Barker is encountered near "the base of the famous Mount Skiddaw". Limping and distraught, the mysterious hiker was bound for Saddleback (now known by its ancient Cumbric name of Blencathra) when he met with a terrible accident. Our narrator and his friend take Barker to their lodgings in Keswick and the weird events of the tale begin to unfold. Skiddaw was a celebrated climb when Bangs was writing, and the Victorian pony trail, the Jenkin Hill Path, remains the most popular route to the blustery summit and its majestic views. If anywhere near Keswick, of course, a trip to Castlerigg is a must—one of Britain's most evocative stone circles, it is situated perfectly, with expansive views of Blencathra, Skiddaw and Helvellyn.

I

My first meeting with Carleton Barker was a singular one. A friend and I, in August, 18—, were doing the English Lake District on foot, when, on nearing the base of the famous Mount Skiddaw, we observed on the road, some distance ahead of us, limping along and apparently in great pain, the man whose subsequent career so sorely puzzled us. Noting his very evident distress, Parton and I quickened our pace and soon caught up with the stranger, who, as we reached his side, fell forward upon his face in a fainting condition—as well he might, for not only must he have suffered great agony from a sprained ankle, but inspection of his person disclosed a most extraordinary gash in his right arm, made apparently with a sharp knife, and which was bleeding most profusely. To stanch the flow of blood was our first care, and Parton, having recently been graduated in medicine, made short work of relieving the sufferer's pain from his ankle, bandaging it about and applying such soothing properties as he had in his knapsack—properties, by the way, with which, knowing the small perils to which pedestrians everywhere are liable, he was always provided.

Our patient soon recovered his senses and evinced no little gratitude for the service we had rendered him, insisting upon our accepting at his hands, merely, he said, as a souvenir of our good-Samaritanship, and as a token of his appreciation of the same, a small pocket-flask and an odd diamond-shaped stone pierced in the centre, which had hung from the end of his watch-chain, held in place by a minute gold ring. The flask became the property of Parton, and to me fell the stone, the exact hue of which I was never able to determine, since it was chameleonic in its properties. When it was placed in my hands by our "grateful patient" it was blood-red; when I looked upon it on the following morning it was of a livid, indescribable hue, yet lustrous as an opal. Today it is colourless and dull, as though some animating quality that it had once possessed had forever passed from it.

"You seem to have met with an accident," said Parton, when the injured man had recovered sufficiently to speak.

"Yes," he said, wincing with pain, "I have. I set out for Saddleback this morning—I wished to visit the Scales Tarn and get a glimpse of those noonday stars that are said to make its waters lustrous, and—"

"And to catch the immortal fish?" I queried.

"No," he replied, with a laugh. "I should have been satisfied to see the stars—and I did see the stars, but not the ones I set out to see. I have always been more or less careless of my safety, walking with my head in the clouds and letting my feet look out for themselves. The result was that I slipped on a moss-covered stone and fell over a very picturesque bit of scenery on to some more stones that, unfortunately, were not moss-covered."

"But the cut in your arm?" said Parton, suspiciously. "That looks as if somebody else had given it to you."

The stranger's face flushed as red as could be considering the amount of blood he had lost, and a look of absolute devilishness that made my flesh creep came into his eyes. For a moment he did not speak, and then, covering the delay in his answer with a groan of anguish, he said:

"Oh, that! Yes—I—I did manage to cut myself rather badly and—"

"I don't see how you could, though," insisted Parton. "You couldn't reach that part of yourself with a knife, if you tried."

"That's just the reason why you should see for yourself that it was caused by my falling on my knife. I had it grasped in my right hand, intending to cut myself a stick, when I slipped. As I slipped it flew from my hand and I landed on it, fortunately on the edge and not on the point," he explained, his manner far from convincing, though the explanation seemed so simple that to doubt it were useless.

"Did you recover the knife?" asked Parton. "It must have been a mighty sharp one, and rather larger than most people carry about with them on excursions like yours."

"I am not on the witness-stand, sir," returned the other, somewhat petulantly, "and so I fail to see why you should question me so closely in regard to so simple a matter—as though you suspected me of some wrongdoing."

"My friend is a doctor," I explained; for while I was quite as much interested in the incident, its whys and wherefores, as was Parton, I had myself noticed that he was suspicious of his chance patient, and seemingly not so sympathetic as he would otherwise have been. "He regards you as a case."

"Not at all," returned Parton. "I am simply interested to know how you hurt yourself—that is all. I mean no offence, I am sure, and if anything I have said has hurt your feelings I apologise."

"Don't mention it, doctor," replied the other, with an uneasy smile, holding his left hand out towards Parton as he spoke. "I am in great pain, as you know, and perhaps I seem irritable. I'm not an amiable man at best; as for the knife, in my agony I never thought to look for it again, though I suppose if I had looked I should not have found it, since it doubtless fell into the underbrush out of sight. Let it rest there. It has not done me a friendly service today and I shall waste no tears over it."

With which effort at pleasantry he rose with some difficulty to his feet, and with the assistance of Parton and myself walked on and into Keswick, where we stopped for the night. The stranger registered directly ahead of Parton and myself, writing the words, "Carleton Barker, Calcutta," in the book, and immediately retired to his room, nor did we see him again that night. After supper we looked for him, but as he was nowhere to be seen, we concluded that he had gone to bed to seek the recuperation of rest. Parton and I lit our cigars and, though somewhat fatigued by our exertions, strolled quietly about the more or less somnolent burg in which we were, discussing the events of the day, and chiefly our new acquaintance.

"I don't half like that fellow," said Parton, with a dubious shake of the head. "If a dead body should turn up near or on Skiddaw tomorrow morning, I wouldn't like to wager that Mr Carleton Barker hadn't put it there. He acted to me like a man who had something to conceal, and if I could have done it without seeming ungracious, I'd have flung his old flask as far into the fields as I could. I've half a mind to show my contempt for it now by filling it with some of that beastly claret they have at the *table d'hôte* here, and chucking the whole thing into the lake. It was an insult to offer those things to us."

"I think you are unjust, Parton," I said. "He certainly did look as if he had been in a maul with somebody. There was a nasty scratch on his face, and that cut on the arm was suspicious; but I can't see but that his explanation was clear enough. Your manner was too irritating. I think if I had met with an accident and was assisted by an utter stranger who, after placing me under obligations to him, acted towards me as though I were an unconvicted criminal, I'd be as mad as he was; and as for the insult of his offering, in my eyes that was the only way he could soothe his injured feelings. He was angry at your suspicions, and to be entirely your debtor for services didn't please him. His gift to me was made simply because he did not wish to pay you in substance and me in thanks."

"I don't go so far as to call him an unconvicted criminal, but I'll swear his record isn't clear as daylight, and I'm morally convinced that if men's deeds were written on their foreheads Carleton Barker, esquire, would wear his hat down over his eyes. I don't like him. I instinctively dislike him. Did you see the look in his eyes when I mentioned the knife?"

"I did," I replied. "And it made me shudder."

"It turned every drop of blood in my veins cold," said Parton. "It made me feel that if he had had that knife within reach he would have trampled it to powder, even if every stamp of his foot cut his flesh through to the bone. Malignant is the word to describe that glance, and I'd rather encounter a rattle-snake than see it again."

Parton spoke with such evident earnestness that I took refuge in silence. I could see just where a man of Parton's temperament—which was cold and eminently judicial even when his affections were concerned—could find that in Barker at which to cavil, but, for all that, I could not sympathise with the extreme view he took of his character. I have known many a man upon whose face nature has set the stamp of the villain much more deeply than it was impressed upon Barker's countenance, who has lived a life most irreproachable, whose every act has been one of unselfishness and for the good of mankind; and I have also seen outward appearing saints whose every instinct was base; and it seemed to me that the physiognomy of the unfortunate victim of the moss-covered rock and vindictive knife was just enough of a medium between that of the irredeemable sinner and the sterling saint to indicate that its owner was the average man in the matter of vices and virtues. In fact, the malignancy of his expression when the knife was mentioned was to me the sole point against him, and had I been in his position I do not think I should have acted very differently, though I must add that if I thought myself capable of freezing any person's blood with an expression of my eyes I should be strongly tempted to wear blue glasses when in company or before a mirror.

"I think I'll send my card up to him, Jack," I said to Parton, when we had returned to the hotel, "just to ask how he is. Wouldn't you?"

"No!" snapped Parton. "But then I'm not you. You can do as you please. Don't let me influence you against him—if he's to your taste."

"He isn't at all to my taste," I retorted. "I don't care for him particularly, but it seems to me courtesy requires that we show a little interest in his welfare."

"Be courteous, then, and show your interest," said Parton. "I don't care as long as I am not dragged into it."

I sent my card up by the boy, who, returning in a moment, said that the door was locked, adding that when he had knocked upon it there came no answer, from which he presumed that Mr Barker had gone to sleep.

"He seemed all right when you took his supper to his room?" I queried.

"He said he wouldn't have any supper. Just wanted to be left alone," said the boy.

"Sulking over the knife still, I imagine," sneered Parton; and then he and I retired to our room and prepared for bed.

I do not suppose I had slept for more than an hour when I was awakened by Parton, who was pacing the floor like a caged tiger, his eyes all ablaze, and labouring under an intense nervous excitement.

"What's the matter, Jack?" I asked, sitting up in bed.

"That d—ned Barker has upset my nerves," he replied. "I can't get him out of my mind."

"Oh, pshaw!" I replied. "Don't be silly. Forget him."

"Silly?" he retorted, angrily. "Silly? Forget him? Hang it, I would forget him if he'd let me—but he won't."

"What has he got to do with it?"

"More than is decent," ejaculated Parton. "More than is decent. He has just been peering in through that window there, and he means no good."

"Why, you're mad," I remonstrated. "He couldn't peer in at the window—we are on the fourth floor, and there is no possible way in which he could reach the window, much less peer in at it."

"Nevertheless," insisted Parton, "Carleton Barker for ten minutes previous to your waking was peering in at me through that window there, and in his glance was that same malignant, hateful quality that so set me against him today—and another thing, Bob," added Parton, stopping his nervous walk for a moment and shaking his finger impressively at me—"another thing which I did not tell you before because I thought it would fill you with that same awful dread that has come to me since meeting Barker—the blood from that man's arm, the blood that stained his shirt-sleeve crimson, that besmeared his clothes, spurted out upon my cuff and coat-sleeve when I strove to stanch its flow!"

"Yes, I remember that," said I.

"And now look at my cuff and sleeve!" whispered Parton, his face grown white.

I looked.

There was no stain of any sort whatsoever upon either!

Certainly there must have been something wrong about Carleton Barker.

II

The mystery of Carleton Barker was by no means lessened when next morning it was found that his room not only was empty, but that, as far as one could judge from the aspect of things therein, it had not been occupied at all. Furthermore, our chance acquaintance had vanished, leaving no more trace of his whereabouts than if he had never existed.

"Good riddance," said Parton. "I am afraid he and I would have come to blows sooner or later, because the mere thought of him was beginning to inspire me with a desire to thrash him. I'm sure he deserves a trouncing, whoever he is."

I, too, was glad the fellow had passed out of our ken, but not for the reason advanced by Parton. Since the discovery of the stainless cuff, where marks of blood ought by nature to have been, I goose-fleshed at the mention of his name. There was something so inexpressibly uncanny about a creature having a fluid of that sort in his veins. In fact, so unpleasantly was I impressed by that episode that I was unwilling even to join in a search for the mysteriously missing Barker, and by common consent Parton and I dropped him entirely as a subject for conversation.

We spent the balance of our week at Keswick, using it as our headquarters for little trips about the surrounding country, which is most charmingly adapted to the wants of those inclined to pedestrianism, and on Sunday evening began preparations for our departure, discarding our knickerbockers and resuming the habiliments of urban life, intending on Monday morning to run up to Edinburgh, there to while away a few days before starting for a short trip through the Trossachs.

While engaged in packing our portmanteaux there came a sharp knock at the door, and upon opening it I found upon the hall floor an envelope addressed to myself. There was no one anywhere in the hall, and, so quickly had I opened the door after the knock, that fact mystified me. It would hardly have been possible for any person, however nimble of foot, to have passed out of sight in the period which had elapsed between the summons and my response.

"What is it?" asked Parton, observing that I was slightly agitated.

"Nothing," I said, desirous of concealing from him the matter that bothered me, lest I should be laughed at for my pains. "Nothing, except a letter for me."

"Not by post, is it?" he queried; to which he added, "Can't be. There is no mail here today. Some friend?"

"I don't know," I said, trying, in a somewhat feminine fashion, to solve the authorship of the letter before opening it by staring at the superscription. "I don't recognise the handwriting at all."

I then opened the letter, and glancing hastily at the signature was filled with uneasiness to see who my correspondent was.

"It's from that fellow Barker," I said.

"Barker!" cried Parton. "What on earth has Barker been writing to you about?"

"He is in trouble," I replied, as I read the letter.

"Financial, I presume, and wants a lift?" suggested Parton.

"Worse than that," said I, "he is in prison in London."

"Wha-a-at?" ejaculated Parton. "In prison in London? What for?"

"On suspicion of having murdered an innkeeper in the South of England on Tuesday, August 16th."

"Well, I'm sorry to say that I believe he was guilty," returned Parton, without reflecting that the 16th day of August was the day upon which he and I had first encountered Barker.

"That's your prejudice, Jack," said I. "If you'll think a minute you'll know he was innocent. He was here on August 16th—last

Tuesday. It was then that you and I saw him for the first time limping along the road and bleeding from a wound in the shoulder."

"Was Tuesday the 16th?" said Parton, counting the days backward on his fingers. "That's a fact. It was—but it's none of my affair anyhow. It is too blessed queer for me to mix myself up in it, and I say let him languish in jail. He deserved it for something, I am sure—"

"Well, I'm not so confoundedly heartless," I returned, pounding the table with my fist, indignant that Parton should allow his prejudices to run away with his sense of justice. "I'm going to London to do as he asks."

"What does he want you to do? Prove an alibi?"

"Precisely; and I'm going and you're going, and I shall see if the landlord here won't let me take one of his boys along to support our testimony—at my own expense if need be."

"You're right, old chap," returned Parton, after a moment of internal struggle. "I suppose we really ought to help the fellow out of his scrape; but I'm decidedly averse to getting mixed up in an affair of any kind with a man like Carleton Barker, much less in an affair with murder in it. Is he specific about the murder?"

"No. He refers me to the London papers of the 17th and 18th for details. He hadn't time to write more, because he comes up for examination on Tuesday morning, and as our presence is essential to his case he was necessarily hurried."

"It's deucedly hard luck for us," said Parton, ruefully. "It means no Scotland this trip."

"How about Barker's luck?" I asked. "He isn't fighting for a Scottish trip—he's fighting for his life."

And so it happened that on Monday morning, instead of starting for Edinburgh, we boarded the train for London at Carlisle. We tried to get copies of the newspapers containing accounts of the crime that had been committed, but our efforts were unavailing, and it was not until we arrived in London and were visited by Barker's attorneys that we obtained any detailed information whatsoever of the murder; and when we did get it we were more than ever regretful to be mixed up in it, for it was an unusually brutal murder. Strange to say, the evidence against Barker was extraordinarily convincing, considering that at the time of the commission of the crime he was hundreds of miles from the scene. There was testimony from railway guards, neighbours of the murdered innkeeper, and others, that it was Barker and no one else who committed the crime. His identification was complete, and the wound in his shoulder was shown almost beyond the possibility of doubt to have been inflicted by the murdered man in self-defence.

"Our only hope," said the attorney, gravely, "is in proving an alibi. I do not know what to believe myself, the chain of evidence against my client is so complete; and yet he asserts his innocence, and has stated to me that you two gentlemen could assist in proving it. If you actually encountered Carleton Barker in the neighbourhood of Keswick on the 16th of this month, the whole case against him falls to the ground. If not, I fear his outlook has the gallows at the small end of the perspective."

"We certainly did meet a Carleton Barker at Keswick on Tuesday, August 16th," returned Parton; "and he was wounded in the shoulder, and his appearance was what might have been expected of one who had been through just such a frightful murder as we understand this to have been; but this was explained to us as due to a fall over rocks in the vicinity of the Scales Tarn—which was plausible enough to satisfy my friend here."

"And not yourself?" queried the attorney.

"Well, I don't see what that has to do with it," returned Parton. "As to the locality there is no question. He was there. We saw him, and others saw him, and we have taken the trouble to come down here to state the fact, and have brought with us the call-boy from the hotel, who can support our testimony if it is not regarded as sufficient. I advise you, however, as attorney for Barker, not to inquire too deeply into that matter, because I am convinced that if he isn't guilty of this crime—as of course he is not—he hasn't the cleanest record in the world. He has bad written on every line of his face, and there were one or two things connected with our meeting with him that mightn't be to his taste to have mentioned in court."

"I don't need advice, thank you," said the attorney, dryly. "I wish simply to establish the fact of his presence at Keswick at the hour of 5 P.M. on Tuesday, August 16th. That was the hour at which the murder is supposed—in fact, is proved—to have been committed. At 5.30, according to witnesses, my client was seen in the neighbourhood, faint with loss of blood from a knife-wound in the shoulder. Barker has the knife-wound, but he might have a dozen of them and be acquitted if he wasn't in Frewenton on the day in question."

"You may rely upon us to prove that," said I. "We will swear to it. We can produce tangible objects presented to us on that afternoon by Barker—"

"I can't produce mine," said Parton. "I threw it into the lake."

"Well, I can produce the stone he gave me," said I, "and I'll do it if you wish."

"That will be sufficient, I think," returned the attorney. "Barker spoke especially about that stone, for it was a half of an odd souvenir of the East, where he was born, and he fortunately has the other half. The two will fit together at the point where the break was made, and our case will be complete."

The attorney then left us. The following day we appeared at the preliminary examination, which proved to be the whole examination as well, since, despite the damning circumstantial evidence against Barker, evidence which shook my belief almost in the veracity of my own eyes, our plain statements, substantiated by the evidence of the call-boy and the two halves of the oriental pebble, one in my possession and the other in Barker's, brought about the discharge of the prisoner from custody; and the "Frewenton Atrocity" became one of many horrible murders, the mystery of which time alone, if anything, could unravel.

After Barker was released he came to me and thanked me most effusively for the service rendered him, and in many ways made himself agreeable during the balance of our stay in London. Parton, however, would have nothing to do with him, and to me most of his attentions were paid. He always had a singularly uneasy way about him, as though he were afraid of some impending trouble, and finally after a day spent with him slumming about London—and a more perfect slummer no one ever saw, for he was apparently familiar with every one of the worst and lowest resorts in all of London as well as on intimate terms with leaders in the criminal world—I put a few questions to him impertinently pertinent to himself. He was surprisingly frank in his answers. I was quite prepared for a more or less indignant refusal when I asked him to account for his intimacy with these dregs of civilisation.

"It's a long story," he said, "but I'll tell it to you. Let us run in here and have a chop, and I'll give you some account of myself over a mug of ale."

We entered one of the numerous small eating-houses that make London a delight to the lover of the chop in the fulness of its glory. When we were seated and the luncheon ordered Barker began.

"I have led a very unhappy life. I was born in India thirty-nine years ago, and while my every act has been as open and as free of wrong as are those of an infant, I have constantly been beset by such untoward affairs as this in which you have rendered such inestimable service. At the age of five, in Calcutta, I was in peril of my liberty on the score of depravity, although I never committed any act that could in any sense be called depraved. The main cause of my trouble at that time was a small girl of ten whose sight was partially destroyed by the fiendish act of some one who, according to her statement, wantonly hurled a piece of broken glass into one of her eyes. The girl said it was I who did it, although at the time it was done, according to my mother's testimony, I was playing in her room and in her plain view. That alone would not have been a very serious matter for me, because the injured child might have been herself responsible for her injury, but in a childish spirit of fear, afraid to say so, and, not realising the enormity of the charge, have laid it at the door of any one of her playmates she saw fit. She stuck to her story, however, and there were many who believed that she spoke the truth and that my mother, in an endeavour to keep me out of trouble, had stated what was not true."

"But you were innocent, of course?" I said.

"I am sorry you think it necessary to ask that," he replied, his pallid face flushing with a not unnatural indignation; "and I decline to answer it," he added. "I have made a practice of late, when I am in trouble or in any way under suspicion, to let others do my pleading and prove my innocence. But you didn't mean to be like your friend Parton, I know, and I cannot be angry with a man who has done so much for me as you have—so let it pass. I was saying that standing alone the accusation of that young girl would not have been serious in its effects in view of my mother's testimony, had not a seeming corroboration come three days later, when another child was reported to have been pushed over an embankment and maimed for life by no less a person than my poor innocent self. This time I was again, on my mother's testimony, at her side; but there were witnesses of the crime, and they every one of them swore to my guilt, and as a consequence we found it advisable to leave the home that had been ours since my birth, and to come to England. My father had contemplated returning to his own country for some time, and the reputation that I had managed unwittingly to build up for myself in Calcutta was of a sort that made it easier for him to make up his mind. He at first swore that he would ferret out the mystery in the matter, and would go through Calcutta with a drag-net if necessary to find the possible other boy who so resembled me that his outrageous acts were put upon my shoulders; but people had begun to make up their minds that there was not only something wrong about me, but that my mother knew it and had tried to get me out of my scrapes by lying—so there was nothing for us to do but leave."

"And you never solved the mystery?" I queried.

"Well, not exactly," returned Barker, gazing abstractedly before him. "Not exactly; but I have a theory, based upon the bitterest kind of experience, that I know what the trouble is."

"You have a double?" I asked.

"You are a good guesser," he replied; "and of all unhanged criminals he is the very worst."

There was a strange smile on his lips as Carleton Barker said this. His tone was almost that of one who was boasting—in fact, so strongly was I impressed with his appearance of conceit when he estimated the character of his double, that I felt bold enough to say:

"You seem to be a little proud of it, in spite of all."

Barker laughed.

"I can't help it, though he has kept me on tenter-hooks for a lifetime," he said. "We all feel a certain amount of pride in the success of those to whom we are related, either by family ties or other shackles like those with which I am bound to my murderous *alter ego*. I knew an Englishman once who was so impressed with the notion that he resembled the great Napoleon that he conceived the most ardent hatred for his own country for having sent the illustrious Frenchman to St Helena. The same influence—a very subtle one—I feel. Here is a man who has maimed and robbed and murdered for years, and has never yet been apprehended. In his chosen calling he has been successful, and though I have been put to my trumps many a time to save my neck from the retribution that should have been his, I can't help admiring the fellow, though I'd kill him if he stood before me!"

"And are you making any effort to find him?"

"I am, of course," said Barker; "that has been my life-work. I am fortunately possessed of means enough to live on, so that I can devote all my time to unravelling the mystery. It is for this reason that I have acquainted myself with the element of London with which, as you have noticed, I am very familiar. The life these criminals are leading is quite as revolting to me as it is to you, and the scenes you and I have witnessed together are no more unpleasant to you than they are to me; but what can I do? The man lives and must be run down. He is in England, I am certain. This latest diversion of his has convinced me of that."

"Well," said I, rising, "you certainly have my sympathy, Mr Barker, and I hope your efforts will meet with success. I trust you will have the pleasure of seeing the other gentleman hanged."

"Thank you," he said, with a queer look in his eyes, which, as I thought it over afterwards, did not seem to be quite as appropriate to his expression of gratitude as it might have been.

III

When Barker and I parted that day it was for a longer period than either of us dreamed, for upon my arrival at my lodgings I found there a cable message from New York, calling me back to my labours. Three days later I sailed for home, and five years elapsed before I was so fortunate as to renew my acquaintance with foreign climes. Occasionally through these years Parton and I discussed Barker, and at no time did my companion show anything but an increased animosity towards our strange Keswick acquaintance. The mention of his name was sufficient to drive Parton from the height of exuberance to a state of abject depression.

"I shall not feel easy while that man lives," he said. "I think he is a minion of Satan. There is nothing earthly about him."

"Nonsense," said I. "Just because a man has a bad face is no reason for supposing him a villain or a supernatural creature."

"No," Parton answered; "but when a man's veins hold blood that saturates and leaves no stain, what are we to think?"

I confessed that this was a point beyond me, and, by mutual consent, we dropped the subject.

One night Parton came to my rooms white as a sheet, and so agitated that for a few minutes he could not speak. He dropped, shaking like a leaf, into my reading-chair and buried his face in his hands. His attitude was that of one frightened to the very core of his being. When I questioned him first he did not respond. He simply groaned. I resumed my reading for a few moments, and then looking up observed that Parton had recovered somewhat and was now gazing abstractedly into the fire.

"Well," I said, "feeling better?"

"Yes," he answered, slowly. "But it was a shock."

"What was?" I asked. "You've told me nothing as yet."

"I've seen Barker."

"No!" I cried. "Where?"

"In a back alley down-town, where I had to go on a hospital call. There was a row in a gambling-hell in Hester Street. Two men were cut and I had to go with the ambulance. Both men will probably die, and no one can find any trace of the murderer; but I know who he is. He was Carleton Barker and no one else. I passed him in the alley on the way in, and I saw him in the crowd when I came out."

"Was he alone in the alley?" I asked. Parton groaned again.

"That's the worst of it," said he. "He was not alone. He was with Carleton Barker."

"You speak in riddles," said I.

"I saw in riddles," said Parton; "for as truly as I sit here there were two of them, and they stood side by side as I passed through, alike as two peas, and crime written on the pallid face of each."

"Did Barker recognise you?"

"I think so, for as I passed he gasped—both of them gasped, and as I stopped to speak to the one I had first recognised he had vanished as completely as though he had never been, and as I turned to address the other he was shambling off into the darkness as fast as his legs could carry him."

I was stunned. Barker had been mysterious enough in London. In New York with his double, and again connected with an atrocity, he became even more so, and I began to feel somewhat towards him as had Parton from the first. The papers next morning were not very explicit on the subject of the Hester Street trouble, but they confirmed Parton's suspicions in his and my own mind as to whom the assassins were. The accounts published simply stated that the wounded men, one of whom had died in the night and the other of whom would doubtless not live through the day, had been set upon and stabbed by two unknown Englishmen who had charged them with cheating at cards; that the assailants had disappeared, and that the police had no clew as to their whereabouts.

Time passed and nothing further came to light concerning the Barkers, and gradually Parton and I came to forget them. The following summer I went abroad again, and then came the climax to the Barker episode, as we called it. I can best tell the story of that climax by printing here a letter written by myself to Parton. It was penned within an hour of the supreme moment, and while it evidences my own mental perturbation in its lack of coherence, it is none the less an absolutely truthful account of what happened. The letter is as follows:

"LONDON, July 18, 18—.

"My Dear Parton,—You once said to me that you could not breathe easily while this world held Carleton Barker living. You may now draw an easy breath, and many of them, for the Barker episode is over. Barker is dead, and I flatter myself that I am doing very well myself to live sanely after the experiences of this morning.

"About a week after my arrival in England a horrible tragedy was enacted in the Seven Dials district. A woman was the victim, and a devil in human form the perpetrator of the crime. The poor creature was literally hacked to pieces in a manner suggesting the hand of Jack the Ripper, but in this instance the murderer, unlike Jack, was caught red-handed, and turned out to be no less a person than Carleton Barker. He was tried and convicted, and sentenced to be hanged at twelve o'clock today.

"When I heard of Barker's trouble I went, as a matter of curiosity solely, to the trial, and discovered in the dock the man you and I had encountered at Keswick. That is to say, he resembled our friend in every possible respect. If he were not Barker he was the most perfect imitation of Barker conceivable. Not a feature of our Barker but was reproduced in this one, even to the name. But he failed to recognise me. He saw me, I know, because I felt his eyes upon me, but in trying to return his gaze I quailed utterly before him. I could not look him in the eye without a feeling of the most deadly horror, but I did see enough of him to note that he regarded me only as one of a thousand spectators who had flocked into the court-room during the progress of the trial. If it were our Barker who sat there his dissemblance was remarkable. So coldly did he look at me that I began to doubt if he really were the man we had met; but the events of this morning have changed my mind utterly on that point. He was the one we had met, and I am now convinced that his story to me of his double was purely fictitious, and that from beginning to end there has been but one Barker.

"The trial was a speedy one. There was nothing to be said in behalf of the prisoner, and within five days of his arraignment he was convicted and sentenced to the extreme penalty—that of hanging—and noon today was the hour appointed for the execution. I was to have gone to Richmond today by coach, but since Barker's trial I have been in a measure depressed. I have grown to dislike the man as thoroughly as did you, and yet I was very much affected by the thought that he was finally to meet death upon the scaffold. I could not bring myself to participate in any pleasures on the day of his execution, and in consequence I gave up my Richmond journey and remained all morning in my lodgings trying to read. It was a miserable effort. I could not concentrate my mind upon my book—no book could have held the slightest part of my attention at that time. My thoughts were all for Carleton Barker, and I doubt if, when the clock hands pointed to half after eleven, Barker himself was more apprehensive over what was to come than I. I found myself holding my watch in my hand, gazing at the dial and counting the seconds which must intervene before the last dreadful scene of a life of crime. I would rise from my chair and pace my room nervously for a few minutes; then I would throw myself into my chair again and stare at my watch. This went on nearly all the morning—in fact, until ten minutes before twelve, when there came a slight knock at my door. I put aside my nervousness as well as I could, and, walking to the door, opened it.

"I wonder that I have nerve to write of it, Parton, but there upon the threshold, clad in the deepest black, his face pallid as the head of death itself and his hands shaking like those of a palsied man, stood no less a person than Carleton Barker!

"I staggered back in amazement and he followed me, closing the door and locking it behind him.

"'What would you do?' I cried, regarding his act with alarm, for, candidly, I was almost abject with fear.

"'Nothing—to you!' he said. 'You have been as far as you could be my friend. The other, your companion of Keswick'—meaning you, of course—'was my enemy.'

"I was glad you were not with us, my dear Parton. I should have trembled for your safety.

"'How have you managed to escape?' I asked.

"'I have not escaped,' returned Barker. 'But I soon shall be free from my accursed double.'

"Here he gave an unearthly laugh and pointed to the clock.

"'Ha, ha!' he cried. 'Five minutes more—five minutes more and I shall be free.'

"'Then the man in the dock was not you?' I asked.

"'The man in the dock,' he answered, slowly, 'is even now mounting the gallows, whilst I stand here.'

"He trembled a little as he spoke, and lurched forward like a drunken man; but he soon recovered himself, grasping the back of my chair convulsively with his long white fingers.

"'In two minutes more,' he whispered, 'the rope will be adjusted about his neck; the black cap is even now being drawn over his cursed features, and—'

"Here he shrieked with laughter, and, rushing to the window, thrust his head out and literally sucked the air into his lungs, as a man with a parched throat would have drank water. Then he turned and, tottering back to my side, hoarsely demanded some brandy.

"It was fortunately at hand, and precisely as the big bells in Westminster began to sound the hour of noon, he caught up the goblet and held it aloft.

"'To him!' he cried.

"And then, Parton, standing before me in my lodgings, as truly as I write, he remained fixed and rigid until the twelfth stroke of the bells sounded, when he literally faded from my sight, and the goblet, falling to the floor, was shattered into countless atoms!"

1910

CROWDY MARSH

Sabine Baring-Gould

The marshes and bogs of the west of England have long inspired literature, perhaps the most famous example being Arthur Conan Doyle's fearsome Grimpen Mire. These remarkable wetland habitats are notoriously difficult to cross, as we can attest, having ended up knee deep in them on a couple of occasions. In "Crowdy Marsh", first published in *The Story-Teller* in January 1910, it is in a remote section of Cornwall's Bodmin Moor that our protagonist loses his way. Following a ghostly encounter with the Wild Hunt, his adventure takes an even stranger turn as he learns the secrets of the marsh's underbelly and a moral lesson to boot.

A slightly righteous tone is not surprising given that Sabine Baring-Gould (1834–1924) was an Anglican priest and noted hymnist ("Onward, Christian Soldiers" being his biggest "hit"). He was also a dedicated antiquarian, folk song collector and prodigious writer of fiction and non-fiction, authoring over a thousand publications in his nine decades on a range of topics, including much about his native West Country. In common with several other noted clerical authors of the period, Baring-Gould was fascinated by the folkloric and strange, producing a book-length study of werewolves and a collection of *Curious Myths of the Middle Ages* that was admired by H. P. Lovecraft.

The place described by Baring-Gould still feels isolated, but is today dominated by Crowdy Reservoir. Popular with birdwatchers, the reservoir has a short walking route mapped from its car park that allows you to get a good feel for the area. In *A Book of Cornwall* Baring-Gould stated that "some of the Cornish bogs are far worse than those on Dartmoor. Crowdy is particularly ugly and dangerous." What remains of Crowdy Marsh lies to the west of the reservoir and is now designated a Special Area of Conservation; it is out of bounds to visitors due to a combination of deep water, ground-nesting birds and cattle with calves. Although the area around Crowdy has produced archaeological finds dating back to the Mesolithic, none of our tale's "faculties" have yet been unearthed.

I believe that one of the most desolate spots in the west is the moor about Brown Willy, and one of the most unpleasant experiences I have encountered is being lost at the fall of night on that moor late in the autumn, and when the days are short and the darkness settles down as a black pall over moor and fen, when even the tors no longer reflect the dying light, and are seen only as black profiles against a sky in which is scarce a ray or only a ghastly glare in the west.

I was out one day at the end of October with my friend Richards, shooting on the Bodmin moors, or to be more exact, we went out with the purpose of shooting blackcock, but saw not one. The fact that we had been unsuccessful tended to make us prolong our tramp, always hoping that we might see one, and always disappointed. At last I said, "Come, Richards, we must turn back; the sun has set, and I don't want to lose my way about Brown Willy and run the risk of stumbling into Crowdy Marsh."

Brown Willy, the highest of the Cornish tors, is not of great height, only 1,375 feet, but with its five-horned head it proves a bold and conspicuous object, and in ancient times it was a beacon; three immense cairns are piled up on the summit on which once blazed fires to warn the country round when foreign sails appeared on the sea, and there was thought to be risk of invasion.

We were bound for Camelford, where is a comfortable hotel, and where we were aware that a good supper was awaiting us.

CROWDY MARSH

But then—how to get there? Now the moor about Brown Willy and his sister, Rough Tor, is peculiarly nasty with bogs, and these bogs are not to be trifled with. On the west of Rough Tor is Stannon Marsh, and below the tor it possesses a little odious morass of its own, Rough Tor Marsh, in which the De Lank river rises. Then under Buttern Hill is another, much bigger, that festers in its own muck, feeding no stream at all. Due north of Rough Tor on Davidstow Moor is a tract of comparatively dry land, lying between the swamp just mentioned and the redoubted Crowdy Marsh, but this measures only two-thirds of a mile in breadth, and Crowdy Marsh throws out a wet and oozy arm into this dry moorland to grip and draw under an incautious wanderer.

Now it is no joke finding one's way by daylight from Brown Willy across this bridle path between morasses into the Camelford Road, and I did not much relish the prospect of venturing on it with night falling. So now I urged Richards to step out, as we had seven miles to walk if we went the way indicated. But there was another way over Lower Moor between Stannon Marsh and Crowdy that was much shorter, but I was not well acquainted with that portion of the moor, and did not like to venture on it in the dark. It was a mistake, as a direct line ran from the monument on Polden Down to Camelford. However, ill-luck attended us all that day, and I chose to push on over Davidstow Moor, where I knew I should strike the high road in two miles and a half, whereas by the other way I would have no main road at all, and I thought I might get lost among lanes when leaving the open moor.

We paced on for some time cheerily, and a certain failing amount of light enabled me to see that we were skirting Rough Tor; and then I said to my companion:

"Now we must look alive, and mind our steps. We have Scylla on one side and Charybdis on the other, and I do not think there is much choice in rotten apples; I would as soon be engulfed in one as in the other. Look alive, man! By Jove! I am in water."

And so I was. I floundered forward and went in to my middle. Then I threw my gun down, cast myself across it, and drew my legs with a tremendous effort out of the slime that sucked at me, and had indeed, by suction, torn off one of my gaiters.

I called out to Richards to keep away from me, and aim for the lightest spot in the sky; as for me, I would find my way out as best I could.

The only possible way of getting out of these bogs is to aim for some point and work steadily forward towards it, for otherwise one shifts from one tussock of grass or mass of grey moss to another, and loses all knowledge of direction, and very often one travels about in a circle.

But just now it was not easy to take a direction; to the north there was nothing conspicuous at which one could aim; and yet, to the north we had to go. How I cursed my folly in taking this course instead of that from the monument. Lanes, bad though they might be and bewildering, could not swallow one up as would these bogs, if they got hold of you. Moreover, the cold of the slimy water was intense, and numbed the legs and feet. At last, creeping forward on my breast with the gun athwart me, I reached a hump of drier ground, and seated myself on it to gather breath before proceeding farther, worming my way through the mire. I called to Richards to go forward; I would follow. But I received no answer. I called again and again, but met with no response.

There was still a long tract of morass very similar in nature to that through part of which I had struggled, and I was fain to get through it in the same manner as before, writhing along like a lizard. Then my strength gave way. The strain on my muscles had been too great, and I turned dizzy. What had become of Richards I did not know. I greatly feared that he had been swallowed up. Exhausted, panting, my brow beaded with sweat, yet at the same time conscious of extreme cold from immersion, I tried to gather my senses together. I was still not out of the morass, I did not know in which direction to worm my way. The stench in my nostrils of the decomposing matter sickened me. As I thus lay prostrate, I heard the peal of a horn. A steely light still lingered in the south west, not enough to enable me to distinguish forms at a distance. Moreover, I could not turn my head where I lay and look in the direction whence came the sound. Then I heard the deep-mouthed baying of hounds and another peal of the horn nearer than before. Next moment, to my ineffable surprise, I saw the dark form of a horseman in full gallop pass near me, over the surface of the morass, followed by a pack. As one of the hounds swept by me, touching me, by a sudden impulse I let go my gun, and threw my arms about the body of the dog. In an instant I was whirled from the tussock of grass on which I lay, and carried forward swift as the wind, ploughing through water, coarse grass and moss blinding me, but I held fast desperately, and in a few moments felt that I was on firm ground, whereupon I relaxed my hold and rolled over on one side. Then I saw before me a rude stone house, thatched doubtless with rushes and heather, before which the huntsman had drawn up, and the hounds were barking about the door. There was either no window to the cottage, or that which existed had been so well closed by shutters as to allow no ray of light to appear; a streak, however, issued from below the door.

The horn rang out again. Then the door was thrown open, and in the doorway, against the red light from a peat fire within, appeared the forms of three women. Their faces I could not see, nor was there light sufficient coming from the house to enable me to distinguish the features of the horseman. But I could make out that he had saddlebags cast over the back of the steed. These, without a word of explanation or salutation, he lifted and cast at the women, who caught them and at once retired within. I could see a table, and on to this the women poured the contents of the bags that glittered, but whether from the reflection of the fire or from phosphoric light in themselves I had no means of judging. Without a word one woman came forth, and threw the empty bags to the huntsman, who caught them dexterously, replaced them over his saddle, sounded another blast, and instantly he, followed by the pack, was off careering over the moor, and the last I saw of him and the hounds was profiled against the dying light in the sky on the shoulder of a tor. The women had shut the door. I had been unnoticed.

I remained where I lay for a few minutes, too exhausted to rise, too perplexed to know what to do. But by degrees I recovered energy and framed resolutions; and, rising to my feet that were stiff and numbed, I went to the door, knocked, and remained awaiting a reply. None came. I knocked again; and then, impatient at the delay, unhasped the door uninvited, and entered.

The spectacle that met my eyes was sufficiently surprising to make me doubt whether I were awake or dreaming. About the table sat the three women, aged, grey and haggard, with long, lean fingers, sorting the contents of the saddlebags heaped upon it. But what that was among which their fingers moved I could not tell. There appeared to be small, flickering lights of various colour, and different degrees of brilliancy; interspersed in the heap were dark particles.

"I am sorry to intrude," said I, as the three women raised their faces and looked at me. They were strangely alike, all much of an age, equally grey, wan and weird, with their hair hanging over their shoulders. All had their sleeves rolled up above their elbows; the nervous arms so lean that their hands at the extremities looked preternaturally large.

"I must apologise," I said. "I sank up to my shoulders in Crowdy Marsh, and I extricated myself with the utmost difficulty, and am so exhausted and so chilled that I am constrained to throw myself on your hospitality, and entreat you to allow me to rest so as to warm myself and get somewhat dry before proceeding on my way."

"You can come in and rest," said one of the sisters.

"Sit by the fire," said the second.

"Drink from the simmering cauldron," said the third.

Then without further regarding me, they proceeded with their work. I took them at their word. I drew towards the hearth, and crouched over the fire. My teeth chattered with cold. On the hob stood a mug and ladle. Without more ado I dipped the long-handled ladle into the pot, and poured the liquid it brought up into the mug and set that to my lips. The draught was fiery; it sent a glow through my arteries and inflamed my brain. It was excellent in flavour and strength, and I felt that it nerved me and enabled me to resist the chill that had invaded my members, and was stealing upon my heart. My garments began to steam. It was not judicious to dry them upon me by the fire, but what else could I do? I felt that I must drive away the numbness, so as to enable me to pursue my course; and the exertion, I trusted, would restore circulation and prevent the ill effects of my immersion in the morass.

I now looked at the sisters—for sisters they certainly were. What could have induced these women to settle on the edge of the ill-savoured and unwholesome marsh? No one with common sense I should have supposed would have done that, but would have selected a habitation on higher ground, above the mists that hung over Crowdy. Possibly the moor-slope was so thickly strewn with granite masses, as to leave only a vacant spot for their hovel and little field near the brim of the morass. This alone could explain their settling in such a spot.

I puzzled my head to make out on what the sisters were engaged.

At one moment I supposed that they were sorting out the crystals that go by the name of Cornish diamonds. At another I conjectured that they were collecting glow-worms; but then, I considered, these insects are not seen in October.

Two of the sisters were gathering what they collected into little heaps at their sides on the board; the third had a pan on the floor at her feet, and I noticed that she picked out and raked together only such particles as showed no light, and these she dropped into the pan.

As my chill passed off, my interest in what proceeded under my eyes increased. I could restrain my curiosity no longer, and, drawing my stool to the table, asked: "Would you mind informing me what those articles are which you are selecting so carefully?"

"Faculties," replied the woman who sat nearest to me.

"Gifts," said the second.

"Talents," said the third.

"I am in no degree enlightened," said I. "Who was the rider who came to your door and surrendered to you his saddlebags?"

"Dewer, the great master," answered the first.

"He gathers up the neglected, the unused, and the misused faculties," explained the second.

"In Nature nothing is lost," said the third.

"Everyone," continued the first, "is given faculties. Such as have been received and by stress of circumstances have not been brought to perfection go into my heap."

"I select all such faculties as are wilfully neglected," said the second. "They go into my heap."

"All such as are misused, turned to evil, I cast into the pan," said the third. "Look yonder where they lie, like slugs sodden in salt water."

"Mine are for redistribution," said the first. "The same with mine," said the second.

"Mine go into Crowdy Marsh," said the third.

She stooped, lifted a trap-door, and shot the contents of her pan into the hole beneath the floor.

"That is the sewer discharging into the morass, and they run down into Crowdy, where they rot and stink."

"Dewer," said the first, "rides over the world, and collects human faculties from the souls of men and women—faculties implanted in them when they come into the world, that have been unused, neglected, or ill-used. In Nature, there is no waste."

"We sort them out for redistribution," said the second.

"Save such as have been ill-used; they go to feed Crowdy," added the third.

I was not much the wiser for their explanation.

"Excuse me," I said, "generalities are beyond my powers of comprehension; come to particulars, and then I get hold of the sense. What, for instance, is that?"

I pointed to a sparklet that the first was handling. It was luminous with a steady ray.

"That," said she, "is the faculty of the strategist. It was implanted in a man, and had circumstances been propitious he would have made a great general—a Wellington, or a Napoleon. Had he been in Parliament he would have been in the Ministry before long, and have been a marvellous man for organising and holding his party together. But circumstances were unfavourable. He was to the end of his days a coalheaver. He is in no degree blameworthy. He had not the chance."

She took up a luminous drop that diffused a soft, sweet radiance.

"This," she said, "is the maternal faculty. It was disposed of to a woman who never had the offer of a man's hand, and died, sorely against her will, as an old maid. She never had the chance."

Then I turned to the other sister.

"Excuse my freedom," said I, "if I say to you what I did to your sister. Do not give me generalities, but particular instances. What is that star you hold between your finger and thumb that has in it all the prismatic colours?"

"That," said she, "is the artist's faculty. He in whom it was lodged as a child showed marked aptitude with his pencil. He could catch a likeness in a moment, and with him every stroke told. His father, like a reasonable man, saw what was the bent of his son's genius, and directed his education in conformity with his taste for art. He sent him to the Royal Academy."

"Which killed the artistic faculty in him," I interrupted.

"No; that was not so. His father died early and left him a competence; he was not rich, but in easy circumstances. He laid aside his brush and palette, and spent his time in golf, cricket, billiards, bridge and poker; in a word, became a loafer and pleasure seeker, and did nothing with the talent that was in him, and which he knew was there, but was too lazy to develop. He had the chance and threw it away. He goes to my heap."

"And that," said I, pointing to another drop.

"It is the modelling faculty," said the second sister. "It was bestowed on a woman."

"What, to make a sculptor of her?"

"No; the moulding of character. She married a very rich man, and had many children—ten in all. She might have shaped their minds and characters. But she was inert. She left them to nurses and governesses, and became a great society lady, neglecting her domestic duties and the direction of her children's future. She had ten chances and threw them all away. This goes into my heap."

"See," exclaimed the third sister; "here is a pile of talents that have been, not neglected, but misused; that have been dedicated to evil only. This," taking up what looked like a dead slug, "this—"

"Stay," I interrupted. "Faculties, talents, turned to bad ends are manifest enough in the world. I have come across many of them, to my cost. I need no special examples; I have seen too many of them already."

Suddenly the sisters cried out: "Throw yourselves down. He comes! He comes! As you value your eyesight do not look up."

I saw the three hags cover up their eyes and drop their faces upon the table. I obeyed, and cast myself down.

Then I heard a rushing sound, and a brilliant light filled the room; so brilliant was it, that although my face was covered, it dazzled me through my fingers and eyelids. I could not have looked up. I should have been blinded.

In a moment the light was gone; the sound had passed away. I rose and resumed my place at the table.

"He has passed through," said one sister.

"Who?" I inquired.

"The Angel of Redistribution," answered the first. "See, my pile has gone. His right hand gathered it up."

"And his left hand took up mine," said the second.

"Of mine he has taken nothing," said the third sister; "all mine goes down the drain into the slough of rottenness."

Then the sisters rose to their feet.

"The moon has risen," said the first. "It is time, stranger, for you to go."

"Keep to the right above the marsh," advised the second.

"They have come out in quest of you," said the third.

I also had risen. I was no more to remain in the cottage. That was obvious. I made my way to the door, but, standing there, I turned for the purpose of thanking the sisters; but instantly the door was slammed in my face and I was shut out.

Presently I heard my name called. I saw lights. Then I was grasped by the hand, and Richards exclaimed:

"By the living Jingo! I thought never to see you again. How did you manage to escape?"

"I escaped in a strange fashion," I replied. "But of that on a future occasion. Hark!"

I heard the blast of the horn and the baying of hounds.

"Look," I cried, as I saw the Wild Hunt sweep over the moonlit side of a tor in mad career.

"I hear nothing and see nothing," said Richards.

"You must see—look yonder. Do you not see them?"

"See what?"

"Dewer and his pack."

"I see nothing but the broken shadows of clouds flying over the face of the moon. On my word, friend! Immersion in Crowdy Mire seems to have quickened your faculties to see and to hear what are unperceived by other eyes and ears."

"It may be so—it must be so," I said meditatively. "I have had strange experiences this night, such as are not given to other men."

1913

THE HILL

R. Ellis Roberts

Richard Ellis Roberts (1879–1953) collected his weird tales in 1923's *The Other End*, although such uncanny pursuits were something of a sideline for the writer. He was primarily a journalist and critic, eventually becoming the *New Stateman*'s literary editor in 1930. A self-described book-lover, Roberts wrote enthusiastically about his favourite authors, including those engaged with weird fiction. He held the pioneering Welsh author, Arthur Machen, in particularly high esteem. *The Other End* was well received upon publication, with the *Liverpool Daily Post* stating that "Mr Roberts is not content with the mere thrill of the strange and uncanny, though he gets that excellently, but rather rests his effect on the sense of the vital reality of these unrecognised powers, whose presence seems, indeed, less an intrusion upon our world than upon theirs." Our favourite story in the book, "The Hill", certainly chimes with this description.

Mark Valentine has identified the "Hill of Sacrifice" at the centre of the strange events in Roberts' tale as Colmer's Hill on the Symondsbury Estate in Dorset. An unusual, conical shape, it stands tall among rolling fields; as Roberts states, it "quarrelled vehemently with the rest of the landscape." The large Scots pine trees at the summit of Colmer's Hill are now part of its recognisable modern form, but would have been absent when Roberts' story was first published in the *English Review* in 1913, having been planted during the

First World War in remembrance of the fallen. Today, a permissive path leads you to Colmer's Hill from the Symondsbury Estate car park. It's a beautiful ramble, with views out to the sea from the hill's summit. But if a strange music starts up on your ascent, and the sky begins to darken, just mind how you go.

It was one of those hard, precise evenings when, before sunset, everything seems to become flat, the fields that lay just in front of me were cut out of cardboard, the long road down to Broad Oak appeared to stretch, not to the country, but to a backcloth; and the trees that overarched the lane to Symondsbury were untouched by any breeze that might give them the illusion of reality. For, when the country takes the decorative note, it is reality which is the illusion: one almost imperceptibly flattens oneself along the hedgerows in order to avoid breaking the perfect truth of the theatre which Nature contrives so much more skilfully than man.

I was tired and walked a little listlessly. I had business to do in Bridport; but I knew I should be there long before seven, and I enjoyed sauntering down the road, while the decadent sun of early April made green tinsel out of the budding larches, while soft little puddles of brown glowed from the ruts and hoofmarks in the sandy soil. I was feeling well in a genially tired way, and quite ready for the walk home again; feeling, however, singularly un-sharp. I mean that my senses, after the exertions of the week, were rather sleep-haunted—I had caught Nature's lesson, and felt all this activity of limb and thought to be the substance of nothing but a rather beautiful dream. My mind was as casual as my walk, and was occupied, so far as I remember, with nothing more arresting than some vaguely pleasant remembrance of a youthful affection.

THE HILL

I dwell on all this because I want to insist that I was not in an observant mood, not at all in the state to make the adventure I had likely. Those to whom I have told this story have all insisted that my "imagination" or "fancy" has made more of the facts than they warrant; that I was deceived by shadows, or misled by reflections; that my eyes were tired and played me tricks, that my memory is false and ill-suited to exact accuracy. So I would insist that such imagination as I have was almost quiescent, that my mind was singularly unalert, and that nothing can explain the extreme vividness of my recollection of that night of April 3rd, except the truth of what I saw. Its very incongruity, not only with my mental condition, but with the actual character of the evening, with the verdant artificiality of that Dorset springtime, when the countryside is rather less actual than the contour on an ordnance map, is a witness to the reality of that experience.

I had indeed forgotten the Hill. I generally used to look out for the first sight of it, when the road begins to run under the shoulder of the wooded height, and to skirt the Hill of Sacrifice. I don't know who gave it that name: whether, indeed, it is more than a modern device of some local journalist; but it suits the Hill. Everyone who passes along the main road from Chideock to Bridport must see it; but its most characteristic aspect is only caught from the road between North Chideock and Symondsbury. It is a curious, conical hill, covered with green grass and generally delivered over to innumerable sheep. It reminds one instantly of those high places on which the ancient Hebrews honoured other gods than Jehovah, the places where Solomon built temples for the family godlings of his heathen queens. Everyone felt this about the Hill, so it does not show any preoccupation of mine that I, too, always connected it with sacrifice, and the stone, square altars of the old faiths. I had never been up the Hill. I never met anyone who had. It was out of the way, and would be, though an easy, an unnecessary little climb for one whom Fleet Street had left without the wind of his youth. The sheep which grazed there belonged to a farm in the valley, and found their own way up and down.

Well, as I said, on that night I had forgotten the Hill; and when I caught my first glimpse of it, I had a shock. I thought at first the shock was due to the vision of a familiar but forgotten object. I think when one, so to speak, re-sees a perfectly familiar object, it has a more active and energising effect on the nerves than contact with something entirely new. Certainly the Hill made me jump. I stood and stared at it. As I stared I realised that the shock I had received was not entirely due to the Hill's re-assertion of its presence to my forgetful mind.

The Hill was different.

I glanced hastily back along the road, and over to my left where the fields stretched idly away; they were the same as they had been a minute ago, comfortable, artificial, flat, with no more atmosphere than a landscape in a modern painting. Then I swerved back to the Hill. It was ominous, alive, clamant with some mystery that I had not guessed. I should explain that though it was the Hill of Sacrifice, no one had associated it with anything mysterious or unusual. It was obviously the servant of some settled, rather courtly, religion, where the priests of the second-century Roman, journeying from Dorchester, had made polite augury at dawn. This evening, all that was changed. The Hill threatened. It quarrelled vehemently with the rest of the landscape. It stood like something or somebody naked and hairy in the middle of a crowd of modish and courtly figures; it was like some primitive, pre-Gothic idol in a French classical temple; or as if you sundered a picture of Watteau's with one of those brown, watchful Tahitians of Gauguin's.

THE HILL

I stood and stared at the Hill. And as I stared I became aware of two things. First, there were no sheep on the Hill. Their absence aided the strange, nude look of the thing. And I began to think that perhaps, after all, the change in the Hill was my fancy. Then, as I looked, the Hill lurched: that, of course, is an exaggeration; but it was the effect made on me by the movement of something that was almost up on the round crown at the top. With that movement the power of the Hill became active: suddenly and as by antagonism, I, too, leapt into mental alertness. The Hill and I were there, enemies, but akin in this, that we were the players in the set scene; still the green fields spread away to the backcloth; still the road ran as a stage road runs to the wings; still the sun, though now faintlier, flickered on green and brown, and turned them to paper and canvas—but now there were two lives on the stage, and the play was begun.

Before starting for the Hill—it is noteworthy that no other course but that of immediate access to my antagonist ever seemed possible—I looked at it once more, for I knew when I had scrambled through the hedge and across the first field, I should lose sight, for a while, of the top: I looked at the spot where the Hill had shuddered, and I saw that it was a figure, apparently human, and heavily burdened, which was now on the top and against the blue-black clouds which the sun was even now burning into angry gold. I was now much too far away—I have always suffered from short-sightedness—to make out clearly whether it was man or woman, or what it was that the figure carried; nor indeed did I greatly care, but I got through the hedge and started as quickly as I could for the summit of the Hill.

In the second field it was darker; and I felt that the atmosphere was a trifle oppressive; and there was a heavy, hot smell in the air, like musk. Of course, by now my imagination was at work; but I was not consciously inventing any explanation of what I saw or felt. I was simply bringing to bear on facts that were obtrusive all I had of perception and sensitiveness. I had not even then definitely decided whether what was abroad was evil or not. I knew it was an enemy—but it was inimical, at present, only in the sense of demanding effort and conflict. I could not proclaim that it was evil. As I climbed towards the lower slopes of the Hill, still hidden from view by a thick hedge, I was not conscious of any definite aim. I knew where I had to go; but I had no idea of what I should find, or what I should do. Just before I reached the final hedge something happened which removed all doubt as to the nature of that which I had to fight. Abruptly, and beginning on one long piercing note, a strange music clove the surrounding silence. After the first shrill rending of the evening's solitary quiet, the music went on with a wicked and luxuriant abandon that recalled to me all that I knew of the vague power of harmony for evil. It was not vulgarly lascivious or alluring; it had in it that higher note of defiance, that keener note of pride and power and of certain, though dishonourable, rule which distinguishes the realm of the devil from that of the world and the flesh. It had in it that perverse ascetic note, that strain of rapture and endeavour and adventure which the sons of Satan achieve no less than the sons of Christ. It gave out no single note of compromise or concession: it was music of the airless heights, of the wilderness, of the great wastes of sand, or the interminable vastness of evil waters where the greater devils meditate and morosely scheme.

When I heard it, all doubt dropped from me. There dropped, too, everything of the present. I knew the music: I knew, somehow, the player; and I knew his instrument. And as I went on up the Hill I knew what task lay before me, and with Whom I was to wrestle. I felt no fear and no confidence. No fear as to the terror or extent of the conflict, and no confidence as to the result. The whole incident, though still to come, seemed a part of my life, not something that I could do, or could not do, so much as something without which I would not be I.

When I was through the hedge the sun was set, but it was still quite light, and I hoped it would not be dark for almost another hour. I looked up to the top of the Hill, and there was the figure I had seen, kneeling and piling stones on one another. He—for it was a young lad—was half turned towards me; but he was stooping over his work, and evidently had no idea of my approach. The music, which was getting louder every moment, seemed to come from the top of the Hill; but I could see no signs of the player: nor, indeed, had I expected to.

I looked carefully to my stick, and wished it had been of some stouter wood than cherry; and then started rapidly up the Hill. As I went on the music altered in character: from defiance it passed to menace, and from menace to a curious thin anger that somehow seemed intended for other ears than mine. It was. The lad looked up, puzzled, and I saw him distinctly say something towards the sound of the music. Then he saw me, recognised me, I think, and started down the Hill. The music stopped.

I went on, and after a few minutes the lad and I met. We were both a little out of breath, and stood for a moment at gaze. He was a singularly beautiful boy, with one of those faces in which it is so hard to discover the lines which will afterwards coarsen and harden. He was about seventeen, and I remember that I had seen him working on some job between Allington and Eype. At the moment his beauty was almost unearthly: it had no intellectual qualities, and little of character, but just that even bloom which marks young animals. There was in his eyes, however, a look far from animal—a look of exultation, of absorption, and combined with it a hardness that showed me my task would not be easy. What he said was in curious contrast with his appearance, and in even odder discordance with what was in our hearts, and in the heart of the Hill, and in the heart of that old musician who this night, at least, was claiming the worship of his ancient altar.

"You be trespassing, Mr O'Brien."

"I suppose I am," I answered. "It's so jolly to be in a country where trespassing doesn't do any harm. It's why I like Dorset, and these great grazing fields."

He looked at me as the country folk do when they don't quite catch what you say, and yet don't want to confess to it.

"No one be allowed up here. I must ask you to go down again, sir."

His tone was very polite; but his eyes were set, and I saw his fingers twitching, and noticed the tremor of his shirt above his scurrying heart.

"Nonsense," I said. "I'm going to the top. Good night to you," and I started to get past him, rather hurriedly, and with little dignity, I am afraid.

With a sharp cry he stepped in front of me. Before he could say anything more, I spoke again, as sharply as I could—for I would have given anything just then to avoid the fight, and for the lad to go home—"What on earth are you doing, boy? You know perfectly well Mr Goodere doesn't mind where I go on his land. Besides, you have no business here: you are not in his employ, and I don't know that he would allow you here. Get out of my way."

For the moment my tone of ordinary annoyance staggered him. He became—for a minute—an ordinary good-looking lad who, through clumsiness, had offended "one of the gentry," and made a fool of himself. I kept hold on myself and waited to see him go away, apologetic and abashed. If this was the fight, I had feared unnecessarily. He began to turn on his heel, muttering some excuse, and I went on upwards, when suddenly the music began again, insistent, defiant, challenging. In a second he rushed round; and with hot, hurried words, clung to my arm, impeding my way—"I was not to go—he was meeting his girl—he wouldn't let me—he would break me if I did—he would—" lies, and appeals, and foul threats followed each other as swift as sin; his face once more took on that strange look of unearthly beauty, of curious exultation, as he asked me not to go up the Hill.

And the music played faster and faster.

After a struggle that lasted, I suppose, but for a few minutes, I broke away from him and ran towards the summit. All pretence was now thrown aside. The lad knew that I was aware of his purpose: knew that I knew Who his companion would be, and what that awful music meant, as it broke the evening quiet of the spring fields with a challenge older and more hideous than any voice of cities or of civilisation.

I got to the top of the Hill, with the lad close on my heels: and when I was at the top I realised suddenly that it was night. Not, I think, that the ordinary world was yet dark, but a mist, acrid and pungent, hung over the top of the Hill, and seemed to settle on the rude altar which the boy had built.

I could not see him, but I heard his breathing close on my right. I thought I would try one last chance to avoid the conflict—for now fear had entered my very marrow. "Come down," I said, trying to make my voice as self-possessed as possible and as ordinary, "Come down and I'll go too."

There was no answer but his quick breathing; and then on a note of the music he began to sing. When he sang there was little trace of Dorset in his speech, and his voice was a beautiful treble, that of a boy whose voice is going to break later than usual. What he sang I cannot put down here. It soared up in unimaginable wickedness, clear and pure as crystal, full of thoughts and words that we believe to have forsaken our world. The music adapted itself to his song and grew subtly and insolently wicked. The psalm of Satan rose up, invitatory, clarion, ascending to heights of sin that I did not know had ever been expressed in human words. The air grew hotter, and the mist glowed with a strange blurred light. The keen, acrid smell grew more intense, and the music shrieked more and more riotously, as though precluding some monstrous apocalypse.

Then, with no warning, there was silence.

I could hear nothing, not even my own breathing; and I could see nothing but the blurred glow that was, I judged, just over the altar. Then I heard a sound. It was a voice, but of an accent not human, and the words it spoke were not English. I remember how, even then, it struck me as odd that one should hear a voice in a Dorset field speaking in tones that belonged neither to the place nor to the age I lived in. It sounded very low, very sure, and very old; old not with any quavering, but with that sacerdotal certainty of age-long experience which people who are very old, or of a great tradition, so frequently possess. Yet any certainty I had caught in human voices seemed but a shadow beside the deep, awful solemnity of this utterance. The voice was magical, ecstatic, assured with an eternal assurance. I strained my ears to listen during the few seconds while the voice continued, but I could distinguish nothing except what I thought possibly was the syllable "Pai," and I wondered if the sentence was in Greek.

My senses by now were singularly acute: I had passed through fear into that strong, wine-glowing condition when one watches everything securely, oneself being external even to the dangers that are threatening one's body or soul. In this state, and in the boldness engendered by it, I took one step towards the glow that still shone over the altar. Long before I could approach, however, I was smitten—or rather not so much smitten as involved in a thick, palpable, and hideous atmosphere. Never have I been so submerged by anything external. The sensation was partly like that caused by a quicksand, which will wrestle with one's leg or arm as though the sand were endowed with life, and when one pulls out the endangered limb, it is as if one sprung out of some being's lively jaws. So with an automatic movement of repulsion, I leapt back and was released. Then the light glowed more brightly and I saw my companion. He was standing stark naked, with his arms outstretched like an Orante's on a Catacomb fresco. His lips were still moving, and his gaze fixed intently on the glow above the rude stones he had piled up. Every moment the glow increased; I was only just over three yards from the altar, but the glow gave no heat, neither was there any smoke. Then as the light grew, in the centre of it there appeared a figure, and yet not so much a figure as a face, nor so much a face as a presence. It had the same beauty, that intolerable and sinful beauty which the boy had; or rather it seemed to *be* that beauty. It was, however, never still, but passed with incredible rapidity from the expression of one sensation to that of another; it had that most singular quality which can occasionally be seen on earthly faces, a complete lack of unity—there was no central and availing character in which the details might inhere, and it was this lack which gave the Presence its extraordinary sense of wrongness, of wickedness, of sin. It is a vulgar comparison, but the mode of its loveliness, the mode of its very expression, reminded me of nothing so much as a cinematograph, that dreadful invention in which the mimicry of Life treads breathlessly and continuously on the heels of Life itself, and yet never attains it. The same absolute lack of peace, of joy, of truth, shone at me from the glow on the Hill of Symondsbury.

As I was looking, feeling numbed and rather sick from my effort to penetrate that infernal barrier which surrounded the altar, the boy stooped down and picked up something which had escaped my notice. When he stood up again I saw it was a spaniel which from the droop of its head was either drugged or dead—I guessed the former. Round its neck was a cord, and at the end of the cord a knife, whose blade glanced in the strange glow, gleaming uneasily in the shadow of the night. Carrying the spaniel the boy stepped forward. I waited anxiously. He, when he was within the circle of the light, not only appeared to feel no discomfort, but looked lighter, more at ease, supremely healthy. If it had not been for the look on his face, and the careless way he carried the dog, one would have judged him walking towards some celestial, instead of an infernal, revelation. As he approached the altar the Presence over it retreated, or rather ascended, and hovered, ominous, giving a sort of benison to what was going to be done.

For the strangest thing about that strange evening was not, perhaps, the events so much as my unhesitating acceptance of them. As I said, I was in no expectant mood when I first saw that movement on the Hill; yet I never doubted that what I saw on the Hill was an altar, never even questioned myself as to what the boy's purpose was, nor Whom it was he was going to worship: nor did he, in spite of the assumed ordinariness of our conversation, ever doubt that I was come to prevent his rites, if and how I could. Why this was, I leave to others; I have only to record the facts.

As he stepped up to the altar, I felt once more that I must take some action, I knew not what. It seemed useless to approach any nearer to the circle of the sacrifice, and it was evident I could do nothing with the boy except by force; and he had on his side powers greater than I had on mine... But, had he? Ashamed, I remembered my faith. Since this ghastly business had begun I had uttered no conscious prayer, taken no steps to set in motion that vast spiritual machinery which is on the side of beauty and holiness. I made quick, in my foolish flurry, to remedy my mistake. Hurriedly I scampered through an "Our Father" and "Hail Mary," and, making the Sign of the Cross, walked towards the altar. Once more I was sucked in—though this time with greater force—and it needed considerable effort, as well as natural revulsion, to pull myself out of the circle; and then I fell back on the clean, dark grass trembling with futile excitement.

As I stumbled out, the Presence laughed, and the boy echoed it. Anything more horrible in its perfection, more cruel in its note of absolute and casual conquest I never expect to hear. I felt not only beaten and baffled, but silly and childish; I felt as though some huge force had been not so much victorious, as possessive, over me. The boy knew, it seemed, that I could offer no resistance, let alone any active interference. Maddened by the laughter, I dashed once more towards the altar, and again was first absorbed and then, by the strong reaction of my body, flung out of the ring, weak and helpless. As I was thus beaten for a third time, the music began again.

This time it had lost its note of gay sinfulness, and was more ceremonial and evocative; but it still kept its undertone of essential vice; the grey of its formal progress was still marked by passages of scarlet and phrases of deep black. With the beginning of the music the boy stooped, laid the dog on the altar, untied the knife, and swiftly cut some string that bound its legs together. As he did so, either because the effect of the drug had passed off or because he touched the poor animal with the knife, the dog gave a little moan. I cannot hope to convey the effect on me of the dog's cry. Quite suddenly I felt that what I had to do was to save the dog. That possibly I should also have to struggle with the boy, and to fight that Presence which still hung over the altar and glowed in the darkness of the night; but that everything else was incidental to saving the dog.

The boy had now begun a new hymn, and this time he, too, used a language which was not English. Once again I stepped forward, and as I moved the dog shrieked loudly, horribly. I rushed forward, and in a moment was involved in the atmosphere of terror and power. This time, however, instead of fighting against it, I tried to ignore it, and simply kept in mind the fact that I must save the dog. I caught the boy's arm just as the knife was about to come down behind the animal's shoulder, and with a quick jerk twisted his wrist, so that the knife flew out of his hand. With a snarl of fury he turned on me—still ignoring him, I caught at the dog and rushed towards the darkness. Then something caught me: the glow buzzed like a million bees, the face of the Thing became altogether blurred with the rapidity of its changes, and loomed once more imminent and horrible. Hands that were not hands plucked at the spaniel, feet that were not feet tried to trip mine; whatever I caught changed and swelled and shrunk and changed until I found myself again and again digging my fingers into my own palms, or clutching in foiled futility at the thick, obscene air. The smell was now rank and poisonous, and though there was no heat I felt the sweat running down my brow. The boy had fallen, apparently in a fit, but still clung tightly to my ankles; and as I pushed and heaved and struggled through the light I dragged his body with me. At first, as I say, the Thing which was there had seemed to attack me; but after a moment this stopped, and, instead of any active attack, I had to contend with what felt like a crushing, inchoate and slime-covered mass. I was near the end of my resources, and there was still more than a yard and a half of that atrocious glow to get through. As I fought on, the dog in my arms moved, gave a little bark and snapped furiously at the air. Strangely enough, the effort of the animal gave me extra strength. I burst out of the clutch that was holding me, and, the dog still barking excitedly, fell exhausted but outside the light. As I fell, my head struck something cold and sharp, and I fainted away.

I woke in the morning to find a small spaniel anxiously licking my hand.

I sat up, and saw some farm-hands approaching with a hurdle. I feebly waved my hand, and noticed that it was covered with blood. My head ached intolerably, and I put up my hand to it and found my hair was caked with dried blood. Then on the ground I saw a knife, with blood on the blade. The men came up. "Are you better, Mr O'Brien?" "Yes, I'm all right," and I tried to struggle to my feet, but my head swam and I had to sit down again, rather ignominiously, on the ground.

"I shan't need that hurdle, I don't think—but thanks very much. How on earth did I—" Then I recollected what my last conscious experience had been, and I could still smell that acrid stench.

"How did'ee get here? Why, we don't know. Farmer Goodere's spaniel bitch brought us up here. She were in a terr'ble to do. Don't 'ee remember aught?"

I did: but nothing I could tell these men. I muttered something about having fallen against a stone; and they looked puzzled.

I got up again, and found I could stand.

Yes; there was the altar, or rather its ruins, for the stones had fallen. I began to walk along with the men, when I noticed some pebbles arranged rather curiously round the altar. I looked more closely at them—and spelled out in Greek letters the words ΠΑΝ, ΠΡΙΑΠΟΣ, ΑΠΟΛΛΩ; and then I knew under what titles the boy had come to sacrifice to Evil, and with Whom I had fought that night. I stooped and caressed the dog, who was frisking at my side in extravagant pleasure.

"'Ee must have a pup of hers, Mr O'Brien—she won't be long now," said one of the men.

That afternoon there was a caller—or rather two—at my cottage. My little maid came and told me that Mrs Toogood would like to see me, and a woman entered whom I knew well by sight. She was evidently in great distress. When she was a little calmer she told me how her boy—who had just begun work as a railway porter—had been rather odd lately, humming to himself, and looking, as she expressed it, "all overish." This morning she had gone to wake him, and found him looking dead white; no effort of hers could rouse him from a slumber that seemed deeper than natural. She made up her mind to send some excuse to the station, and ran round for the doctor. When he came the boy was awake. "He seemed, Mr O'Brien, to be a child again. He just put his arms round me and kissed me—which he hasn't done for three weeks—but he can't speak."

"Can't speak," I echoed.

"Not a word," she sobbed. "The doctor says he's had a shock." Here she broke down again and wept.

I sat wondering. "I suppose, Mrs Toogood, you don't know whether he was out last night?"

"Out? No, sir. I still go up and see him after he's in bed—and he was in at half after nine. He was very curious, though, and didn't say a word to me, though I knew he was awake."

THE HILL

"Ah! but earlier in the evening—about sunset?"

"No, sir. He was home to supper, though he didn't eat a bit and wouldn't speak a word. But it's this morning, sir. Though he's so kind and nice and happy, he had such odd ideas. He got a slate and wrote on it, 'I belong to Mr O'Brien'—"

"What," I said—"I belong—!"

"Yes, sir; that's what I'm telling you. And the doctor said we mustn't excite him, though he doesn't get annoyed like he used; and so I've brought him up here. I thought you might help me, sir."

"Where is he?"

"Outside, sir." She rose eagerly. "May I have him in?"

"Yes," I answered.

In a minute she was back with her son. There was no doubt about it. It was the same boy. He was not less beautiful than I had thought; but this morning there was nothing sinister or evil about his beauty. He saw me and then, with a grace very rare in an English boy, knelt and kissed my hand. I hastily drew it away, and asked him—

"What do you want?"

With a smile that was quite jolly and boylike, he darted into a corner, where there was a pair of old boots of mine, and went through the motions of polishing them. Then looked, first at me, then at his mother, with an air of plaintive request.

Well, after some discussion that lasted longer than it needed, the boy became my servant. He was perfectly sane, though more childlike than most country boys. He has never recovered his voice, but is so quick that one hardly realises his dumbness. I can give no explanation of how he was on the Hill of Sacrifice at the same time that he was at home eating his supper; but would suggest that there is more than modern incredulity will admit in those old stories of the Sabbath when demons assumed the places of men and women who were temporarily absent from their homes, entangled in the lures of the Devil.

Farmer Goodere had to give me, not a puppy, but Jessie herself: for she ran to my cottage that evening, and has lived with me ever since.

1919

THE GARDEN THAT WAS DESOLATE

Ulric Daubeny

Ulric Daubeny (1888–1922) published his only volume of fiction in 1919, three years before his tragic early death at the age of 34. Aside from one other known supernatural tale, *The Elemental* contains all of his weird fiction, including his most read story, "The Sumach", a botanical spin on the vampire legend. An academic who wrote on the history of woodwind instruments and Cotswold churches (worthy Jamesian enterprises both), Daubeny drew on his knowledge of the Cotswolds for "The Garden That Was Desolate". Here, Philip Cranham (perhaps named for the Gloucestershire village close to the story's setting) is walking between the "Cotswold eyrie" of Birdlip and the "forgotten town of Painswick" when he stumbles upon Ralf Cook and his strange walled garden. What, or who, could such high walls be keeping out?

Today, a walking route between Birdlip and Painswick forms part of the Cotswold Way, one of Britain's most idyllic long-distance trails. From Birdlip the path winds through beech woods and past Great Witcombe Roman Villa, before visiting Cooper's Hill, the terrifying descent at the heart of the famous cheese-rolling event held every spring bank holiday. The whole Cotswold Way follows the Cotswold Edge escarpment mentioned by Daubeny, and provides the walker with wonderful panoramas. However, if the tale of Ralf Cook is anything to go by, it's perhaps best not to become too enchanted by the view.

The country to the south of Birdlip, a Cotswold eyrie close on Roman Ermine Street, is, if scarcely wild, at least bleak, austere, and sparsely populated. It is a region of prehistoric burial mounds, of straggling British trackways, of Roman roads, Norman churches, ancient farm buildings, ruinous cottages; a drywall country, sharply undulating, its bleak downs relieved by occasional secretive woods of larch or beech. In striking contrast is the Cotswold "Edge", a precipitous drop of several hundred feet into the fertile Severn Valley, where a kaleidoscopic vista of irregularly shaped and parti-coloured fields spreads out in a level tract, for a distance of some thirty miles. Close to Birdlip, the high-road skirts this "edge", and there, for the space of several minutes, Philip Cranham lingered, watching the play of sunlight over the jagged chine of Malvern, pale and beautiful in the shimmering distance.

"What a position for a house!" he mused, turning reluctantly, and continuing at a brisk walk, for the air on these heights is chilly, even towards the end of June. His way bore to the south-west, in the direction of the forgotten town of Painswick, which was to be the last stage of his tour.

A lover of the unconventional in walking, Philip deserted the usual high road through the woods, striking across a strip of common, and over several fields, until he met a narrow lane, which promised to lead him in the right direction. Deeply rutted by former traffic, it was long since grass-grown, scattered with mossy boulders, and enclosed on either side by a straggling bramble hedge. A veritable picture of desolation, thought Philip, glancing uneasily at the approaching heavy clouds, for the tremulous mutter of thunder had assailed his ears, and he looked in vain for a place of shelter. This was an upper rampart of the Cotswolds, a ridge bleak and desolate, set apart from all things hospitable, where there was no course but to throw one's weight against the wind, and face the threatened downpour. The lane, overgrown and serrulated, continued for some distance until, quite unexpectedly, the hedge was succeeded by a wall, dry-built as is the custom of the district, and strengthened by a massive cornice. Philip marvelled at its height, for it stood at least twelve feet; it looked to be of recent building, and still retained that bright, cream colour, peculiar to the local limestone, when freshly dug. Near the middle, the wall was broken by a gateway, flanked by massive pillars, on which hung double doors, palpably amateurish in construction. One of these had been unhooked, and dragged into the enclosure, where an elderly man was busy strengthening it with pieces of rough timber.

"'Afternoon!" he volunteered, after a nervous scrutiny of Philip, who had come to a halt before the gateway. "Going to have a storm!"

He needed to be no prophet, for already great, bloated drops of rain were falling, heralded by a resounding clap of thunder. Philip cast an apprehensive glance skywards, and commenced to unstrap his mackintosh.

"Yes. We are in for it," he agreed, with the pointed addition, "Unpleasantly exposed, up here. Not even a decently thick hedge to shelter under!"

There was a noticeable hesitation before the stranger answered, and when he did, it was with a certain shy reluctance.

"Come inside. You can shelter in my room, until the rain stops."

Philip required no second bidding. Half-a-dozen steps, and he was viewing an extensive garden, consisting first of a rough lawn, backed by currant and gooseberry bushes, young fruit trees, a yew hedge industriously trimmed, and then divers beds and footpaths, disappearing over the sloping hillside. Signs of any habitable building, there were none.

"Come along!" enjoined the stranger, advancing hastily across the spacious lawn. "I live over there, in the look-out post."

For the first time, Philip noticed, built against and forming part of the left-hand boundary wall, a kind of miniature watch-tower, with pyramidal stone roof, terminated by a central chimney. A flight of steps led them to the doorway, for the place was built upon a mound, with floor-level half way up, and sloping roof considerably above the wall. Within there was a single room, possibly twelve feet square, having a fireplace in one corner, a narrow window cut through the outer wall, and another, a very large one, facing down the garden, and over the lovely Vale of Severn.

"What a glorious view!" exclaimed Philip, despite himself.

"Damned view! Damned view! Wish I had never set eyes upon it!"

Philip turned in open-mouthed astonishment, but his companion paid no heed, though he continued in a quieter tone.

"I am a slave to that view. I can sit, and look at it for hours. I worship it—yet all the while I hate it!... Like to hear the story of all this?"

With rather an abandoned gesture, he swept his hand about, to indicate the tiny house, the garden, and the towering outer walls.

"I should like to know why there are immensely high walls on three sides—or rather, two, for the third is incomplete—and yet—"

"To keep out undesirables, my dear Sir; to keep out undesirables!" interrupted the stranger, with uncontrolled impatience. "The walls and the tall gates, which I am busy strengthening."

"But—excuse me," continued Philip, obstinately bent on satisfying his curiosity, "the third wall, as I say, is but partially built, while no barrier of any kind protects the bottom of the garden!"

A long silence ensued, broken only by the drumming of the rain upon the unceiled roof, and an occasional echoing burst of thunder. Philip lounged thoughtfully near the open window, while his companion stood irresolute, chewing at his moustache, and with close-knit brows, as if striving to recapture some elusive or forgotten memory. Presently his expression cleared, and as quickly changed to one of crafty eagerness.

"Come, come, Sir. Come, come! You cannot expect everything, *all* at once! Do you know, every stone of those walls—yes, even of this house—I built myself?"

Philip nodded encouragingly. At times the man seemed sane enough, and yet he was decidedly peculiar.

"The reason for all this," he continued, repeating the gesture which embraced the whole of the surroundings, and ended with the larger window. "The reason of it all, is that. The view. More than seven years ago, I camped here, while on a holiday from London. After all the noise and smoke and racket, this place seemed like Paradise; and the view—I simply could not tear myself away! It ended in my purchasing the land, for I had determined to erect a house here. There was some trouble with a woman, who held part as an allotment, and claimed the place as hers, but she could produce no legal title, so the lawyer and I bundled her out, between us. Vindictive old harridan, she was—"

He ceased abruptly, creeping across to the rickety door, which he slowly opened, and after a stealthy glance around, closed, with an exclamation of relief. Philip watched narrowly. The manner was so ridiculously furtive as to point without a doubt to lunacy; it was becoming distinctly creepy, this sheltering from a thunderstorm, in the cottage of a maniac!

"Where was I?" the man resumed, seating himself by the empty fireplace. "What? Ah, yes! I had determined, as you say, to build a house here. Seven years ago, it was, this very day, that half-a-dozen labourers commenced to turn the sods, for the foundations. A month later I was all alone. Nobody would work for me, though I had men up from Stroud, Gloucester, Cheltenham, finally from London. Will you credit me, when I tell you that the beastly old hag who claimed the place had frightened 'em all away? I admit that there were several distressing accidents. The first day, a man was bitten by an adder, and another crushed beneath a heavy stone-cart. The Cheltenham foreman tripped up in a rabbit hole, and broke a leg, and his successor suddenly went mad, but—Fools! Idiots! They actually believed the crude tales of the country folk, who said that the ranting old woman was a witch! They took to their heels, and ran, the dirty cowards!"

"What happened after that?"

"They left me, to build the house as best I might; and build it, I swore I would, in face of Beelzebub! Witch or no witch, she did not frighten me, though often enough she came and threatened; yes, cursed and threatened... So I started right away, to build the highest wall I could, to keep her out!"

"Has it taken seven years to do all this?"

"Yes. I could only build at intervals, for the garden had to be planted, and I practically live on its contents. In two years' time, I hope to have the defensive walls completed, and then the ill-omened old faggot will be shut out from my property for ever!"

"But, pardon me once more," insisted Philip, bent on settling the question of the stranger's sanity. "Why did you not run up a medium wall all round, sufficient to exclude unwelcome visitors, and then raise and strengthen it at your leisure?"

The recluse made no reply. Instead, he sprang towards the door, tore it open, and halted on the threshold, quivering with rage. Facing him was a wizened, bent old woman, clad in an assortment of dirty rags, leaning heavily upon a stick. Her face was stained and wrinkled like a winter walnut, and inexpressibly malignant was the look that shot from beneath the overhanging eyebrows.

"What is it, you old devil?" choked the man, his voice pitched high in apprehension. "Why do you stand gibbering at me like that?"

She made no immediate answer, but pointing a skinny talon, uttered a husky chuckle.

"Ha, ha! Ralf Cook! What did I tell 'ee? What did I tell 'ee, these seven years agone?"

"Stand back there. Stand back. Don't you dare to molest me, woman!"

"Why don't ye answer, Ralf Cook? Is it that ye are afeard, or can it be that ye don't remember? Seven years I gev thee; seven years, I said, and then—Are ye leavin', Ralf Cook, leavin' here this very day?"

"No, you old fool! You won't frighten me by your threats and curses. I bought this land, and paid for it, and—by glory!—I mean to stay here, in face of you or anybody!"

"Then, Ralf Cook, by all the Powers—"

Her arms were raised in vehement imprecation, but before the words could leave her lips, the man had dealt her a smashing blow across the face. She swayed helplessly for a moment, and then staggered backwards, falling heavily to the ground. A sudden vivid flash of lightning transfixed the two men, but as the echoes of the thunder died away, Philip pushed through the open doorway, and bounded down the steps. One glance was sufficient to convince him that the old woman's neck was broken. Awestricken by the sight, he looked back, to meet a pair of fiend's eyes, madman's eyes—homicidal maniac's eyes. Then blank, unreasoning panic overtook him; he fled blindly, in his terror taking what appeared to be a different route across the garden. Here the grass grew rank, a yew hedge was pitifully unkempt, the fruit trees were old and straggling, the pathway all but indistinguishable. At last the boundary wall: but it was stained by the flight of many winters, and near a crumbling gateway lay one wooden door, rotting amid the weeds, while the other hung perilously upon its rusted hinges. When at last he checked his pace, Philip found himself in the grass-grown lane, and on looking back, felt relieved that the walls of the accursed garden were no longer visible.

With the memory so fresh upon him, Philip's judgment lost its normal balance. To witness, perhaps in some measure to be a mute accomplice in the murder of an old woman by a maniac, might well upset the strongest nerves, and he could not forget that his own life must have hung in fearful jeopardy. So alarming was the thought of giving evidence in the witness-box, that by the time Philip had reached Painswick, he was fully determined to say no word to the police. Instead, he gave himself to headlong flight, catching the late motor bus to Stroud, and the evening train to London. Months went by, but although he kept in anxious touch with local news, no hint came that the murder had been detected. At times Philip suffered considerable pangs of conscience, and on more than one occasion he was on the point of going to the police, only to be deterred by the anticipation of considerable official censure, for so long concealing knowledge of the crime. Later, his engagement, and then the happiness of marriage put a period to further vain recriminations, but the memory of that awful afternoon, a secret even from his wife, was seldom from him.

Two years passed before he again set foot in Cotswold, this time with his wife and sister, viewing the romantic beauty of the district from a comfortable motor. It had been entirely Philip's proposition, this re-visiting of scenes with which he had been familiar since his youth, and if the suggestion had not entirely sprung from sentiment, the other reason was such that he refused to admit it, even to himself.

It fell out that they stayed a while at Painswick, and then it was that Philip, throwing further self-deception to the winds, determined to satisfy his pent-up curiosity. Explaining that he wished to make enquiries of an old acquaintance, they one day motored over, approaching the garden from the direction by which he had so precipitately left it. A passable road led past the entrance to the grass-grown lane, and there, near a cottage, they drew up. Philip, in a happy moment of inspiration, crossed to the cottage, with a view to making some discreet enquiries.

A typical Cotswold woman answered to his knock, tanned and healthy, but prematurely grey.

"Good afternoon," he greeted her. "Can you tell me anything about the house—that is, the garden up the lane? Mr Ralf Cook, I think, was the owner's name," he added, seeing that the woman preserved a stolid silence.

"I'll ask father to come," she answered, regarding him with questioning eyes. "Will you step inside, Sir?"

Philip followed into the neatly furnished parlour, and was presently joined by a corduroyed rustic, very old and lame.

"Ralf Cook?" repeated the latter, on becoming acquainted with the business. "Yes, zur, I can tell 'ee zurnmat about he, to be zure I can. Ralf Cook, o' Cook's Folly, we called un; ay, and fule he were right 'nough, when he tried to be upsides o' Mother Gaskin! 'T'were a bad day for he when he went up theere, zur, an' no mistake, not but what I allus said as how—"

"Is the building complete?" ventured Philip, breaking in upon the old fellow's ponderous garrulity. "Are the walls finished?"

"Nowe, o' coourse not. *She* seed to that, bless ye! Why, I can yet mind the day, zur, when he began a-buildin. Six men he brought wi' un, and what o' that? One were crushed beneath a waggin, 'nother broke his leg, the foreman—"

"Yes. Yes. I know about that. What I really wanted to ask was, of Mr Cook himself. Is he still living there?"

The old man glared at Philip in open-mouthed astonishment.

"*Still theere?*" he at last gasped. "Lor' sakes, an' he old 'nough to be my own feyther when he came, mor'n forty years back!"

"What do you mean? Forty years! Mr Cook told me that he had been there about seven."

"He—he *towld you?*"

"Yes. Don't you understand? I was here the summer before last, and had a long conversation with him."

Instead of making a direct reply, the old man shuffled to the door, and called his daughter. His voice was distinctly tremulous, when he began to question her.

"Polly. Can ye mind the time when Ralf Cook were a-livin' up at the Folly?"

"Why, no, father," she replied, obviously puzzled. "You know, I wasn't born then. Not till several years later."

"Ah, ye be thirty-vour, now, baint ye? This here gen'leman—but no matter, Polly. Ye can run along!"

Left alone, the two men regarded each other in moody silence.

"What became of him?" asked Philip presently.

"Hung 'isself—leastways so t'were said, but people do hold as how Mother Gaskin did it vur un. She allus was a rum un, was Mother Gaskin. Folks don't rightly know what became o' her, though some vows she went off a-ridin' upon her broomstick, and got took up inter the moon. O' course that bain't rightly possible, leastways, not to my way o' thinkin'."

There was no more to be learnt, so Philip, curiously unconvinced, hurried back towards the motor. This was empty, and realising that the girls had wandered off alone, he decided to seize the opportunity, and put an end to further doubt by private personal investigation. Accordingly he set off up the lane, ruminating all the while on the extraordinary tales he had just heard. Could the old man have been weak-witted, and was he backed up by his daughter merely to preserve appearances before a stranger? It seemed quite probable, more probable than that he must disbelieve the evidence of his own senses. Yes, of course, how could he have doubted! There, ahead of him, stood the garden wall, bright and new looking, and the massive, dry-built gateway, with one door still unhooked! A few steps more, and he had come to a standstill before the familiar entrance.

"'Afternoon!" greeted an elderly man, who was at work mending the dismantled gate with pieces of odd timber. "Going to have a storm!"

A heavy echo of thunder came, as if to confirm his supposition, and then the rain began to fall, in isolated, swollen drops.

"Yes, we are in for it!" Philip found himself repeating, as a person in a dream. "Unpleasantly exposed up here. Not even—"

Then he was running, racing madly away from the accursed spot. Horror in its most primitive form pursued him, and he fled until, soaked with perspiration and painfully short of breath, he found himself clambering on board the waiting motor. Presently his wife and sister came into view, approaching from the entrance to the grass-grown lane. Both were somewhat breathless, and a trifle pale.

"Oh, Philip!" the former panted, as soon as they had reached the motor. "We've found such a horrid place! Joyce suggested walking up that lane, just to see where it led, and we came across a kind of deserted garden, surrounded by enormous walls. They looked old and dilapidated, and there was a tumbled-down gateway—Oh, all so sad and dreary. Everything inside was wild, and overgrown, and there was a curious little house, built against the wall, which looked as if it had not been touched for years.

"Suddenly, as we were wandering around, we both had an impression that somebody was watching us. I don't know why, but it quite gave us the horrors, and we simply had to run—What is the matter, dear? You look quite ill!"

"Oh, nothing. Perhaps the thunder. It was quite a heavy clap."

"When? We heard nothing! Have you seen your friend?"

"Yes—No, I mean. He has left this neighbourhood. Shall we be making a move homewards?"

1920

THE MYSTIC TUNE

Marie Corelli

The English novelist Marie Corelli (1855–1924) was a powerhouse of late-nineteenth and early-twentieth-century literature. Although sneered at by Victorian and Edwardian critics, her books regularly outsold those of her lauded (and often male) contemporaries, and she was admired by figures as diverse as Oscar Wilde and Queen Victoria. Corelli's popular tales, such as those collected in *The Love of Long Ago and Other Stories* (1920), often combined occult, mystical elements, including reincarnation and clairvoyance, with a moralistic flavour and an ornate style. A flamboyant, eccentric character, she was known to enjoy boating in an imported Venetian gondola near her home in Stratford-upon-Avon, whose historic buildings she campaigned to preserve in her later years.

On an unnamed island among the Outer Hebrides, Corelli's wanderer in "The Mystic Tune" is drawn towards the haunting sound of a violin in a seemingly empty landscape. This is a place of mist-crowned hills and rose-purple heather, certainly not unlike the area around Gearrannan Blackhouse Village on the Isle of Lewis. The restored crofting township features cottages similar to that described by Corelli in her tale. With the awe-inspiring Calanais Standing Stones nearby, there is some excellent walking in the area—perfect in late summer with the heather in bloom.

There are certain parts of the Western Hebrides where one may walk for many miles without meeting a human being save, possibly, a solitary shepherd or belated fisherman tramping slowly homeward to some village hidden among the mist-crowned hills. It is easy to lose one's way but more than difficult to find it, especially if, as is often the case, the eyes of the mind become bewildered by the weird and almost tragic beauty of the natural scenery. The very ability to think is, in a sense, hypnotised out of practical considerations into a passive state of dreamy sufferance. In such a condition one may wander far, almost unconscious of time or distance—and so it chanced to me one late summer evening, when, after a day of persistent rain and drifting mist, the clouds suddenly cleared and the heavens seemed, as it were, torn open to display a wild glory of scarlet and gold flaring round the sinking sun. I found myself on the slope of a hill crowned with heather, glowing rose-purple in all the light flung broadcast by the western clearing of the sky—and all suddenly, as I stood watching the vibrating splendour, I heard the distant sound of a violin. The plaintive wail of the strings shivered through the air like the cry of a bird wounded in its flight, and I listened with a sense of pain that was akin to fear. For there was no one in sight—all the land lay bare and gleaming wet in the sunset glow, and on the sea there loomed a darkness of angry shadows contesting with broken teeth of white foam; but there was not a boat returning from the herring fishing, and not a sign of any habitation from which the call of the quivering strings could come. Still listening intently, I heard the music take a richer form—a tune of exquisite sweetness and irresistible appeal unfolded itself on the air like the petals of a flower, and its beauty enthralled me. I could not stay there on the hill and allow so divine and haunting a melody to escape me—I resolved that I must follow it and find the player. With this impulse upon me I ran down the hill, and still continued running for a time, the magic tune still sounding and going on before me as a guide, though I knew not, and thought not, as to where it might lead me. The sun was slowly sinking, and I felt that soon I might be more a lost wanderer than before if darkness fell before I could discover any shelter—but the Tune called me on, and its irresistible, melancholy sweetness filled my soul, leaving no room for prudence concerning my own personal guidance or safety. Breathless with running, I presently slackened my heedless pace through the wet heather which tangled itself about my feet, and contented myself with a steady rapidity of walking, which brought me to a narrow path winding across a moor. Here the Tune seemed to grow louder and more persistent, and though I now began to think it was a fantastic illusion of sound in my own imagination I still went on, impelled almost unconsciously. All at once I perceived a small dull light twinkling microscopically among the gathering evening shadows, and making my way toward it, I came close upon a crofter's cottage, set by itself, as it were, in a wilderness—the twinkling light gleaming like an eye from one opening of either a window or a door. As I quickened my steps and drew nearer the Tune came out, as it seemed, to meet me—it stretched its beautiful arms of melody forth to embrace and draw me to itself, and in the dying flares of the sunset I found I had reached my goal.

The figure of a man, dimly silhouetted against the wall of the cottage, gradually took shape—a man, playing a violin of exquisite tone and power—such an instrument as any connoisseur would at once have envied. I checked myself in my hurried walk, and only ventured on, step by step, till I came within a few feet of the mysterious player who continued playing the same mysterious tune. There was still enough light in the sunset sky for us to see each other, and as I approached he looked at me without any apparent surprise or curiosity, drawing his bow across the strings with steady tenderness and purity. He had not the appearance of a native of the country—he wore the clothes of a man accustomed to cities and social observances, and his slim, well-poised figure gave an impression of athletic force and symmetry. I longed to speak—to ask if I might take shelter in the cottage, or haply find a guide to show me the way back to the village my walk had left so far behind me, but I dared not break the flowing of the Tune! All at once a voice, low and penetrating, spoke to me across the swaying melody—

"When she is asleep I will come to you."

I could not understand this, but was content to wait, and gradually my eyes, becoming accustomed to the shadows gathered round and about the cottage, were able to see a little through the open door. There, by the glimmering embers of a peat fire, sat a woman, deeply sunk in an armchair, her feet supported on a wooden stool, and her hands moving up and down rhythmically were beating mechanical time to the Tune. I could not discern her features, but she seemed old and feeble, and the hands that never ceased their swaying motion were ghostly thin and spectral. I drew a few steps nearer the door and looked in more closely. There was something desolate and unearthly about that huddled figure—an embodied hopelessness, a helpless pitifulness, that chilled my blood and filled me with awe as well as compassion—surely, thought I, here was a human wreck cast aside and left to be broken up by the tide of cruel circumstance and yet—the Tune! Like a living thing of tenderest sympathy it caressed all the air round that lonely and aged creature, giving light as it were to the deepening darkness, and speaking in soft accents of wordless rhythm which suggested a speech higher than human; and while I waited, leaning against the open door and listening, a long, shivering sigh came breathing out on the air, and a faint wailing voice murmured—

"He does not sing it as he used to sing! There is something gone—gone—gone!"

The spectral old hands waved beseechingly and then fell inert. The Tune, hovering in the evening mists like a winged creature, paused, and seemed to tremble—then went on softly, and yet more softly, while the player moved out of the shadows and, still playing, came to the door of the cottage and looked in. Watchfully he studied the huddled figure in the chair, drawing the bow delicately across the strings of his violin till the weary head fell back—then, with another long sigh of exhaustion, all movement ceased in a sleep that resembled more of a swoon than slumber. The player ceased, and the sudden silence in the darkening evening created a sense of such weird emptiness and desolation that it was almost unbearable. My eyes filled with tears, and I hesitated to speak. The man with the violin addressed me.

"You have missed your way?" he asked, gently. "I am sorry to have been so long without speaking to you, but I could not interrupt the Tune till she slept."

He waited, but still I could say nothing. He flicked a string or two of the violin with one finger half mechanically, and presently went on—

"She lost her grandson in the war—he was a friend of mine. And he was all she had—a bright, handsome lad of great musical genius. The tune I played was his favourite tune—it is a very old Gaelic melody. He used to whistle it, and above all, to sing it in a voice that would have made his fortune had he ever had the chance. He went out to Flanders as a gunner, and the very first day he took the field he was killed—just blown to bits like a handful of paper. She could never understand it. She does not believe he is dead. Since the armistice I have visited her regularly—she is all alone except for one woman of the moorlands who looks after her. All she cares for is the Tune. I play it for her whenever I can."

"And you," I said at last, "you are no relation?"

"No. I am a violinist by profession—I play in Paris, London, Berlin—you may have heard my name."

He gave that name—one of the greatest renown in the European musical world.

"Oh!" I exclaimed. "*You* are that wonderful genius! *You*—"

He deprecated my enthusiasm by a slight wave of the hand.

"Not at all!" he said. "I am no genius, for I cannot even play the tune as *he* sang it!" He bent toward the sad and aged figure in the chair. "Yes, she is fast asleep now," he continued. "And so she will forget—for a time! I have a professional engagement in Glasgow, and as long as it lasts, I shall come and play to her in all my spare hours. It is the only thing I can do for *his* sake!" He paused, then laid the violin down on a chair with the bow beside it. "Let me show you the way across the moor—you must have missed the direct path."

"I followed the Tune!" I said. "It seemed to *pull* me toward it!"

He smiled gravely.

"Yes? I am not surprised. It is a wonderful tune. It had its birth in the past, among the Highland bards of old, and no doubt it is weighted with many memories. But this last one is as poignant as any—glorious and hopeful youth struck down by the devilish wickedness of war, leaving helpless old age desolate and broken-hearted. The governments of this world have much to answer for—the Tune could tell them that its sorrow is only one of millions!"

We had walked away from the hut, and my companion put me on the straight road where I could see in the deepening shadows the twinkling lights of the little wayside hotel I had strayed from. I held out my hand, which he pressed warmly and kindly.

"When I hear you play again at Queen's Hall," I said, "I shall know your heart is even greater than your genius! I shall think of your goodness and sympathy for this poor, lonely old woman, and whatever you play, whether it be of Beethoven or any other great composer, I shall feel that the Tune is your real masterpiece!"

"The only masterpiece that is never mastered!" he replied, gently, with a smile. "For it has the soul of the dead in its melody, and however well I may try to play it, I fail!—for she will always say it is not as *he* sang it!"

1920

THE WIND IN THE WOODS

Bessie Kyffin-Taylor

Bessie Kyffin-Taylor (1880–1922) remains a relatively obscure figure in the history of the weird tale, but her 1920 collection, *From Out of the Silence*, contains some real gems. "The Wind in the Woods" develops in the vein of several of E. F. Benson's "spook stories"—a traumatic event leaves its sinister imprint upon the environment and somehow resonates into the present.

The tale takes place in Wales, with our narrator telling us only that its location is a "very well-known district, within only an hour's journey from a large manufacturing town", with hills "high enough to lift one up from life's little worries, but not high enough to be awe-inspiring". If Merthyr Tydfil, once the "iron capital of the world", fits the bill for the manufacturing town, then perhaps the story's hills now lie somewhere within the Bannau Brycheiniog (Brecon Beacons) National Park, which covers some 520 square miles of South and Mid Wales.

There are many places to experience "Silent Wood" vibes in the national park—large, non-native conifer plantations were once thought ideal for the banks of the area's reservoirs and unpromising agricultural land. Several of these forested spots now feature walking trails, although future generations may see fewer conifers, the tide having happily turned from planting mute, monocultural blocks to restoring and expanding native woodland.

To say I was an artist would be giving myself too high-sounding a name, yet my days were spent in trying, and at times succeeding, in depicting scenes as I saw them—not people! I never attempted portraits, for the expression on human faces more often irritated me, than interested—every nine out of ten wore such a worried, harassed look, as if, in the race for gain, or pleasure, they had lost sight of all things conducive to rest or repose; I had no wish to paint such things, nor did I wish them to come and pose in their best garments, with a smile such as one and all would, I knew, adopt.

Fortunately for me, I was not dependent upon my efforts with brush and pencil, though I confess I made quite a nice income by them; but it was always joy to me to remember, if I did not want to paint, I need not, for my meals were forthcoming, whether I made the price of them or not.

I was the owner of a charming flat in London. This was my anchorage, and here I was looked after and cared for by an old family servant, a woman well on in years, who had been for long years a faithful friend and servant in my family, and now, in her later years, had constituted herself my factotum, ruling my small domain, and incidentally myself, with a firm hand, never by any chance seeming to realise that I really was grown up, but bestowing the same thought upon the changing of my socks on a wet day as she had done when I was nine or ten. Her name was "Merry"—Mrs Merry. As children, we had all adored her; as a middle-aged man, I respected and looked up to her, glad to ask and take her wise advice on many issues of the day.

Mrs Merry was well used to my vagabondish ways, though at times she was wont to say I should be much happier if I married and settled down! I always laughed at her, for my only love-story was buried fathoms deep in the dust-heap of forgotten things; and the very words "settle down" sent a cold shiver down my spine—it, the "settling down" process, would mean a wholesale giving up of all those ways I held so dear. No more sudden trêkings at a moment's notice, or coming home any day or any hour, as sure of welcome as I was sure of being safe from questions as to my doings. Mrs Merry *never* questioned, though she was always delighted when told where I had been, or what I had done. Sometimes I had sketches to show to her, but as often I had none; in either case, she was convinced of my talent and ability, and her faith and loyalty never wavered.

It was early in July when a sudden desire for trees, rivers, and growing things caused me to drop the work I was on, call Mrs Merry, and request a small Gladstone bag should be packed as quickly as possible, that I was going away. The old lady looked at me keenly, remarking—

"You don't look ill!"

I laughed.

"Nor am I," I said; "but it is hot in the town; also, I feel as if I must see trees instead of people for a while."

"That will mean strong boots and knickers, I suppose, sir?" was her next remark.

"Yes, Merry, dear, it will; also plenty of pipes, baccy, books, and a stick. I may paint, or I may not; in any case, expect me back a month from tomorrow, for sure, unless I send you word; and if you don't hear, why then," I added, laughing—"some one had better begin to look for me."

"I do wish you would settle down, Mr Wilfred," was the old dame's parting shot, as she went out to do my behests.

Settle down, I mused, filling a much-used old briar, never, now, though my thoughts went back to those days of joy, when I and a sweet-faced girl with dark eyes and a little fair head just reaching to my shoulder, talked in twilight hours of a home that was to be. If she had passed to the "Great Beyond," I could have borne it better than the tale of treachery and cunning, which ended in my dark-eyed love leaving me on the morning, which should have been my wedding-day, merely announcing, by wire, that she had married my best chum, Kirk Compton, in London, that morning.

Trouble of that kind takes one of two lines, it either sends a man, or woman, to the bad—that is, to drink, gambling—anything of a wild, riotous kind of existence to, as they think, help them to forget—or it sends them into themselves, to more or less live a life of solitude, finding companionship in books or hobbies, fearful of making friends, lest they, too, should prove unfaithful; one's faith in goodness shattered, it is years, if ever, before one comes into one's own, realising that there is infinitely more in life than the shallow so-called love of one girl. And so, as I was not addicted to drink or cards, I became a recluse, or almost. I had a few friends, was voted a good chap, but a cynic, and gradually left to my own devices. I was happy as the years went on, finding my books and work all sufficient, while my fervent love of nature proved the healing of my sore, and I was content.

July 20th stared me in the face from a large lettered calendar, as I woke for my early cup of tea, on the day I was starting for a whole month, somewhere in Wales.

THE WIND IN THE WOODS

There is not any object in making a mystery of my destination, except the small fact that my chosen haunt was a very well-known district, within only an hour's journey from a large manufacturing town; therefore, it is possible that there are people who might recognise and locate the district if I gave more than a mere hint of its place on the map. It has been for years a very favourite corner of mine; the hills which surround it are not so high as to be unclimbable, they are heather clad, though here and there one came upon an oasis of sprongy turf and golden bracken—what I call, in my own mind, "kind hills"—high enough to lift one up from life's little worries, but not high enough to be awe-inspiring, or to frown down upon us puny mortals. The rivers are fishable after rain, otherwise one can inspect the stones, which form the beds of these mountain streams, and decide among the dry stones which place might best conceal a trout, when the next rain comes; personally, I am quite willing to believe that once there were fish in plenty in the stream, but that lean years had driven the farm folks to catch them the best way they could.

Perhaps the chief beauty of the place lay in the charm of its many and varied woods—at least, this was to me the magnet which drew me here generally once or twice in a year.

Up on the hillsides the woods seemed to open out, one into another, ever revealing fresh beauties of trees, from the tender green of the sapling birch to the hoary old beech or oak of many years old; beneath their green arms, the ground was carpeted with soft tiny wild thyme, wild mint, and little flowers of many kinds whose names were unknown to me. Most of my hours were spent deep in the heart of these woods, which never failed to hold me entranced with their ever-varying lights and shades.

Below, nearer to the river, there were woods also, but of quite a different nature, there, high pine trees of sombre hue towered above you, each one seeming to say: "Let me stretch up to the blue sky and leave the gloom of this wood beneath me." For gloom there undoubtedly was, yet I have liked that gloom; sometimes, on a hot summer's day, I have enjoyed lying on a soft, dry heap of pine needles, listening to the gentle coo of wood-pigeons, nesting high above me. "Silent Wood," as I called it, was always sheltered from wind, for the pine trees were close together, and beyond a soft sighing wind in the tree tops I never remember feeling the wind from any quarter. The sunlight seldom penetrated the "Silent Wood," save only in single shafts between the pines, or, maybe, in some clear patch where a tree had fallen or been cut down; but, even lacking sunshine, it was always warm and dry.

One side of the wood was bounded by a path, the other side by the stream—at least in autumn and winter it was—for in summer it dried up or trickled away to reappear a mile or so further on, as if it had tumbled into some old mine shaft, and later, changed its course and returned.

"Silent Wood" was *not* my favourite, but it had a fascination for me, difficult to describe; and on this July morning, when I bid farewell to dear old Merry, and started for my holiday, "Silent Wood" was much in my mind as a quiet place to rest in, before I tackled longer, steeper walks, or began to think of taking canvas and paints with me.

My journey was long, also suffocatingly hot, dusty, and tedious; many people were travelling, and my compartment was well packed with bundles and packages, as well as people, so I hailed my last change with a sigh of relief, for soon the hills and trees would surround me instead of the bricks and mortar I had grown so tired of.

A broken-down trap, drawn by a fat Welsh pony, met me at my station; from thence we crawled up four long miles of hill ere

I reached my favourite quarters, an old farmhouse in which I was always a welcome guest, and where two cheery rooms were always at my disposal. The peacefulness of that first evening will linger in my memory for many a day. To be able to gaze around, seeing nothing but hills, fields, trees, and sky, instead of houses, chimneys, motors, and people, was pure joy to me; and when, after a simple meal, I lit my pipe, I felt content to linger in the warm, hay-scented air indefinitely.

There are those to whom the contemplation of such a holiday, as the one I thought lay before me, would have been a dire penalty, those to whom solitude and nature would spell boredom and weariness; and I pity all those natures, for they know not what they miss.

I passed a gloriously restful night, and was up early, with a long day of golden sunshine ahead of me. I had never been here in July before, early spring or September had been my usual seasons; but to be here in July, in radiant warmth and beauty, was a treat I was prepared to revel in.

Day by day slipped away, in almost complete idleness, until a week had vanished, almost unnoticed by me, for calendars had been left behind me, and I, more often than not, forgot to wind up my watch—I had no use for time. I ate when I felt hungry, and slept when I was tired; but the end of this week found me thinking of brush and canvas, so I decided to take lunch in my pocket, trusting to luck for some tea if I desired it, and prepared for a long day's sketching.

"Which way do you think of going, sir?" asked my hostess, more, I fancy, from politeness than from any real interest in my goings and comings.

"Oh, I don't know," I answered, "but probably I shall wander to the woods."

"Which, sir?" she next enquired, a little to my surprise.

"Probably the shadiest," I replied, smiling, "the one below with the pine trees, and silence, is the one I most fancy today."

"The higher woods are nicer, sir, don't you think?" was her next remark.

"No, I don't," I said. "I like the pine woods, they are always so intensely silent; one never feels any wind there, and there is a breeze today."

"That is true, sir," said Mrs Hughes. "There isn't any wind there—*as a rule*."

"As a rule?" I echoed. "Why, I've never felt it there, not even in autumn."

"No, sir, you wouldn't then, but you may now; and I'd go to the upper woods if I were you."

Now Mrs Hughes had never, to my knowledge, taken the slightest interest in my doings previously, and her persistence this morning simply had the effect of making me feel perverse, as is the way of men; so, smilingly, I bade her good morning, determined, in my own mind, that "Silent Wood" should be my destination for that day. The good lady ventured no further remarks, but turned away to busy herself with farm duties, leaving me free to set off without further questioning.

There was a slight breeze, just enough to make walking more pleasant, but rather more than I liked for sketching purposes, so I was glad when I dipped down from the path by the river-side to the edge of my pet woods. They were, as ever, still, dark, and airless, just as I had pictured them many, many times as I smoked my pipe beside my studio fire while busy London surged on, beneath my windows.

In those woods, I have always felt as if I must tread softly. I do not remember ever to have sung or whistled there; yet, there was never anything to disturb, for I have never seen even a rabbit, it seemed too sombre a place for animal life; moreover, there was nothing but dry pine needles for them to eat. I don't remember ever *seeing* the wood-pigeons I occasionally heard above my head; so, lacking animal life, the place was even more silent than deep woods usually are.

It suited me in my present mood, however, and in the intense silence lay its greatest charm. Somewhere in the world there are a few kindred spirits, I have no doubt, to whom such perfect silence and freedom from every jar would appeal, as it appeals to me—those who often crave for just one hour's unbroken silence, and who find it one of the most difficult things to attain; those to whom the incessant opening and shutting of doors, clattering of things, ringing of bells, voices, and the coming and going of people have to be endured with a smile, though every nerve may be on edge, and the aching for quietness is almost more than can be borne—those people, and those only, will enter into and fully understand the intense charm to me of "Silent Wood."

I entered it, as usual, on this morning as on many previous ones, walking softly as if not wanting to disturb its peace by so much as a snap of a dry twig, and as I walked deeper and deeper into the shadows it seemed to grow stiller and more silent. The scent of the pines was soothing, and the warm, dry air seemed to draw it out and intensify it.

About the centre of the wood I paused to look and listen. Not a sound broke the stillness, save only the faintest cooing of the wood-pigeons; so there, in the patch of sunlight, I drew together heaps of pine needles to form a couch, stretching myself on it in complete enjoyment, canvas and brushes idle by my side.

The natural outcome of such an environment and such quiet calm was to fall soundly asleep—a glorious, restful sleep—knowing that there could not be any early knocking at my door, no engagements to keep, nothing, no one for whom I need wake until I had slept all I desired. I woke at long length, with the softest of breezes blowing gently on my face, so softly as to make me wonder, in my half-asleep state, if it also were part of my dreams; but no! there it was again, soft and cold, and this time a little stronger. I opened my eyes. Surely it must be night! I thought. How many hours had I slept? It seemed dark, yet high up between the pine-tree tops I could catch a glimpse of blue sky. Then it is not late, I thought, but how dark it is here under the trees. I must see the time, and shake myself into a more reasonable state of mind, for, truly, I feel almost nervy! So my thoughts ran as I raised myself from my pine-needle couch, and stood up.

I glanced round and could scarcely believe it was my beloved "Silent Wood," it seemed so chill and dark, not the soft gloom I was accustomed to there, but an eerie darkness as of a gathering storm; but ever and anon a little moaning wind swept past me, each just seeming more chill and dank.

"Horrible!" I murmured, fastening up my coat before preparing to pick up my little knapsack of odds and ends, "horrible! I never thought the place could be so chilly; I'll get out as speedily as I can for it must be late."

I peered at my watch, which was difficult to see in the gloom, to find I had, as usual, forgotten to wind it.

"It is probably about four!" I said aloud, "but it's like night!"

I spoke aloud, and my voice seemed to come back to me in mocking echo from the far side of the wood, "like night."

"I never knew there was an echo," I thought. "I'll try again tomorrow," I said clearly, and back from the distance came the echo—"tomorrow"—and a hoarse laugh came with it.

I started, I had not laughed! Then, who? "Oh, you idiot," I murmured, giving myself a shake, "it's some country yokel answering you back, making a fool of you; pull yourself together and get off home—you require your tea."

So, with a last look round, I turned my face towards home, and tea, but my feet seemed weighted, and seemed as if I could not leave the wood, eager as I was to reach the daylight.

I seemed to have already dragged myself double the distance I had to go ere I found myself at the edge of the wood, shivering in every limb, chilled to the bone, unnerved, as I could not believe possible, over—nothing at all! In the warmth of the sun I speedily recovered, and was ready to laugh at my own stupidity; to prove this to my own satisfaction, I gaily shook my fist at the woods behind me, calling back—"tomorrow," and, far away in the distant darkness, I fancied—for it could only have been fancy—I heard a mocking echo and a faint sound of laughter, as if the word "tomorrow" floated back to me; fancy or not, it served to hasten my steps, and the farm kitchen with its cheery tea-table, which I hurried to reach, quickly dispelled any lingering fear I might have felt.

For the first time, since my holiday began, I passed a restless night, burdened, when I slept at all, by dreams of mocking voice and laughter. My first thought on waking was one of dire vengeance, on some one, for causing me to lose a night's precious sleep. I would repay them, I vowed, as I sprang up, preparing to dress as rapidly as possible.

"Will you be in, sir, for lunch, or will you take it out?" asked my hostess, as soon as I had finished a wonderful breakfast of home-cured ham, fresh eggs, scones, and home-made jam.

"I will take it out, please, Mrs Hughes," I replied. "Some of that fine ham, and some bread and butter, if you will be so good. Don't make it into those abominations called sandwiches though, it would utterly spoil both bread and ham. I never can enjoy food done up in that way, the bread tastes of ham and the ham only tastes of bread, and both are dry and worn out by the time you want your lunch; so separately, please—if you love me."

Mrs Hughes eyed me as if uncertain whether to laugh or scold at what she termed my oddities—the laugh triumphed, and she went off chuckling over the ways of faddy men-folks. Presently, the good lady reappeared with a neat parcel, which she handed to me, with the remark—

"There you are, sir, *separately*, and I hope you will enjoy your lunch. Which way will you be going, sir?"

So again my destination seemed to be of interest to the worthy dame, but this time I wasn't going to let her off so easily.

"Why do you ask, Mrs Hughes?" I enquired.

"Well, sir, it's Tommy, it's Tommy," she said hesitatingly. "Seems like the lad likes to be on the look-out for you, sir, and always pesters me to say which way you've gone, sir."

As the good lady was speaking she edged nearer and nearer the door, and her final words were uttered as the door closed between her and myself, leaving me looking rather blankly at the door, and quite unable to reconcile Tommy's present anxiety as to my whereabouts, seeing the lad had not apparently noticed my existence up to now.

However, they were none the wiser—no one, save myself, knew whither I was bound, and if I changed my mind, no one would know, or care.

I debated a few moments as to whether to burden myself with sketching materials or not, and, finally, a happy thought struck me, I would take my kodak, it was ready loaded with new and highly-sensitive films, so, if I liked, I could take special bits, and later, if I wished, sketch or enlarge from them in the quiet of my studio. So with my camera on my shoulder, my lunch in a handy pocket, I set off, prepared for another happy peaceful day in "Silent Wood." Yet now I had started, I wondered if it really would give me the pleasure I had anticipated to fulfil my vow of vengeance on Him, Her, or It, who had mocked me the previous day. I was *quite* determined, on one point, that I would discover the hiding place of my mocking friend, and rid myself of the disturber of my sanctuary. To begin with I would not enter the woods by my usual path, I had a fancy to inspect the far side of it, which was as yet unknown to me, and which I had often thought of exploring, but so far had been too lazy to do so; it had been sufficient for me to get into the still warmth, and there to stay—resting, dreaming, or reading; but today I felt energetic, braced up, ready for anything, so instead of taking the lower path by the river to the woods, I struck off higher up, crossed a few fields and some tiresome fences, heavily loaded with barbed wire as if to keep out some invading enemy and not the three or four cows it guarded. My plan had led me higher than the woods, which now lay stretched below me in a large triangle, thick and dense, possibly half-a-mile in length, not more, I shouldn't think; looked at from where I stood it appeared quite an insignificant patch of dark trees surrounded by fields of waving corn, or haycocks, late in being carted home. Here and there, men and women were working in the fields; I could hear a reaper busy somewhere, and voices of children at play sounded clearly in the distance.

It was gloriously sunny, not a breath of wind stirred the leaves or grasses, yet, in spite of its beauty and brilliance, the dark trees lying below seemed to call me. I could see the waving branches of the pine trees, as if they were arms beckoning me to come, to rest in their shade. I knew I had to go; I knew in my heart I wanted to go, yet I lingered, drinking in the beauty of fields and sunshine as I strolled along, until, descending gradually, I found myself near the edge of the woods, at exactly the opposite corner from my usual point of entrance.

One more fence, a thick one of briars, thorns, and undergrowth, and I was in my beloved woods. It wasn't quite so dark on this side as the other, yet it felt more desolate, more cheerless somehow, possibly fewer people came this way, which might account for it; anyway, here I was, and now to explore. First, I quietly skirted the wood for a little way, but this proved uninteresting, so I struck in under the pines, and almost at once was conscious again of the warm scenty feeling of the air.

"Glorious," I murmured; "how peaceful, how still, but I will not rest yet, I want to look round first." Presently, I caught a glimpse of what appeared to be a building. Funny place for a house, I thought; I wonder if anyone lives there, if so, my friend of the mocking laughter is now unearthed; so, with a smile at my own smartness, I marched on until I reached the building, at least what I thought was a building—now, alas! a ruin. Two ends and one side were almost intact, the rest, except one chimney, was just piles of rough, grey stones. It had every appearance of having been deserted many years, for the tumbled-down stones were moss-grown, with here and there little ferns protruding between the crevices; the spot must once have been a lonely corner, though now it looked utter desolation.

Laying my camera and lunch down, I strolled to have a nearer inspection of the lonely ruin before I sat down. There was not any trace to be found of how many rooms the cottage had once contained, though probably three or four was the limit; what must once have been a fireplace faced me as I entered, and on one side, about two yards from the ground, were five stone stairs; evidently there had been a stone staircase or steps leading to an upper room or rooms, though no sign of any floor above remained now. I couldn't imagine a stone house falling to pieces so completely, it gave one the impression more of having been hurled down stone after stone, nothing else would have demolished it so utterly.

There being nothing more to inspect, I strolled back to my belongings, but the sight of my camera reminded me that, after all, I could get a picture of so battered a domicile without the fag of sketching it; it would be interesting, I thought, to have a photograph of those five curious stone steps, and battered walls, so I quickly found my focus, taking the picture from a little distance to get a big pine in as well. It was a curious tree, at least half of it had apparently been shattered at some time. I then went closer, focussing for the stone steps only. It was shady within the walls so I gave a little longer time, and hoped for success, though I felt sorry I had not even yet succeeded in getting exactly the point of view I wanted. I had one film left; I would wait until the sun lit up the far side, and would take that also. That was enough for now, and I had earned both lunch and rest.

Somehow, my moss cushion did not give me the comfort I liked, though to try to say why, was beyond me, apparently it left nothing to be desired, my back was against a pine as I faced the deeper shade of the woods in front of me. There was not any wind to disturb me, and no sound of any kind, all was quiet, serene, peaceful, and yet—

Again, and yet again, I found myself involuntarily turning to look over my shoulder at the heap of grey stones behind me. I didn't *want* to look at it, I had seen enough of it, yet turn I must and did, I was getting fanciful, for I could have sworn I saw a shadow of some person flit past the one-time doorway. Surely I had not missed a part of the place in my search, and there was someone hiding there. I would make sure. To this end I walked right round the place, looking well among the old bushes and holly trees—no sign of life—so I went back to my cushion and my rest.

One pipe I smoked, falling asleep ere I had finished it, to wake with a violent start, springing from my seat, sure, positive then, as I shall always be, that someone had laid a hand on my face. I tried to imagine a crawling thing had wandered over my face, I imagined a leaf falling, even tried the effect by closing my eyes and dropping a leaf on to my cheek, it was useless, no amount of thinking could make me believe that touch was aught but a hand.

Ghosts! I didn't believe in, I always looked on yarns of such things as the results of too heavy a supper, or a too vivid imagination, so was inclined to laugh at what I struggled so hard to minimise. I tried to whistle, but if you try to whistle with the corners of your mouth turned down, you will understand that effort ended in failure. I tried to hum a song, which resulted in a species of quavering dirge, I got up, I stamped, I beat the soft, unoffending turf with my stick, I did everything I could think of to shake off a creepy feeling that was fast getting a firmer hold of me, anything to avoid turning round as I felt impelled to do—all was useless, I might as well give in, but had now quite made up my mind I had had enough of the remains of the cottage, I would leave it to its solitude, first taking one more photo, then I would go on straight through the deep shades I loved, and out at the side I knew best. Just once, I admit it, I looked towards the fence and bank down which I had come, almost furtively, I glanced that way, as if in my heart I would rather have returned by the same path, but it was only momentary, for I knew that through "Silent Wood" was the way I should go.

I picked up my camera for my final snapshot, choosing the far side of the ruined place, now in the sunshine, and exposed my film. As the shutter clicked, the sunlight vanished, as if a heavy cloud had suddenly obscured it, and the camera in my hand shook, as if it had been hit—*my* hands were perfectly steady, I am positive of that, yet I had all but dropped my precious toy!

Someone must have thrown a stone I decided, but who the someone was, or where they were, I did not venture to look into, enough for me that I had got my pictures, and was ready to start through the woods, and so home to tea.

I was probably halfway, having long passed out of sight of the ruins, when I remembered my long forgotten ham and bread. I had better eat it, I supposed, so feeling happy again, now I was in the warm gloom of my favourite place, I made for myself another cosy seat, and proceeded with the now somewhat belated lunch. I was just about to bury the paper wrapping, as is my way, when it suddenly whisked away in a sudden gust of wind.

"Wind!" I ejaculated. "Here! Impossible!"

As I spoke, another little gust whirled past me, scattering the pine needles, and whirling a little crowd of dried bits round my feet. It really is most remarkable, I murmured to myself, the times without number I have been in these woods and never felt the smallest breath of wind until yesterday and today. I'd best be moving, it may rain, though I'll be dry enough here if it does, all the same I'll go. As I rose, another and another draught of cold air swept by me, and then a sudden quietness fell, and all around me seemed to be growing darker, and still darker, little whispering winds seemed chattering above my head, and colder and more chilly it seemed to grow.

I started off hurriedly, only to find, in the gathering darkness, I had missed my way. On and on I plunged, deeper and deeper the blackness grew, colder and colder the wind, now rising almost to a gale, anon, dying away with a moaning sound. Bravely I struggled, wildly endeavouring to locate one familiar tree or stone.

The wind, now icily cold, seemed to lash me, buffeting me, as if I, strong man as I was, had been but a weak puny child.

Suddenly I stopped, determined to find my bearings, determined I would *not* be driven along as I was. I raised my face; my eyes were streaming with water, in the smarting cold of the lashing wind.

Gloom, black gloom, met me on every side. Pines, once familiar, now seemed twice their original size, standing out rigid, gaunt, and black, no glimmer of light anywhere.

"My God, I am utterly lost," I said, aloud.

"Utterly lost," came back a voice from far away, and with the words, making my blood freeze and heart stand still, a shriek of hideous laughter.

With a valiant effort, I steadied my voice, and shouted aloud:

"Who are you? Come to my help."

"To my help," rang out the voice, and I shuddered as a shrill peal of laughter followed it.

"Won't you come?" I cried once more.

"You come," echoed the voice, and the laughter that came with it seemed of many voices—the gruff, hoarse laughter of a man, the shrill, cackling laugh of women, and even, I was sure, the laughter of children.

On, on, I plunged! gasping now for breath, praying, hoping for deliverance; lost, but blindly struggling to reach some haven of refuge. A more vicious bang of the tearing wind suddenly sent me forward, and I seemed to have reached grass at last. With a sob of relief, I raised my eyes, thinking to see the grass at the edge of the wood, but was frozen stiff with horror and amazement, to find myself on the clearing, with the ruined cottage before me.

"Ruined cottage," I called it, ruined no longer! To my amazed eyes it appeared intact: a door stood ajar, a window on each side of it, through each of which glimmered a faint light; two windows above, from one of which peered a white, tearful face—a man with an evil, sinister face, stood beneath the lone pine, holding a wailing child by its hair with one hand, and in the other—Oh God, the horror of it!—a long, sharp knife, which glistened as the glimmer from the windows struck it.

I didn't faint, I didn't fall, so rooted to the spot was I, I seemed as if made of stone. The wind had all but died away; and, but for the fact that, in my now frenzied brain, I *knew* I had seen the place desolate and ruined, I should have thought I was faced with a workman's dwelling, peopled by real beings. I *knew* it was NOT so. Fascinated, horrified, I gazed. The man moved, with a muttered curse, dragging the child with him up to the door; as he reached it, the wind redoubled its fury, howling, shrieking, like every evil let loose. I fell on my knees, powerless now to even pray; and hiding my face in my hands, I waited, for some awful thing, I knew, was to come.

It came, with a wild scream of awful horror, the scream from an upstairs window! and then a second, the shrill, awful scream of a child! Agonised, I knelt, and saw the man lurch through the door, reeling, join a group of waiting people hitherto unseen by me. As he came up to them, one of the women spoke to him, and then began to laugh. Oh God! the unspeakable horror of that laugh. One after another of the group spoke to the man, and each, as they moved off, laughed or chuckled, even two small boys who were with them burst into shrill laughter. I cannot describe it, save, only in one way, it sounded like fiends from Hell, so vile, so malicious, so diabolical were those awful sounds. As I knelt, unable to move, I struggled to keep a hold of myself, I found I was striving to explain away what I knew in my heart was totally inexplicable. I whispered to myself, "That laughter *is* real, *is* human, hideous as it is," but I knew it was neither real nor human. Always, to my dying day, it will ring in my ears, laughter such as no human creature could be responsible for.

Quite suddenly, there came a lull in the wind, a stillness in the air, the laughter died away. Could I, dare I move, rise, and venture to look? But even as I thought of it, the wind, with redoubled fury, broke forth again, causing me to crouch still lower as it swept over me. An awful crash sounded, a crash that echoed and re-echoed through the woods. The wind had seized and felled, as if with giant hand, the pine that had been standing at the far side of the cottage. So terrific was the blow that the end of the cottage, where it hit, fell like a house of cardboard! To demolish the rest of it seemed but child's play, as, with one whistling shriek, the wind tore beneath the now shattered roof, ripping it off, and almost the remainder of the walls, with a deafening roar, high above which rang out peal after peal of hideous laughter! until it, too, died away as now the wind was dying, dying fitfully, with an angry gust, and then a sobbing wail, until at length a long low wail seemed to pass through the woods and fade into silence, a long silence.

At last I moved, raised my head, looked, listened. Nothing, no sound broke the stillness; the ruined cottage was as I had first seen it, just a worn, weather-beaten heap of grey stones, a semblance of a fireplace, five stone stairs, that was all. I ventured nearer, trying to persuade myself I had dreamed the horrible scene. I must have dreamed it, for it had been dark, pitch dark, when the wind had begun to rise, and yet, by what light then had I witnessed this awful thing, for light of some kind there surely had been. Who were those people I had seen, from whom came that awful laughter? I was trembling yet, shaken, feeling desperately ill, no dream had brought me to this pass—then what?

Visitants from "Beyond"? But to what end, for they and their works were evil? I turned abruptly, with one thought in my head, to get out of the wood, and home. I glanced at my watch, having made a point this time of winding and setting it right—only five o'clock. I must be mad, I had gone through hours of dark night; how could it possibly be but five! I supposed, long afterwards, when I reviewed these hours, that it was the knowledge that it was only five o'clock, and not perhaps, as I expected, many hours later, that gave me the fillip of courage, which led me to linger still another moment near the ruins, and gaze, as if to print the thing on my mind. I stood possibly three yards from the ruined doorway, and said aloud "It was a murder!" Away through the woods came the mocking answer "A murder." "Oh God!" I gasped, "not again, for they are fiends from Hell!"—"From Hell!" came back the answer, and again the awful sound of laughter of many voices—

I turned and fled, holding my hands over my ears as I strove to run. I remember knocking violently against something, and falling, falling, falling, endlessly, or so it seemed, and then nothingness until I opened my eyes three weeks later, to find myself in bed in my quaint room at the farm, and beside my bed, placidly knitting, sat Mrs Merry.

"Merry!" I whispered, and the sound, or want of sound, in my own voice startled me.

"Yes, it's me, sir," answered the dear soul, "and high time too; but we are not talking, sir, if *you* please, it is medicine time and then you'll sleep."

I only too gladly obeyed, unquestioningly, as I obeyed for many weeks, the quiet, though firm, commands of Mrs Merry. I was far too weak to fight, even had it been of the slightest use; indeed, it was very little less than six weeks ere I was permitted to ask a question or have my own way in anything; but at length a day came when I was allowed to sit in a chair by the window, from which the view was something only expressed by colour, words could not do it. I gazed for a long time in silence, then said:

"I am well now, Merry, tell me what brought you, what has been wrong with me, where was I, everything—I must know."

She looked at me, then put her glasses on—she always did that if she meant to talk severely, then she said abruptly:

"You'd been missing for two days when they found you."

"Missing for two days?" I asked, incredulously, "But where was I?"

"You were at the bottom of an old lead mine," she answered, "on a big heap of dead leaves and ferns. Luckily, it wasn't one of the deep mines, and also the leaves and ferns saved you, though how they got there is a mystery," she added.

"But how on earth—" I began.

"Quite so, sir," she went on, "that's what we all want to know, how on earth, unless you were mooning along and wandered into a weak place in the ground above the mine. That's where you were, anyway, in one of the small shafts close to the old ruined cottage. You were quite unconscious; you must have had your camera in your hand, sir, because it was beside you, though how it wasn't broken is another mystery."

"Bring me my camera, Merry dear," I said.

"Very well, sir," she answered. "That can't do you no harm"; and off she went, to return presently, gingerly holding my kodak, as if fearful of it.

She was right. By some marvel it was unhurt; moreover the number of the film I had last turned to stood clearly forth. I would have them developed at once. I felt curious, but I had not yet asked all my questions:

"Who found me, Merry?" I next asked.

"Tommy Hughes, sir."

"Tommy Hughes!" I said. "What made him look for me?"

"Well, sir," answered the old lady, "they do say as he found another gentleman once in the same place, and when you didn't come home, he set off to look for you."

"Was the other chap hurt, Merry?" I asked.

"No, sir—at least not hurt, sir, because he was lying on ferns and leaves just the same. Oh no! he wasn't hurt, sir, not his body!"

"What do you mean?" I asked. "Tell me, please."

"Oh, dear sir, how you do worrit, and it's time for your soup, anyway."

"Tell me first, Merry," I said.

She glanced at me, to see if I was in earnest, and then, seemingly, decided that for the moment, at least, I was boss.

"His body was all right, sir, it was, his head, at least his wits, sir; he's been in a lunatic place ever since, so they say," she amended, with a sniff which, I knew, meant utter disbelief in gossip or village yarns.

I did *not* so entirely disbelieve, for, as the fragments of memory began to join together, I shuddered as I recalled my experience, and could only too readily believe that a very little weaker minded individual than I would very easily lose his reason if he went through all I had done. I would, however, leave further questioning until the next day, for I had observed the snap with which my dear old Merry had closed her lips.

The following day my doctor paid me a visit, one of his many, but this time he came in less professional manner, in fact he had every appearance of spoiling for a gossip, I could have wagered my last sou on it, so wasn't surprised when he accepted my offer of tea, and a smoke, with alacrity. The tea disposed of, he did not beat about the bush, but asked me if I could give him any light at all on my accident.

"I am curiously interested," he said, "because you are not my first case to have a very similar accident."

"Did your other patient make as good recovery, doctor?" I asked, instead of, as politeness demanded, answering his question.

"No, he did not," he replied. "He never recovered and never will in my opinion. He is mentally deranged, though all searching has failed to reveal a cause. He is quiet generally, and peaceable, but in a high wind he becomes frenzied, utterly distraught, his attendants are unable to cope with him, often he shrieks and yells, for the most part unintelligible rubbish. One night, in a furious gale, a man was blown over in the grounds, and the attendants were laughing about it when, without apparent reason, the poor insane chap fell on the luckless attendant and half-killed him, shouting all the time:

"'Stop laughing, will you!' It's always the same if the wind blows. They take him to a more sheltered room when it blows hard now.

"Tell me, will you, what preceded your fall—there must be some sort of link between the two, because, in your delirium, you raved of the wind, though we've had no wind to speak of since your arrival."

"I'll tell you the story, doctor, though you will be inclined to put me with your other patient, *unless* I can convince you, and this I may perhaps do, if my camera depicts what I saw."

I told him my experiences during two days in the woods I loved, I gave him every detail, even to the taking of the snapshots of the place, and he listened, silently puffing at his pipe, until I ended by telling him of how I struck something violently and fell, remembering nothing more until I found myself in my room.

There was a long pause as I finished, he seemed unable to speak, so I asked him how Mrs Merry came upon the scene.

"She arrived after you had lain long unconscious, saying you had said if you were not home in a month to come and look for you—not hearing, she came and found you, as I have said, and has since nursed you devotedly."

"What does it all mean, doctor?" I then said.

His answer disconcerted me.

"I do not know, though I have heard strange stories told of the pine woods, which you are pleased to call 'Silent,' but I confess I have hitherto put them down to an extra glass or two of beer. Now, for the first time, I am bound to think more seriously of them, having on my hands first, the strange maniac, and then you, found in the same spot, under similar conditions, and—strangest of all—*on the same day* of the year!

"I don't know the tale, but no doubt your worthy host does, ask him, and, meanwhile, develop your snapshots, though I do not hope for much in the way of proofs from them.

"I will look in tomorrow, you had better rest now," and my matter-of-fact materialistic doctor picked up his hat and departed.

I sat at my window for a long time, thinking much, hearing again, in fancy, the roar of wind, the laughter of fiends, the crash of the tree. As it grew dark, I was possessed with the desire, at all costs, to develop those films, so, calling Mrs Merry, I told her I was tired, and was going to bed, that there was nothing I required, so, bidding her "Good night," I made my rough and ready preparations, lacking all the essentials of a proper dark room, but in these days, tabloids of developers, a jugful of water, a candle-lamp, with a crimson silk scarf tied round it, would serve me very well.

The first negative came up beautifully, just an ordinary common or garden broken-down cottage.

The second was a different story, and I watched it fearfully. There was distinctly, unmistakably, a form of a man going into the doorway!

The third film, taken from the other side of the cottage, showed me a lower window, more or less unbroken, in the frame of which was the face of a man—so much I could see, but to me that meant much, for *I knew* that I was alone, horribly alone at that moment of taking the photo.

Next morning, I was up earlier than had been permitted for some time, and a very few minutes sufficed to print a rough print from each negative. I stared at them, stared, with my eyes nearly starting from my head. They were good photos, clear, sharply defined, no woolly-looking details, so easily mistaken for other than the actual things I intended to take, except the figure, and the face. Those I neither saw, nor intended to portray, yet there they were, and, as is so often the case, the camera lens depicted what the human eye did not see. The figure, tall, gaunt, seemed as if going into the house, but the face! the *face* in the frame of the window was unmistakably the face of the man who passed me, who entered the house, from which issued those screams of agony, the man who later joined the group of people to whom he spoke, the people who made the air hideous with their horrible laughter.

I kept my own counsel, hiding the photos also, until late in the afternoon, the doctor made his appearance. He studied them carefully, and then said:

"I should have laughed at your story, my friend, laughed at your photos of your so-called empty cottage, last evening, but tonight I cannot. I made a few enquiries after I left you, and the outline of what I gleaned was this:

"The cottage was built when the lead mines were working, for the use of the men, and was subsequently taken possession of by a foreman. He was a glum, taciturn brute, given to drink and gambling. He brought with him to the cottage, known as Leadmine Cottage, a very pretty young girl as his wife, though gossips say she was not. He seemed passionately attached to the girl, and also to a little child of three, said to be his niece's child. The man, by name Woodrow, led an almost double life, one half of which was spent with a gang of men and women, with whom he was said to drink and gamble, and who used to jeer at him for what they spoke of as his milksop life, in the company of his so-called wife. When with her, he was simply a devoted husband, and when sober always refused to associate with the gang who other times attracted him. Finally, the gang of criminals—I can call them nothing better—tried to embitter him against the girl, whom they thought was getting a firmer hold on him. One or other of them started to fill his mind with suspicions of the girl, telling him that chance visitors found Leadmine Cottage attractive. They used to follow him home, for the fiendish joke of hearing him abuse the girl and threaten her with worse things if she was untrue to him. These fiends finally plotted, and eventually sent a young doctor out there, saying someone was ill in the cottage. The unsuspecting doctor called late one evening, and Woodrow was persuaded to hide in the trees and watch. It was, I am told, a wild, stormy evening, one of those sudden storms that come in these mountain districts in summer, and break down corn, lash rivers to fury, and hurl trees and branches to the ground.

"Woodrow watched, and saw the doctor enter, saw him speak to the girl, saw her smile at him, and laughing, give him her hand as she might do to a doctor, who desired to feel her pulse; though this was apparently not the construction put upon her innocent action by her husband, goaded to madness by drink, as well as by his uncontrollable jealous nature. He waited until the doctor had gone, and then entered the cottage, murdered his wife and child, afterwards rejoining his fellow-criminals, whom, it is said, received his news with jest and laughter, glorying in the success of the vile plot which they guessed would give him wholly back to them and their evil ways.

"The cottage and all trace of the crime was effaced, so 'tis said, by the sudden rising of the wind, bringing down a tree, which fell athwart the house, shattering it to bits. The gang are believed to have fled the country, all but one, who later died in hospital after giving the story to a medical man there, whom, by a curious coincidence, if indeed there be such things, wrote it to a colleague of mine, whom I met last night at a dinner. It is a strange story, and one, in the light of your recent experience, not to be gainsaid. The story goes on to say, that in the same month every year, the murder takes place, with every detail complete, even to the rising wind; and that those who know the story and the wood, shun it as the plague, during that month. At any other time, I believe, it justifies your name for it of 'Silent Wood.'

"That is the story, my friend, make of it what you will. I have also taken the liberty of asking an aged miner to look in this evening. I want you to be good enough to start chatting casually of the wood, your fall, etc., and show him your photos. Don't give him any other lead. Now, I will see if he has come. He is very old, but can see pretty well. His little grandchild is bringing him to see me here, to save time, and the old boy wants a dose for a cough."

With this, the doctor vanished, to return almost at once, leading an old man by the arm.

They tell me folks live long up here, and surely it must be so if this is a specimen, for the old man looked ninety, and hale at that, though bent and withered. I gave him a chair and baccy, but instead of filling his pipe, he stared at me with clear, penetrating eyes, and mumbled:

"So you're the gent that fell down the mine."

"Yes," I said, "I'm that unfortunate man."

"Did you fall, or were yer put there?" he questioned, sniggering to himself.

"I don't know," I said.

"No, my boy, but I do," he wheezed, pointing a claw-like finger at me. "I do, yer were put there, my lad, put there, look you, and so will others be, if they do not keep away from the pines in July!"

"I took a picture of it," I said, after a pause.

"A picture—whatever—" answered the aged being, "show me the picture. I once worked there."

"Hurry," whispered the doctor, "he quickly fails."

I handed him the picture, holding a powerful magnifying glass over it as I did so.

"Aye, aye! there's Johnny Woodrow's house," he muttered, "all in a heap, all in a heap."

"This is another," I said.

"My God!" burst from his shaking lips. "My God, there's Johnny Woodrow, Johnny Woodrow, my old pal. Why, I thought him was dead, he is dead, I knows he's dead, how could he live after murdering his wife and little child—murdered them, he did, in the cottage by the pines, and them as interferes with the cottage, he'd put 'em down the mine—he said he would put 'em in the mine to starve, if they move a stone or meddle with wot 'e calls her grave. He told me he'd do it afore he went away, 'is very words were 'Living or dead, I'll do it, Bob,' and wot Johnny says he'll do, he *will* do."

His old head fell forward on his breast as he finished speaking, so we did not speak, save in a whisper.

"He sleeps," said the doctor. "Presently he will wake, but will not remember. We will leave him. Mary will take him home, and

I'll send him some stuff in the morning. The old boy is nearly through," he added, "but I am glad he was here to give you what you wanted—proof!" though proof of what, or for what reason, I cannot pretend to fathom.

We parted a little later, my doctor and I—he to go on with his work for sick humanity; I, on the morrow, to return to my studio in London, back to the turmoil of town, back to live among the haunts of men, to leave the beauty of hills and rivers; but in some quiet hour in my studio, maybe during some winter night of wind and storm, I shall hear again the hideous laughter, shall dream of the scent of the pines—nay, perhaps I shall even try to forget the horror of all I went through, and may memory, sometimes kind, only recall the peace, the scent, the perfect still quietness of the woods I loved best, when I knew them only as

"SILENT WOOD."

1922

BRICKETT BOTTOM

Amyas Northcote

The seventh son of Sir Stafford Northcote, Earl of Iddesleigh, Amyas Northcote (1864–1923) could trace a lineage in his family's home county of Devon back to 1103. However, despite his aristocratic ties to England, Amyas emigrated to the bright lights of Chicago as a young man, eventually running a business and penning articles on life in the US for a British audience. His single volume of stories was published after returning to the UK—*In Ghostly Company* appeared in 1922, not long before his death.

"Brickett Bottom" is often cited as the finest of Northcote's stories, a simple, yet decidedly eerie, tale concerning two sisters and a mysterious house spied on a country walk. Written in Northcote's spare style, the narrative's uncertain location adds to its dreamlike quality; we only know that "Overbury is a small and very remote village in one of our most lovely and rural counties", and that this is a place of downland, sheep tracks and isolated valleys.

Many parts of the South Downs would make a good fit for Brickett Bottom. Beginning in Winchester and finishing up in Eastbourne, the 100-mile South Downs Way takes the long-distance rambler through some of England's finest chalk downland. On the section of the trail that runs near the small town of Steyning, it's easy to imagine stumbling across a "narrow glen" like the one described by Northcote. There are some good circular routes to be plotted from the town, including walks that take in the wonderful, storied prehistoric hill fort of Chanctonbury Ring.

The Reverend Arthur Maydew was the hard-working incumbent of a large parish in one of our manufacturing towns. He was also a student and a man of no strong physique, so that when an opportunity was presented to him to take an annual holiday by exchanging parsonages with an elderly clergyman, Mr Roberts, the Squarson of the Parish of Overbury, and an acquaintance of his own, he was glad to avail himself of it.

Overbury is a small and very remote village in one of our most lovely and rural counties, and Mr Roberts had long held the living of it.

Without further delay we can transport Mr Maydew and his family, which consisted only of two daughters, to their temporary home. The two young ladies, Alice and Maggie, the heroines of this narrative, were at that time aged twenty-six and twenty-four years respectively. Both of them were attractive girls, fond of such society as they could find in their own parish and, the former especially, always pleased to extend the circle of their acquaintance. Although the elder in years, Alice in many ways yielded place to her sister, who was the more energetic and practical and upon whose shoulders the bulk of the family cares and responsibilities rested. Alice was inclined to be absent-minded and emotional and to devote more of her thoughts and time to speculations of an abstract nature than her sister.

Both of the girls, however, rejoiced at the prospect of a period of quiet and rest in a pleasant country neighbourhood, and both were gratified at knowing that their father would find in Mr Roberts' library much that would entertain his mind, and in Mr Roberts' garden an opportunity to indulge freely in his favourite game of croquet. They would have, no doubt, preferred some cheerful neighbours, but Mr Roberts was positive in his assurances that there was no one in the neighbourhood whose acquaintance would be of interest to them.

The first few weeks of their new life passed pleasantly for the Maydew family. Mr Maydew quickly gained renewed vigour in his quiet and congenial surroundings, and in the delightful air, while his daughters spent much of their time in long walks about the country and in exploring its beauties.

One evening late in August the two girls were returning from a long walk along one of their favourite paths, which led along the side of the Downs. On their right, as they walked, the ground fell away sharply to a narrow glen, named Brickett Bottom, about three-quarters of a mile in length, along the bottom of which ran a little-used country road leading to a farm, known as Blaise's Farm, and then onward and upward to lose itself as a sheep track on the higher Downs.

On their side of the slope some scattered trees and bushes grew, but beyond the lane and running up over the farther slope of the glen was a thick wood, which extended away to Carew Court, the seat of a neighbouring magnate, Lord Carew. On their left the open Down rose above them and beyond its crest lay Overbury.

The girls were walking hastily, as they were later than they had intended to be and were anxious to reach home. At a certain point at which they had now arrived the path forked, the right hand branch leading down into Brickett Bottom and the left hand turning up over the Down to Overbury.

Just as they were about to turn into the left hand path Alice suddenly stopped and pointing downwards exclaimed: "How very curious, Maggie! Look, there is a house down there in the Bottom, which we have, or at least I have, never noticed before, often as we have walked up the Bottom."

Maggie followed with her eyes her sister's pointing finger.

"I don't see any house," she said.

"Why, Maggie," said her sister, "can't you see it! A quaint-looking, old-fashioned red brick house, there just where the road bends to the right. It seems to be standing in a nice, well-kept garden too."

Maggie looked again, but the light was beginning to fade in the glen and she was short-sighted to boot.

"I certainly don't see anything," she said, "but then I am so blind and the light is getting bad; yes, perhaps I do see a house," she added, straining her eyes.

"Well, it is there," replied her sister, "and tomorrow we will come and explore it."

Maggie agreed readily enough, and the sisters went home, still speculating on how they had happened not to notice the house before and resolving firmly on an expedition thither the next day. However, the expedition did not come off as planned, for that evening Maggie slipped on the stairs and fell, spraining her ankle in such a fashion as to preclude walking for some time.

Notwithstanding the accident to her sister, Alice remained possessed by the idea of making further investigations into the house she had looked down upon from the hill the evening before; and the next day, having seen Maggie carefully settled for the afternoon, she started off for Brickett Bottom. She returned in triumph and much intrigued over her discoveries, which she eagerly narrated to her sister.

Yes. There was a nice, old-fashioned red brick house, not very large and set in a charming, old-world garden in the Bottom. It stood on a tongue of land jutting out from the woods, just at the point where the lane, after a fairly straight course from its junction with the main road half a mile away, turned sharply to the right in the direction of Blaise's Farm. More than that, Alice had seen the people of the house, whom she described as an old gentleman and a lady, presumably his wife. She had not clearly made out the gentleman, who was sitting in the porch, but the old lady, who had been in the garden busy with her flowers, had looked up and smiled pleasantly at her as she passed. She was sure, she said, that they were nice people and that it would be pleasant to make their acquaintance.

Maggie was not quite satisfied with Alice's story. She was of a more prudent and retiring nature than her sister; she had an uneasy feeling that, if the old couple had been desirable or attractive neighbours, Mr Roberts would have mentioned them, and knowing Alice's nature she said what she could to discourage her vague idea of endeavouring to make acquaintance with the owners of the red brick house.

On the following morning, when Alice came to her sister's room to inquire how she did, Maggie noticed that she looked pale and rather absent-minded, and, after a few commonplace remarks had passed, she asked:

"What is the matter, Alice? You don't look yourself this morning."

Her sister gave a slightly embarrassed laugh.

"Oh, I am all right," she replied, "only I did not sleep very well. I kept on dreaming about the house. It was such an odd dream too the house seemed to be home, and yet to be different."

"What, that house in Brickett Bottom?" said Maggie. "Why, what is the matter with you, you seem to be quite crazy about the place?"

"Well, it is curious, isn't it, Maggie, that we should have only just discovered it, and that it looks to be lived in by nice people? I wish we could get to know them."

Maggie did not care to resume the argument of the night before and the subject dropped, nor did Alice again refer to the house or its inhabitants for some little time. In fact, for some days the weather was wet and Alice was forced to abandon her walks, but when the weather once more became fine she resumed them, and Maggie suspected that Brickett Bottom formed one of her sister's favourite expeditions. Maggie became anxious over her sister, who seemed to grow daily more absent-minded and silent, but she refused to be drawn into any confidential talk, and Maggie was nonplussed.

One day, however, Alice returned from her afternoon walk in an unusually excited state of mind, of which Maggie sought an explanation. It came with a rush. Alice said that, that afternoon, as she approached the house in Brickett Bottom, the old lady, who as usual was busy in her garden, had walked down to the gate as she passed and had wished her good day.

Alice had replied and, pausing, a short conversation had followed. Alice could not remember the exact tenor of it, but, after she had paid a compliment to the old lady's flowers, the latter had rather diffidently asked her to enter the garden for a closer view. Alice had hesitated, and the old lady had said, "Don't be afraid of me, my dear, I like to see young ladies about me and my husband finds their society quite necessary to him." After a pause she went on: "Of course nobody has told you about us. My husband is Colonel Paxton, late of the Indian Army, and we have been here for many,

many years. It's rather lonely, for so few people ever see us. Do come in and meet the Colonel."

"I hope you didn't go in," said Maggie rather sharply.

"Why not?" replied Alice.

"Well, I don't like Mrs Paxton asking you in that way," answered Maggie.

"I don't see what harm there was in the invitation," said Alice.

"I didn't go in because it was getting late and I was anxious to get home; but—"

"But what?" asked Maggie.

Alice shrugged her shoulders.

"Well," she said, "I have accepted Mrs Paxton's invitation to pay her a little visit tomorrow."

And she gazed defiantly at Maggie.

Maggie became distinctly uneasy on hearing of this resolution. She did not like the idea of her impulsive sister visiting people on such slight acquaintance, especially as they had never heard them mentioned before. She endeavoured by all means, short of appealing to Mr Maydew, to dissuade her sister from going, at any rate until there had been time to make some inquiries as to the Paxtons. Alice, however, was obdurate.

What harm could happen to her? she asked. Mrs Paxton was a charming old lady. She was going early in the afternoon for a short visit. She would be back for tea and croquet with her father and, anyway, now that Maggie was laid up, long solitary walks were unendurable and she was not going to let slip the chance of following up what promised to be a pleasant acquaintance.

Maggie could do nothing more. Her ankle was better and she was able to get down to the garden and sit in a long chair near her father, but walking was still quite out of the question, and it was with some misgivings that on the following day she watched Alice depart gaily for her visit, promising to be back by half-past four at the very latest.

The afternoon passed quietly till nearly five, when Mr Maydew, looking up from his book, noticed Maggie's uneasy expression and asked:

"Where is Alice?"

"Out for a walk," replied Maggie; and then after a short pause she went on: "And she has also gone to pay a call on some neighbours whom she has recently discovered."

"Neighbours," ejaculated Mr Maydew, "what neighbours? Mr Roberts never spoke of any neighbours to me."

"Well, I don't know much about them," answered Maggie. "Only Alice and I were out walking the day of my accident and saw or at least she saw, for I am so blind I could not quite make it out, a house in Brickett Bottom. The next day she went to look at it closer, and yesterday she told me that she had made the acquaintance of the people living in it. She says that they are a retired Indian officer and his wife, a Colonel and Mrs Paxton, and Alice describes Mrs Paxton as a charming old lady, who pressed her to come and see them. So she has gone this afternoon, but she promised me she would be back long before this."

Mr Maydew was silent for a moment and then said:

"I am not well pleased about this. Alice should not be so impulsive and scrape acquaintance with absolutely unknown people. Had there been nice neighbours in Brickett Bottom, I am certain Mr Roberts would have told us."

The conversation dropped; but both father and daughter were disturbed and uneasy and, tea having been finished and the clock striking half-past five, Mr Maydew asked Maggie:

"When did you say Alice would be back?"

"Before half-past four at the latest, father."

"Well, what can she be doing? What can have delayed her? You say you did not see the house," he went on.

"No," said Maggie, "I cannot say I did. It was getting dark and you know how short-sighted I am."

"But surely you must have seen it at some other time," said her father.

"That is the strangest part of the whole affair," answered Maggie. "We have often walked up the Bottom, but I never noticed the house, nor had Alice till that evening. I wonder," she went on after a short pause, "if it would not be well to ask Smith to harness the pony and drive over to bring her back. I am not happy about her—I am afraid—"

"Afraid of what?" said her father in the irritated voice of a man who is growing frightened.

"What can have gone wrong in this quiet place? Still, I'll send Smith over for her."

So saying he rose from his chair and sought out Smith, the rather dull-witted gardener-groom attached to Mr Roberts' service.

"Smith," he said, "I want you to harness the pony at once and go over to Colonel Paxton's in Brickett Bottom and bring Miss Maydew home."

The man stared at him.

"Go where, sir?" he said.

Mr Maydew repeated the order and the man, still staring stupidly, answered:

"I never heard of Colonel Paxton, sir. I don't know what house you mean."

Mr Maydew was now growing really anxious.

"Well, harness the pony at once," he said; and going back to Maggie he told her of what he called Smith's stupidity, and asked her if she felt that her ankle would be strong enough to permit her to go with him and Smith to the Bottom to point out the house.

Maggie agreed readily and in a few minutes the party started off. Brickett Bottom, although not more than three-quarters of a mile away over the Downs, was at least three miles by road; and as it was nearly six o'clock before Mr Maydew left the Vicarage, and the pony was old and slow, it was getting late before the entrance to Brickett Bottom was reached. Turning into the lane the cart proceeded slowly up the Bottom, Mr Maydew and Maggie looking anxiously from side to side, whilst Smith drove stolidly on looking neither to the right nor left.

"Where is the house?" said Mr Maydew presently.

"At the bend of the road," answered Maggie, her heart sickening as she looked out through the failing light to see the trees stretching their ranks in unbroken formation along it. The cart reached the bend. "It should be here," whispered Maggie.

They pulled up. Just in front of them the road bent to the right round a tongue of land, which, unlike the rest of the right hand side of the road, was free from trees and was covered only by rough grass and stray bushes. A closer inspection disclosed evident signs of terraces having once been formed on it, but of a house there was no trace.

"Is this the place?" said Mr Maydew in a low voice.

Maggie nodded.

"But there is no house here," said her father. "What does it all mean? Are you sure of yourself, Maggie? Where is Alice?"

Before Maggie could answer a voice was heard calling "Father! Maggie!" The sound of the voice was thin and high and, paradoxically, it sounded both very near and yet as if it came from some infinite distance. The cry was thrice repeated and then silence fell. Mr Maydew and Maggie stared at each other.

"That was Alice's voice," said Mr Maydew huskily, "she is near and in trouble, and is calling us. Which way did you think it came from, Smith?" he added, turning to the gardener.

"I didn't hear anybody calling," said the man.

"Nonsense!" answered Mr Maydew.

And then he and Maggie both began to call "Alice. Alice. Where are you?" There was no reply and Mr Maydew sprang from the cart, at the same time bidding Smith to hand the reins to Maggie and come and search for the missing girl. Smith obeyed him and both men, scrambling up the turfy bit of ground, began to search and call through the neighbouring wood. They heard and saw nothing, however, and after an agonised search Mr Maydew ran down to the cart and begged Maggie to drive on to Blaise's Farm for help leaving himself and Smith to continue the search. Maggie followed her father's instructions and was fortunate enough to find Mr Rumbold, the farmer, his two sons and a couple of labourers just returning from the harvest field.

She explained what had happened, and the farmer and his men promptly volunteered to form a search party, though Maggie, in spite of her anxiety, noticed a queer expression on Mr Rumbold's face as she told him her tale.

The party, provided with lanterns, now went down the Bottom, joined Mr Maydew and Smith and made an exhaustive but absolutely fruitless search of the woods near the bend of the road.

No trace of the missing girl was to be found, and after a long and anxious time the search was abandoned, one of the young Rumbolds volunteering to ride into the nearest town and notify the police.

Maggie, though with little hope in her own heart, endeavoured to cheer her father on their homeward way with the idea that Alice might have returned to Overbury over the Downs whilst they were going by road to the Bottom, and that she had seen them and called to them in jest when they were opposite the tongue of land.

However, when they reached home there was no Alice and, though the next day the search was resumed and full inquiries were instituted by the police, all was to no purpose. No trace of Alice was ever found, the last human being that saw her having been an old woman, who had met her going down the path into the Bottom on the afternoon of her disappearance, and who described her as smiling but looking "queerlike."

This is the end of the story, but the following may throw some light upon it.

The history of Alice's mysterious disappearance became widely known through the medium of the Press and Mr Roberts, distressed beyond measure at what had taken place, returned in all haste to Overbury to offer what comfort and help he could give to his afflicted friend and tenant.

He called upon the Maydews and, having heard their tale, sat for a short time in silence. Then he said:

"Have you ever heard any local gossip concerning this Colonel and Mrs Paxton?"

"No," replied Mr Maydew, "I never heard their names until the day of my poor daughter's fatal visit."

"Well," said Mr Roberts, "I will tell you all I can about them, which is not very much, I fear."

He paused and then went on: "I am now nearly seventy-five years old, and for nearly seventy years no house has stood in Brickett Bottom. But when I was a child of about five there was an old-fashioned, red brick house standing in a garden at the bend of the road, such as you have described. It was owned and lived in by a retired Indian soldier and his wife, a Colonel and Mrs Paxton. At the time I speak of, certain events having taken place at the house and the old couple having died, it was sold by their heirs to Lord Carew, who shortly after pulled it down on the ground that it interfered with his shooting. Colonel and Mrs Paxton were well known to my father, who was the clergyman here before me, and to the neighbourhood in general. They lived quietly and were not unpopular, but the Colonel was supposed to possess a violent and vindictive temper. Their family consisted only of themselves, their daughter and a couple of servants, the Colonel's old Army servant and his Eurasian wife. Well, I cannot tell you details of what happened, I was only a child; my father never liked gossip and in later years, when he talked to me on the subject, he always avoided any appearance of exaggeration or sensationalism.

"However, it is known that Miss Paxton fell in love with and became engaged to a young man to whom her parents took a strong dislike. They used every possible means to break off the match, and many rumours were set on foot as to their conduct—undue influence, even cruelty were charged against them. I do not know the truth, all I can say is that Miss Paxton died and a very bitter feeling against her parents sprang up. My father, however, continued to call, but was rarely admitted. In fact, he never saw Colonel Paxton after his daughter's death and only saw Mrs Paxton once or twice. He described her as an utterly broken woman, and was not surprised at her following her daughter to the grave in about three months' time. Colonel Paxton became, if possible, more of a recluse than ever after his wife's death and himself died not more than a month after her under circumstances which pointed to suicide. Again a crop of rumours sprang up, but there was no one in particular to take action, the doctor certified Death from Natural Causes, and Colonel Paxton, like his wife and daughter, was buried in this churchyard. The property passed to a distant relative, who came down to it for one night shortly afterwards; he never came again, having apparently conceived a violent dislike to the place, but arranged to pension off the servants and then sold the house to Lord Carew, who was glad to purchase this little island in the middle of his property. He pulled it down soon after he had bought it, and the garden was left to relapse into a wilderness."

Mr Roberts paused.

"Those are all the facts," he added.

"But there is something more," said Maggie.

Mr Roberts hesitated for a while.

"You have a right to know all," he said almost to himself; then louder he continued: "What I am now going to tell you is really rumour, vague and uncertain; I cannot fathom its truth or its meaning. About five years after the house had been pulled down a young maidservant at Carew Court was out walking one afternoon. She was a stranger to the village and a newcomer to the Court. On returning home to tea she told her fellow-servants that as she walked down Brickett Bottom, which place she described clearly, she passed a red brick house at the bend of the road and that a kind-faced old lady had asked her to step in for a while. She did not go in, not because she had any suspicions of there being anything uncanny, but simply because she feared to be late for tea.

"I do not think she ever visited the Bottom again and she had no other similar experience, so far as I am aware.

"Two or three years later, shortly after my father's death, a travelling tinker with his wife and daughter camped for the night at the foot of the Bottom. The girl strolled away up the glen to gather blackberries and was never seen or heard of again. She was searched for in vain—of course, one does not know the truth—and she may have run away voluntarily from her parents, although there was no known cause for her doing so.

"That," concluded Mr Roberts, "is all I can tell you of either facts or rumours; all that I can now do is to pray for you and for her."

1928

WAILING WELL

M. R. James

Montague Rhodes James (1862–1936) defined the English literary ghost story as we have come to know it. Building on Victorian foundations, James cemented the genre's move from Gothic cliché to a more unsettling plane, and in the process provided a useful template for future writers. In many of James' tales an unassuming scholar (perhaps a proxy for Monty himself) is faced with a malign supernatural presence, often following the unearthing of a strange, ancient object or document. This narrative pattern, reinforced through several wonderful television adaptations of his stories, has become as much a part of the fabric of the ghost story as *A Christmas Carol*.

James' ghost stories are often seen as a kind of brilliant side hustle for a man intensely engaged with both serious research and administrative duties at Cambridge and Eton. Nonetheless, the writer took a great deal of time and care over his tales, drawing upon his wide reading and work as a medievalist to lend an uncanny verisimilitude to the antiquarian curiosities and arcane practices encountered by his protagonists. James was also a keen cyclist and walker, enjoying travels in Britain and mainland Europe, and his knowledge of the English countryside informed many of his stories, including "Wailing Well".

"Wailing Well" is an unusual tale for James, both in its humorous first half and the swiftness with which it descends into horror. He wrote the story to be read to the Eton Boy Scouts when they were camping near Worbarrow Bay in Dorset, and his letters tell us that he visited the campsite on the night of 27 July, 1927. James' obituary recounted the trip, noting that "several boys had a somewhat disturbed night, as the scene of the story was quite close to camp."

Worbarrow Bay is today owned by the Ministry of Defence, with its own ghosts, in the form of the abandoned village of Tyneham, nearby. A time capsule of a place, Tyneham was evacuated in 1943 and its land given over to military training. It has remained in the hands of the MOD ever since. Access to Tyneham is limited, but the site is usually open at weekends and public holidays (check online before visiting). From the village car park, you can walk the mile or so to Worbarrow Bay, which makes for a cracking picnic spot with magnificent views.

I n the year 19— there were two members of the Troop of Scouts attached to a famous school, named respectively Arthur Wilcox and Stanley Judkins. They were the same age, boarded in the same house, were in the same division, and naturally were members of the same patrol. They were so much alike in appearance as to cause anxiety and trouble, and even irritation, to the masters who came in contact with them. But oh how different were they in their inward man, or boy!

It was to Arthur Wilcox that the Head Master said, looking up with a smile as the boy entered chambers, "Why, Wilcox, there will be a deficit in the prize fund if you stay here much longer! Here, take this handsomely bound copy of the *Life and Works of Bishop Ken*, and with it my hearty congratulations to yourself and your excellent parents." It was Wilcox again, whom the Provost noticed as he passed through the playing fields, and, pausing for a moment, observed to the Vice-Provost, "That lad has a remarkable brow!" "Indeed, yes," said the Vice-Provost. "It denotes either genius or water on the brain."

As a Scout, Wilcox secured every badge and distinction for which he competed. The Cookery Badge, the Map-making Badge, the Life-saving Badge, the Badge for picking up bits of newspaper, the Badge for not slamming the door when leaving pupil-room, and many others. Of the Life-saving Badge I may have a word to say when we come to treat of Stanley Judkins.

You cannot be surprised to hear that Mr Hope Jones added a special verse to each of his songs, in commendation of Arthur Wilcox, or that the Lower Master burst into tears when handing him the Good Conduct Medal in its handsome claret-coloured case: the medal which had been unanimously voted to him by the whole of Third Form. Unanimously, did I say? I am wrong. There was one dissentient, Judkins *mi.*, who said that he had excellent reasons for acting as he did. He shared, it seems, a room with his major. You cannot, again, wonder that in after years Arthur Wilcox was the first, and so far the only boy, to become Captain of both the School and of the Oppidans, or that the strain of carrying out the duties of both positions, coupled with the ordinary work of the school, was so severe that a complete rest for six months, followed by a voyage round the world, was pronounced an absolute necessity by the family doctor.

It would be a pleasant task to trace the steps by which he attained the giddy eminence he now occupies; but for the moment enough of Arthur Wilcox. Time presses, and we must turn to a very different matter: the career of Stanley Judkins—Judkins *ma*.

Stanley Judkins, like Arthur Wilcox, attracted the attention of the authorities; but in quite another fashion. It was to him that the Lower Master said with no cheerful smile, "What, again, Judkins? A very little persistence in this course of conduct, my boy, and you will have cause to regret that you ever entered this academy. There, take that, and that, and think yourself very lucky you don't get that and that!" It was Judkins, again, whom the Provost had cause to notice as he passed through the playing fields, when a cricket ball struck him with considerable force on the ankle, and a voice from a short way off cried, "Thank you, cut-over!" "I think," said the Provost, pausing for a moment to rub his ankle, "that that boy had better fetch his cricket ball for himself!" "Indeed, yes," said the Vice-Provost, "and if he comes within reach, I will do my best to fetch him something else."

As a Scout, Stanley Judkins secured no badge save those which he was able to abstract from members of other patrols. In the cookery competition he was detected trying to introduce squibs into the Dutch oven of the next-door competitors. In the tailoring competition he succeeded in sewing two boys together very firmly, with disastrous effect when they tried to get up. For the Tidiness Badge he was disqualified, because, in the Midsummer schooltime, which chanced to be hot, he could not be dissuaded from sitting with his fingers in the ink: as he said, for coolness' sake. For one piece of paper which he picked up, he must have dropped at least six banana skins or orange peels. Aged women seeing him approaching would beg him with tears in their eyes not to carry their pails of water across the road. They knew too well what the result would inevitably be. But it was in the life-saving competition that Stanley Judkins's conduct was most blameable and had the most far-reaching effects. The practice, as you know, was to throw a selected lower boy, of suitable dimensions, fully dressed, with his hands and feet tied together, into the deepest part of Cuckoo Weir, and to time the Scout whose turn it was to rescue him. On every occasion when he was entered for this competition Stanley Judkins was seized, at the critical moment, with a severe fit of cramp, which caused him to roll on the ground and utter alarming cries. This naturally distracted the attention of those present from the boy in the water, and had it not been for the presence of Arthur Wilcox the death-roll would have been a heavy one. As it was, the Lower Master found it necessary to take a firm line and say that the competition must be discontinued. It was in vain that Mr Beasley Robinson represented to him that in five competitions only four lower boys had actually succumbed. The

Lower Master said that he would be the last to interfere in any way with the work of the Scouts; but that three of these boys had been valued members of his choir, and both he and Dr Ley felt that the inconvenience caused by the losses outweighed the advantages of the competitions. Besides, the correspondence with the parents of these boys had become annoying, and even distressing: they were no longer satisfied with the printed form which he was in the habit of sending out, and more than one of them had actually visited Eton and taken up much of his valuable time with complaints. So the life-saving competition is now a thing of the past.

In short, Stanley Judkins was no credit to the Scouts, and there was talk on more than one occasion of informing him that his services were no longer required. This course was strongly advocated by Mr Lambart: but in the end milder counsels prevailed, and it was decided to give him another chance.

So it is that we find him at the beginning of the Midsummer Holidays of 19— at the Scouts' camp in the beautiful district of W (or X) in the county of D (or Y).

It was a lovely morning, and Stanley Judkins and one or two of his friends—for he still had friends—lay basking on the top of the down. Stanley was lying on his stomach with his chin propped on his hands, staring into the distance.

"I wonder what that place is," he said.

"Which place?" said one of the others.

"That sort of clump in the middle of the field down there."

"Oh, ah! How should I know what it is?"

"What do you want to know for?" said another.

"I don't know: I like the look of it. What's it called? Nobody got a map?" said Stanley. "Call yourselves Scouts!"

"Here's a map all right," said Wilfred Pipsqueak, ever resourceful, "and there's the place marked on it. But it's inside the red ring. We can't go there."

"Who cares about a red ring?" said Stanley. "But it's got no name on your silly map."

"Well, you can ask this old chap what it's called if you're so keen to find out." "This old chap" was an old shepherd who had come up and was standing behind them.

"Good morning, young gents," he said, "you've got a fine day for your doin's, ain't you?"

"Yes, thank you," said Algernon de Montmorency, with native politeness. "Can you tell us what that clump over there's called? And what's that thing inside it?"

"Course I can tell you," said the shepherd. "That's Wailin' Well, that is. But you ain't got no call to worry about that."

"Is it a well in there?" said Algernon. "Who uses it?"

The shepherd laughed. "Bless you," he said, "there ain't from a man to a sheep in these parts uses Wailin' Well, nor haven't done all the years I've lived here."

"Well, there'll be a record broken today, then," said Stanley Judkins, "because I shall go and get some water out of it for tea!"

"Sakes alive, young gentleman!" said the shepherd in a startled voice, "don't you get to talkin' that way! Why, ain't your masters give you notice not to go by there? They'd ought to have done."

"Yes, they have," said Wilfred Pipsqueak.

"Shut up, you ass!" said Stanley Judkins. "What's the matter with it? Isn't the water good? Anyhow, if it was boiled, it would be all right."

"I don't know as there's anything much wrong with the water," said the shepherd. "All I know is, my old dog wouldn't go through

WAILING WELL

that field, let alone me or anyone else that's got a morsel of brains in their heads."

"More fool them," said Stanley Judkins, at once rudely and ungrammatically. "Who ever took any harm going there?" he added.

"Three women and a man," said the shepherd gravely. "Now just you listen to me. I know these 'ere parts and you don't, and I can tell you this much: for these ten years last past there ain't been a sheep fed in that field, nor a crop raised off of it—and it's good land, too. You can pretty well see from here what a state it's got into with brambles and suckers and trash of all kinds. *You've* got a glass, young gentleman," he said to Wilfred Pipsqueak, "you can tell with that anyway."

"Yes," said Wilfred, "but I see there's tracks in it. Someone must go through it sometimes."

"Tracks!" said the shepherd. "I believe you! Four tracks: three women and a man."

"What d'you mean, three women and a man?" said Stanley, turning over for the first time and looking at the shepherd (he had been talking with his back to him till this moment: he was an ill-mannered boy).

"Mean? Why, what I says: three women and a man."

"Who are they?" asked Algernon. "Why do they go there?"

"There's some p'r'aps could tell you who they *was*," said the shepherd, "but it was afore my time they come by their end. And why they goes there still is more than the children of men can tell: except I've heard they was all bad 'uns when they was alive."

"By George, what a rum thing!" Algernon and Wilfred muttered: but Stanley was scornful and bitter.

"Why, you don't mean they're deaders? What rot! You must be a lot of fools to believe that. Who's ever seen them, I'd like to know?"

"*I've* seen 'em, young gentleman!" said the shepherd, "seen 'em from near by on that bit of down: and my old dog, if he could speak, he'd tell you he've seen 'em, same time. About four o'clock of the day it was, much such a day as this. I see 'em, each one of 'em, come peerin' out of the bushes and stand up, and work their way slow by them tracks towards the trees in the middle where the well is."

"And what were they like? Do tell us!" said Algernon and Wilfred eagerly.

"Rags and bones, young gentlemen: all four of 'em: flutterin' rags and whity bones. It seemed to me as if I could hear 'em clackin' as they got along. Very slow they went, and lookin' from side to side."

"What were their faces like? Could you see?"

"They hadn't much to call faces," said the shepherd, "but I could seem to see as they had teeth."

"Lor'!" said Wilfred, "and what did they do when they got to the trees?"

"I can't tell you that, sir," said the shepherd. "I wasn't for stayin' in that place, and if I had been, I was bound to look to my old dog: he'd gone! Such a thing he never done before as leave me; but gone he had, and when I came up with him in the end, he was in that state he didn't know me, and was fit to fly at my throat. But I kep' talkin' to him, and after a bit he remembered my voice and came creepin' up like a child askin' pardon. I never want to see him like that again, nor yet no other dog."

The dog, who had come up and was making friends all round, looked up at his master, and expressed agreement with what he was saying very fully.

The boys pondered for some moments on what they had heard: after which Wilfred said: "And why's it called Wailing Well?"

"If you was round here at dusk of a winter's evening, you wouldn't want to ask why," was all the shepherd said.

"Well, I don't believe a word of it," said Stanley Judkins, "and I'll go there next chance I get: blowed if I don't!"

"Then you won't be ruled by me?" said the shepherd. "Nor yet by your masters as warned you off? Come now, young gentleman, you don't want for sense, I should say. What should I want tellin' you a pack of lies? It ain't sixpence to me anyone goin' in that field: but I wouldn't like to see a young chap snuffed out like in his prime."

"I expect it's a lot more than sixpence to you," said Stanley. "I expect you've got a whisky still or something in there, and want to keep other people away. Rot I call it. Come on back, you boys."

So they turned away. The two others said, "Good evening" and "Thank you" to the shepherd, but Stanley said nothing. The shepherd shrugged his shoulders and stood where he was, looking after them rather sadly.

On the way back to the camp there was great argument about it all, and Stanley was told as plainly as he could be told all the sorts of fools he would be if he went to the Wailing Well.

That evening, among other notices, Mr Beasley Robinson asked if all maps had got the red ring marked on them. "Be particular," he said, "not to trespass inside it."

Several voices—among them the sulky one of Stanley Judkins— said, "Why not, sir?"

"Because not," said Mr Beasley Robinson, "and if that isn't enough for you, I can't help it." He turned and spoke to Mr Lambart in a low voice, and then said, "I'll tell you this much: we've been asked to warn Scouts off that field. It's very good of the people to let us camp here at all, and the least we can do is to oblige them—I'm sure you'll agree to that."

Everybody said, "Yes, sir!" except Stanley Judkins, who was heard to mutter, "Oblige them be blowed!"

Early in the afternoon of the next day, the following dialogue was heard. "Wilcox, is all your tent there?"

"No, sir, Judkins isn't!"

"That boy is *the* most infernal nuisance ever invented! Where do you suppose he is?"

"I haven't an idea, sir."

"Does anybody else know?"

"Sir, I shouldn't wonder if he'd gone to the Wailing Well."

"Who's that? Pipsqueak? What's the Wailing Well?"

"Sir, it's that place in the field by—well, sir, it's in a clump of trees in a rough field."

"D'you mean inside the red ring? Good heavens! What makes you think he's gone there?"

"Why, he was terribly keen to know about it yesterday, and we were talking to a shepherd man, and he told us a lot about it and advised us not to go there: but Judkins didn't believe him, and said he meant to go."

"Young ass!" said Mr Hope Jones, "did he take anything with him?"

"Yes, I think he took some rope and a can. We did tell him he'd be a fool to go."

"Little brute! What the deuce does he mean by pinching stores like that! Well, come along, you three, we must see after him. Why can't people keep the simplest orders? What was it the man told you? No, don't wait, let's have it as we go along."

And off they started—Algernon and Wilfred talking rapidly and the other two listening with growing concern. At last they reached that spur of down over-looking the field of which the shepherd had spoken the day before. It commanded the place completely; the well inside the clump of bent and gnarled Scotch firs was plainly visible, and so were the four tracks winding about among the thorns and rough growth.

It was a wonderful day of shimmering heat. The sea looked like a floor of metal. There was no breath of wind. They were all exhausted when they got to the top, and flung themselves down on the hot grass.

"Nothing to be seen of him yet," said Mr Hope Jones, "but we must stop here a bit. You're done up—not to speak of me. Keep a sharp look-out," he went on after a moment, "I thought I saw the bushes stir."

"Yes," said Wilcox, "so did I. Look… no, that can't be him. It's somebody though, putting their head up, isn't it?"

"I thought it was, but I'm not sure."

Silence for a moment. Then:

"That's him, sure enough," said Wilcox, "getting over the hedge on the far side. Don't you see? With a shiny thing. That's the can you said he had."

"Yes, it's him, and he's making straight for the trees," said Wilfred.

At this moment Algernon, who had been staring with all his might, broke into a scream.

"What's that on the track? On all fours—O, it's the woman. O, don't let me look at her! Don't let it happen!" And he rolled over, clutching at the grass and trying to bury his head in it.

"Stop that!" said Mr Hope Jones loudly—but it was no use. "Look here," he said, "I must go down there. You stop here, Wilfred, and look after that boy. Wilcox, you run as hard as you can to the camp and get some help."

They ran off, both of them. Wilfred was left alone with Algernon, and did his best to calm him, but indeed he was not much happier himself. From time to time he glanced down the hill and into the field. He saw Mr Hope Jones drawing nearer at a swift pace, and then, to his great surprise, he saw him stop, look up and round about him, and turn quickly off at an angle! What could be the reason? He looked at the field, and there he saw a terrible figure—something in ragged black—with whitish patches breaking out of it: the head, perched on a long thin neck, half hidden by a shapeless sort of blackened sun-bonnet. The creature was waving thin arms in the direction of the rescuer who was approaching, as if to ward him off: and between the two figures the air seemed to shake and shimmer as he had never seen it: and as he looked, he began himself to feel something of a waviness and confusion in his brain, which made him guess what might be the effect on someone within closer range of the influence. He looked away hastily, to see Stanley Judkins making his way pretty quickly towards the clump, and in proper Scout fashion; evidently picking his steps with care to avoid treading on snapping sticks or being caught by arms of brambles. Evidently, though he saw nothing, he suspected some sort of ambush, and was trying to go noiselessly. Wilfred saw all that, and he saw more, too. With a sudden and dreadful sinking at the heart, he caught sight of someone among the trees, waiting: and again of someone—another of the hideous black figures—working slowly along the track from another side of the field, looking from side to side, as the shepherd had described it. Worst of all, he saw a fourth—unmistakably a man this time—rising out of the bushes a few yards behind the wretched Stanley, and painfully, as it seemed, crawling into the track. On all sides the miserable victim was cut off.

Wilfred was at his wits' end. He rushed at Algernon and shook him. "Get up," he said. "Yell! Yell as loud as you can. Oh, if we'd got a whistle!"

Algernon pulled himself together. "There's one," he said, "Wilcox's: he must have dropped it."

So one whistled, the other screamed. In the still air the sound carried. Stanley heard: he stopped: he turned round: and then indeed a cry was heard more piercing and dreadful than any that the boys on the hill could raise. It was too late. The crouched figure behind Stanley sprang at him and caught him about the waist. The dreadful one that was standing waving her arms waved them again, but in exultation. The one that was lurking among the trees shuffled forward, and she too stretched out her arms as if to clutch at something coming her way; and the other, farthest off, quickened her pace and came on, nodding gleefully. The boys took it all in in an instant of terrible silence, and hardly could they breathe as they watched the horrid struggle between the man and his victim. Stanley struck with his can, the only weapon he had. The rim of a broken black hat fell off the creature's head and showed a white skull with stains that might be wisps of hair. By this time one of the women had reached the pair, and was pulling at the rope that was coiled about Stanley's neck. Between them they overpowered him in a moment: the awful screaming ceased, and then the three passed within the circle of the clump of firs.

Yet for a moment it seemed as if rescue might come. Mr Hope Jones, striding quickly along, suddenly stopped, turned, seemed to rub his eyes, and then started running *towards* the field. More: the boys glanced behind them, and saw not only a troop of figures from the camp coming over the top of the next down, but the shepherd running up the slope of their own hill. They beckoned, they shouted, they ran a few yards towards him and then back again. He mended his pace.

Once more the boys looked towards the field. There was nothing. Or, was there something among the trees? Why was there a mist about the trees? Mr Hope Jones had scrambled over the hedge, and was plunging through the bushes.

The shepherd stood beside them, panting. They ran to him and clung to his arms. "They've got him! In the trees!" was as much as they could say, over and over again.

"What? Do you tell me he've gone in there after all I said to him yesterday? Poor young thing! Poor young thing!" He would have said more, but other voices broke in. The rescuers from the camp had arrived. A few hasty words, and all were dashing down the hill.

They had just entered the field when they met Mr Hope Jones. Over his shoulder hung the corpse of Stanley Judkins. He had cut it from the branch to which he found it hanging, waving to and fro. There was not a drop of blood in the body.

On the following day Mr Hope Jones sallied forth with an axe and with the expressed intention of cutting down every tree in the clump, and of burning every bush in the field. He returned with a nasty cut in his leg and a broken axe-helve. Not a spark of fire could he light, and on no single tree could he make the least impression.

I have heard that the present population of the Wailing Well field consists of three women, a man, and a boy.

The shock experienced by Algernon de Montmorency and Wilfred Pipsqueak was severe. Both of them left the camp at once; and the occurrence undoubtedly cast a gloom—if but a passing one—on those who remained. One of the first to recover his spirits was Judkins *mi*.

Such, gentlemen, is the story of the career of Stanley Judkins, and of a portion of the career of Arthur Wilcox. It has, I believe, never been told before. If it has a moral, that moral is, I trust, obvious: if it has none, I do not well know how to help it.

1935

GIBBET LANE

Anthony Gittins

Anthony Gittins (1910–1998) wrote short stories for *The Evening Standard*, *The Strand Magazine* and *Esquire* in the 1930s. "Gibbet Lane" is his most anthologised tale, and was first published in the Hutchinson collection *50 Years of Ghost Stories* in 1935. The narrative follows two interwar iterations of the hipster hiker on a weekend wander in the Surrey countryside. After taking a little-used lane in search of refreshment, the duo have a markedly strange encounter.

In *Literary Hauntings*, Rosalie Parker suggests that Gittins was inspired by Surrey's Gibbet Hill, which stands above the natural amphitheatre of the Devil's Punch Bowl near Hindhead. When a sailor was murdered in 1786 on the old London to Portsmouth road, the three men who assailed him were hanged on Gibbet Hill, near the scene of the crime, and left to swing as a warning to others. An eighteenth-century memorial stone marking the site of the murder can still be seen.

In the years following the incident, Gibbet Hill acquired a fearful, haunted reputation, and a Celtic cross was erected at the summit by a local politician in 1851 in an apparent attempt to exorcise the spot. The area is now managed by the National Trust and an easy walking trail takes you along the edge of the Devil's Punch Bowl, past the Sailor's Stone and up to Gibbet Hill with its views of the distant

London skyline. The unfortunate, anonymous sailor was buried in the tranquil village of Thursley nearby, and his headstone can be found in the churchyard of St Michael and All Angels.

They walked together down the road with a purposeful but laboured stride which, in addition to their farcically large and elaborate rucksacks (every pastime has its panache), marked them as town-dwellers on a weekend hike.

Their movements and pace, schooled to a pavement scuttle, lacked rhythm. They fatigued themselves much more by swinging fast downhill than by plodding uphill, and their long periods of silence were due to this fatigue, and not to any absorption or even interest in the scenery.

Conclusive proof that they came from the noisome intestines of a large town was afforded by their pale faces and a complete ignorance of the purpose of gate-fasteners. And as they were in Surrey (where the country timidly begins south of the latitude through Guildford), and as they expected any and every farmhouse to supply them with tea ("we're quite willing to pay"), and as they behaved with a transatlantic disregard for other people's property, it was evident that they were Londoners.

The taller one, who had a wart (described by his mother as a birthmark and by his father as a damned pimple) on his forehead and sheepish eyes, was a Mr Gollen, aged thirty-two, and he worked in the Chancery Lane office of the Belladonna Insurance Company. His friend, Mr Pounceby, aged thirty-seven, had a large head and rather short hair, and also worked in the Chancery Lane office of the Belladonna Insurance Company. They both had the unimpressionable and sceptical nature common to all insurance agents, and also that deficiency of imagination which is normal in business men.

In fine, they were stolid creatures; material in outlook; daring jesters at the expense of the League of Nations ("damned old mothers' meeting," Mr Pounceby would say); no less daring in their censure of politicians ("start every war, they do," Mr Gollen would observe); and raucously contemptuous of the supernatural ("ghosts? All bosh and eyewash!" they would chorus disdainfully).

It is particularly important to remember that they were so scornful about psychic phenomena. Had they been windy old men, or neurotics, or journalists, no genuine authority could have attached to this story of theirs.

They had just, for the fourth time, unsuccessfully requested tea at a farmhouse.

"Frightfully unsociable people round here," remarked Mr Pounceby, as they trudged on, their huge limp rucksacks likening them to parched camels searching for an oasis.

"Yes, frightfully," agreed Mr Gollen. "Dash it all, you'd think they'd be jolly glad to make a tanner out of two cups of tea."

"Or two cups of tea out of tanner—I mean, tannin," rejoined Mr Pounceby wittily.

"I wish I could think of things like that as quickly as you do, George," said Mr Gollen with intense admiration. "You know, you ought to write a play. I'll bet you could do that Noel Coward sort of dialogue as easy as pat."

"Oh, I don't know," said the gratified Mr Pounceby, desperately cranking his mind in the hope of churning out another witticism. But it was like winding an empty sausage-machine. Nothing emerged.

He did try a pun on "Coward" and "pat", but even in his own eyes it was a dismal failure, so he hastily revived their original topic.

"No, they're not so hospitable as people in Town," he declared, just as if he were in the habit of dropping into houses in, say, the Cromwell Road and offering the residents threepence for a cup of tea. "Hullo, there's someone ahead, up by that signpost. We'll ask him where the nearest pub is."

They covered the intervening distance in silence.

The man who stood near the old, discoloured signpost, occasionally swiping with his stick at the long grass, had a pale, oval face with bright eyes set in dark pits and a thin, curved nose which came forth like an unexpected challenge from his meek and otherwise regular features.

He was about fifty, and wore a brown tweed shooting hat (back to front) with a small feather in one side, very old breeches and dull green stockings, a soiled white cotton scarf tied round his neck and tucked into his faded yellow corduroy waistcoat, and a comparatively new, heather-mixture Norfolk jacket. The clothes did not hang well on him: it was as if, at one time and another, he had been given each garment by a different employer, for they were oddly contrasted and all of better material than probably he himself could afford.

Altogether, with his rough apparel and sensitive features, he cut an unusual figure. He might have been a poet forced to earn his living on the land, and would, indeed, have been less conspicuous at the Café Royal than he was here.

Mr Pounceby, however, was not of this opinion.

"Typical countryman," he remarked as they approached.

"Yes," agreed Mr Gollen, wishing that he had been the first to make this astute observation. "Shall I ask him, or will you?"

Mr Pounceby said he would. He straightened his back and tried to look as if he had walked thirty miles that day and was enjoying it, whereas he had only walked seven and was loathing it. "Which is the way to the nearest public house?" he called out.

The man stopped swiping at the grass with his stick and looked at them. Before replying he deftly decapitated a small clump of rushes. "There's one at Felday," he said.

"Which way's that? Oh, I see it's on the signpost," said Mr Pounceby.

"If you go by that signpost," rejoined the man, "it'll be the English Channel you'll reach before Felday. It swings round with the wind. See?" He grasped it with one hand and twisted it. "Now it's right."

"Thanks," said Mr Gollen.

"Not that it'll help you any better, even now, to find Felday," said the man, "if you're strange to these parts." He began chewing a reed. "I see you are," he added.

This huffed Mr Pounceby, who, though proud of being a townee, always hoped to pass unidentified as such in the country because, as he candidly confessed, "they'll do much more for you, you know, if they think you're one of their sort". Unfortunately he always failed to pass as "one of their sort" because he believed that, to do in Rome as the Romans do, it was only necessary to wear a toga and sandals.

"Isn't it rather a waste of the taxpayers' money," he said, "to put up signposts which are of no use?"

"Squire's orders. Nothing to do with the taxpayers," replied the man. "Very few people use this lane, anyway."

And in his tone there was something which implied that the lane was rarely frequented, not because it was out of the way but because it had an unpleasant history.

He threw away the reed he had been chewing, and moved the post again until it was upright. Then he noted the shadow which it cast. The sun was disappearing behind a muddle of dark clouds, and the dim, attenuated shadow struck the base of an oak in the opposite hedge. "Ten minutes to five," he observed. "You've got about a mile and a half to go."

"Well, thanks," said Mr Gollen again, for he was no conversationalist at the best of times, and having noticed the lowering sky he was anxious to reach shelter before it rained.

He shook hands with the man and moved towards the lane, which was little more than a path, leading to Felday.

Mr Pounceby also awarded the stranger a handshake, and at the same time was about to express his thanks when (and Mr Pounceby afterwards remained positive on this point) the man said:

"I'll come some of the way with you."

"Well, thanks very much," said Mr Pounceby, and caught up with his friend Gollen, while the man fell into step on the outside of Mr Pounceby.

"There's a use for everything, you see," said the man. (Gollen and Pounceby, appalled by the prospect of another mile and a half, had abruptly subsided into one of their periodic silences). "Take that signpost. As a signpost it's useless. It should say how far it is to Felday. It should say that this lane's called Gibbet Lane. It should quite reasonably always point in the same direction. It doesn't do any of these things. But all the same it's a pretty good sort of sundial."

He spoke swiftly, smoothly, giving scant opportunity for question or comment.

"When poor old Jasey had such a terrible fright up here—over a year ago, that was—I thought it was that signpost that did it. Until

I got home I did, anyway. Jasey's my dog—red setter. It does look a bit queer in this dull light, don't you think?"

Mr Pounceby glanced back over his shoulder.

"Come on," growled Mr Gollen, who was concerned about the rapidly darkening sky.

"Like a gallows, rather," added the man, without waiting for a reply. "Actually, there was a gallows there once. The last man they hanged on it was a farmer named Colter—James Colter. Case of wife murder. Two hours after he was dead they found he was innocent. The next morning the gibbet was down—struck by lightning, some said. But there were six people in the neighbourhood who swore they'd seen James Colter during the night."

He paused for a moment. Low in the sky the last pale strand of the sun disappeared, and a small, unexpected wind murmured a requiem in the trees. Then there was silence. The man's voice became more subdued.

"That's why this lane is called Gibbet Lane, and, whatever people may say, there's something mighty queer about it. I never bring Jasey up here now, but I often wonder what he could tell about that afternoon he took fright up here.

"It was like this. We were walking together down this lane. Jasey was two or three yards in front of me. Mind you, he isn't a nervous dog, and never has been. But he suddenly stopped dead and looked round. His eyes were focused about where I was, but he didn't seem to see me. God only knows what did catch his eye, for I've never seen such fear in the look of beast or man as I did then. The hair on his back went straight up, and he began edging away as if hell and all the devils were there.

"I clicked my finger two or three times and called out quietly, but it didn't have any effect. Then he let out a yell and bolted. My God, how he bolted! He went slap down this lane faster than a greyhound could have done, I reckon, and howling all the way."

The man nodded ahead to where the gable of a farmhouse was visible. The window under the gable faced up the lane, which was dead straight and, for the most part, hemmed in by high rocky banks, as if it had once been the bed of a stream. There was no grass, no plant life, no vegetation at all on either bank. It was a sombre gully, and shadows were now huddling into the crannies and fissures of its barren sides.

"That's where I used to live, with my sister. It's empty now. My sister died last March. Well, Jasey was back there in a flash and had jumped the gate into the yard before my sister had time to run downstairs and open it for him. You see, she'd not only heard him coming but had been looking out of her bedroom window—that's the one you can see from here—when he'd started behaving so queerly. She'd seen it all.

"A couple of minutes later I got back, wondering whether that queer-looking signpost had had anything to do with it or whether the dog had seen something strange. It's said they're more susceptible than human beings to—well, to anything psychic. They can sense the presence of death, too. Anyway, I asked my sister what her opinion was. She said: 'Oh, he must have taken fright at some noise. If you'd been with him at the moment...'

"'But I was with him,' I said. 'Just behind him.'

"'*With* him? When he bolted?'

"'Yes. In fact, I was with him all the way down until he ran off like that.'

"My sister looked at me rather curiously, and asked if I'd been drinking. She knew very well, though, that I never do drink, and I told her so. She fixed her eyes very queerly on me, then.

"'I saw you come some of the way down,' she said. 'Then I attended to something in the room. When I looked out again I... Dick, I'm frightened,' she said suddenly, and caught hold of my arm. 'You're telling me the truth, aren't you? Swear to me you were in the lane when...'

"'Nancy,' I said. 'I give you my oath that I was with the dog every step of the way till he bolted from me. Why do you ask?'

"She went very white then, and I thought she was going to faint. 'I don't understand it!' she cried. 'I can see every inch of that lane from my window, and as God's my witness I swear there was not a soul in it when Jasey took fright. The dog was absolutely alone!'

"You can imagine what a shock that gave me," continued the man after a moment's pause. "For I remembered that the dog had been looking where I was, and yet... yet," he said very slowly, "there was something about me—shall I say, something *in* me—so horrible that it sent an animal half-mad with fear. It's the sort of thing that can easily turn a man's reason, isn't it, if he thinks about it... much?"

At this point the man stopped abruptly, and Mr Pounceby, more perturbed than he cared to show, realised that the story was at an end. He realised also, with genuine uneasiness, that they were now walking down the very lane where this peculiar incident had taken place. At that moment he wished he was miles from the spot. Subsequently, he wished most emphatically that he had never gone down the lane at all. It served him as a perennial topic of conversation, of course, but the whole of that afternoon's experience was one that he would never have voluntarily undergone again.

"What a remarkable thing!" he said, mastering his uneasiness.

"What's remarkable?" asked Mr Gollen, speaking for the second time since leaving the signpost.

ny shadows formed by a dark conspiracy of
on light. Westward, the rain was already

y this gentleman has just told us," retorted Mr

r Gollen looked about him with a perplexed frown, and then stared very hard at his friend. "What the dickens d'you mean?" he demanded in bewilderment. "What story? What gentleman?"

Mr Pounceby glanced sharply to his right, stopped dead; and remained as rigid as if he had just awoken from a nightmare. His mouth sagged open; his skin turned the colour of chalk.

"My God!" he exclaimed. And again, slowly, almost in a whisper: "My... God!"

He wheeled round and peered up the dim perspective of the lane.

Beside the signpost, which stood gauntly against a dado of pale clouds, was a man—an indistinct but recognisable figure—swiping with a stick at the long grass.

An hour later, the two of them were in the pub at Felday, and had related their experience to the barman. Mr Pounceby was still considerably shaken.

Outside, the rain was sousing every inch of ground, and mists had descended as if to hold unholy communion with the deep cold lake among the pines.

"Grindlay," said the barman, and spelt it out. "Mr Oliver Grindlay—that's who it was. It's a mercy he'd gone when you went back. Why? Because that story about him and the dog is true, every word. It turned him up pretty bad—he's never been the same man since. And if he knew that something of the sort had happened again today...

"We don't talk about it much in these parts. It was a G[...] you know, that murdered James Colter's wife and had Colter h[...] for it on that spot where the signpost is now. That's another qu[...] thing, the way Mr Grindlay is always up alone by that signpost. Seem[...] to sort of fascinate him.

"You can't explain these things, though, and it's my belief that it's wisest not to think about 'em. But there's some would like to know—though they don't care to hang about Gibbet Lane and find out," said the barman slowly—"just what that dog of his saw which sent him hell-for-leather back home, pretty near stark mad with fear."

Mr Pounceby, who was paler than usual, glanced at his own blurred reflection in the dark, rain-slashed window.

"I shouldn't," he said, and ordered two more double whiskies.

They passed into gloomy shadows formed by a dark conspiracy of elms and the failing afternoon light. Westward, the rain was already sheeting the skyline.

"Why, the story this gentleman has just told us," retorted Mr Pounceby.

Mr Gollen looked about him with a perplexed frown, and then stared very hard at his friend. "What the dickens d'you mean?" he demanded in bewilderment. "What story? What gentleman?"

Mr Pounceby glanced sharply to his right, stopped dead; and remained as rigid as if he had just awoken from a nightmare. His mouth sagged open; his skin turned the colour of chalk.

"My God!" he exclaimed. And again, slowly, almost in a whisper: "My... God!"

He wheeled round and peered up the dim perspective of the lane.

Beside the signpost, which stood gauntly against a dado of pale clouds, was a man—an indistinct but recognisable figure—swiping with a stick at the long grass.

An hour later, the two of them were in the pub at Felday, and had related their experience to the barman. Mr Pounceby was still considerably shaken.

Outside, the rain was sousing every inch of ground, and mists had descended as if to hold unholy communion with the deep cold lake among the pines.

"Grindlay," said the barman, and spelt it out. "Mr Oliver Grindlay—that's who it was. It's a mercy he'd gone when you went back. Why? Because that story about him and the dog is true, every word. It turned him up pretty bad—he's never been the same man since. And if he knew that something of the sort had happened again today..."

"We don't talk about it much in these parts. It was a Grindlay, you know, that murdered James Colter's wife and had Colter hanged for it on that spot where the signpost is now. That's another queer thing, the way Mr Grindlay is always up alone by that signpost. Seems to sort of fascinate him.

"You can't explain these things, though, and it's my belief that it's wisest not to think about 'em. But there's some would like to know—though they don't care to hang about Gibbet Lane and find out," said the barman slowly—"just what that dog of his saw which sent him hell-for-leather back home, pretty near stark mad with fear."

Mr Pounceby, who was paler than usual, glanced at his own blurred reflection in the dark, rain-slashed window.

"I shouldn't," he said, and ordered two more double whiskies.

1939

CURIOUS ADVENTURE OF MR BOND

Nugent Barker

The sight of a country inn has always been welcomed by the weary rambler. In Nugent Barker's "Curious Adventure of Mr Bond", however, generous hospitality is soon tainted with a strange, oppressive atmosphere, as the titular traveller tries to make sense of his unusual hosts at a series of three connected, and deeply peculiar, inns. The tale is a remarkable, darkly humorous, slice of horror from a writer who deserves to be more widely known.

Nugent Barker (1888–1955) was born into a wealthy London family. His father was a member of the Stock Exchange, while his mother, Rosetta Nugent, was descended from the Irish aristocratic family that inspired the writer's first name. The biographical notes to his only published collection of stories state that at school "he distinguished himself at drawing and essay writing and at nothing else whatsoever." Therefore, it perhaps makes sense that following his education he took on illustration work, before beginning to write fiction for magazines in the late 1920s and continuing throughout the 1930s—this story was first published in *Cornhill Magazine* in July 1939. His sole book, *Written with My Left Hand*, was published in 1951.

The setting that Barker created for the brothers Sasserach and their weird hostelries put us in mind of Scotland's remaining forest-scapes. The seemingly endless wall of trees that offers the promise of escape from the high plateau could certainly be matched to Galloway Forest Park, the UK's largest forest. There's a whole host of trails to explore in its 300 square miles, and as a designated Dark Sky Park, the moonlight should be as bright for you as it was for the unfortunate Mr Bond.

Mr Bond climbed from the wooded slopes of the valley into broad moonlight. His Inverness cape, throwing his portly figure into still greater prominence against the floor of tree-tops at his back, was torn and soiled by twigs and thorns and leaves, and he stooped with prim concern to brush off the bits and pieces. After this, he eased his knapsack on his shoulder; and now he blinked his eyes upon the country stretching out before him.

Far away, across the tufted surface of the tableland, there stood a house, with its column of smoke, lighted and still, on the verge of a forest.

A house—an *inn*—he felt it in his very bones! His hunger returned, and became a source of gratification to him. Toiling on, and pulling the brim of his hat over his eyes, he watched the ruby gleam grow bigger and brighter, and when at last he stood beneath the sign, he cried aloud, scarcely able to believe in his good fortune.

"The Rest of the Traveller," he read; and there, too, ran the name of the landlord: "Crispin Sasserach."

The stillness of the night discouraged him, and he was afraid to tap at the curtained window. And now, for the first time, the full weight of his weariness fell upon the traveller. Staring into the black mouth of the porch, he imagined himself to be at rest, in bed, sprawled out, abundantly sleeping, drugged into forgetfulness by a full stomach. He shut his eyes, and drooped a little under his Inverness cape; but when he looked again into the entrance, there stood Crispin Sasserach, holding a lamp between their faces. Mr Bond's was plump and heavy-jawed, with sagging cheeks, and eyes that scarcely reflected the lamplight; the other face was smooth and large and oval, with small lips pressed into a smile.

"Come in, come in," the landlord whispered, "*do* come in. She is cooking a *lovely* broth tonight!"

He turned and chuckled, holding the lamp above his head.

Through the doorway of this lost, upland inn, Mr Bond followed the monstrous back of his host. The passage widened and became a hall; and here, amongst the shadows that were gliding from their lurking-places as the lamp advanced, the landlord stopped, and tilted the flat of his hand in the air, as though enjoining his guest to listen. Then Mr Bond disturbed the silence of the house with a sniff and a sigh. Not only could he smell the "lovely broth"—already, in this outer hall, he tasted it… a complex and subtle flavour, pungent, heavy as honey, light as a web in the air, nipping him in the stomach, bringing tears into his eyes.

Mr Bond stared at Crispin Sasserach, at the shadows beyond, and back again to Crispin Sasserach. The man was standing there, with his huge, oval, hairless face upturned in the light of the lamp he carried; then, impulsively, as though reluctant to cut short such sweet anticipation, he plucked the traveller by the cape and led him to the cheerful living-room, and introduced him, with a flourish of the hand, to Myrtle Sasserach, the landlord's young and small and busy wife, who at that very moment was standing at a round table of great size, beneath the massive centre-beam of the ceiling, her black hair gleaming in the light of many candles, her plump hand dipping a ladle soundlessly into a bowl of steam.

On seeing the woman, whose long lashes were once more directed towards the bowl, Mr Bond drew his chin primly into his neckcloth, and glanced from her to Crispin Sasserach, and finally he fixed his eyes on the revolutions of the ladle. In a moment, purpose fell upon the living-room, and with swift and nervous gestures the landlord seated his guest at the table, seized the ladle from his wife, plunged it into the bowl, and thrust the brimming plate into the hands of Myrtle, who began at once to walk towards the traveller, the steam of the broth rising into her grave eyes.

After a muttered grace, Mr Bond pushed out his lips as though he were whispering "spoon".

"Oh, what a lovely broth!" he murmured, catching a drip in his handkerchief.

Crispin Sasserach grinned with delight. "I always say it's the best in the world." Whereupon, with a rush, he broke into peals of falsetto laughter, and blew a kiss towards his wife. A moment later, the two Sasserachs were leaving their guest to himself, bending over their own platefuls of broth, and discussing domestic affairs, as though they had no other person sitting at their table. For some time their voices were scarcely louder than the sound of the broth-eating; but when the traveller's plate was empty, then, in a flash, Crispin Sasserach became again a loud and attentive host. "Now then, sir—another helping?" he suggested, picking up the ladle, and beaming down into the bowl, while Myrtle left her chair and walked a second time towards the guest.

Mr Bond said that he would, and pulled his chair a little closer to the table. Into his blood and bones, life had returned with twice its accustomed vigour; his very feet were as light as though he had soaked them in a path of pine needles.

"There you are, sir! Myrtle's coming! Lord a'mighty, how I wish I was tasting it for the first time!" Then, spreading his elbows, the landlord crouched over his own steaming plateful, and chuckled again. "This broth is a wine in itself! It's a wine in itself, b'God! It staggers a man!" Flushed with excitement, his oval face looked larger than ever, and his auburn hair, whirled into bellicose corkscrews, seemed to burn brighter, as though someone had brought the bellows to it.

Stirred by the broth, Mr Bond began to describe minutely his journey out of the valley. His voice grew as prosy, his words as involved, as though he were talking at home amongst his own people. "Now, let me see—where was I?" he buzzed again and again. And later: "I was very glad to see your light, I can tell you!" he chuckled. Then Crispin jumped up from the table, his small mouth pouting with laughter.

The evening shifted to the fireside. Fresh logs cracked like pistol shots as Crispin Sasserach dropped them into the flames. The traveller would wish for nothing better than to sit here by the hearth, talking plangently to Crispin, and slyly watching Myrtle as she cleared away the supper things; though, indeed, among his own people, Mr Bond was thought to hold women in low esteem. He found her downcast eyes modest and even pretty. One by one she blew the candles out; with each extinguishment she grew more ethereal, while reaping a fuller share of the pagan firelight. "Come and sit beside us now, and talk," thought Mr Bond, and presently she came.

They made him very comfortable. He found a log fire burning in his bedroom, and a bowl of broth on the bedside table. "Oh, but they're overdoing it!" he cried aloud, petulantly; "they're crude, crude! They're nothing but school-children!"—and seizing the bowl, he emptied it on to the shaggy patch of garden beneath his window. The black wall of the forest seemed to stand within a few feet of his eyes. The room was filled with the mingled light of moon, fire, and candle.

Mr Bond, eager at last for the dreamless rest, the abandoned sleep, of the traveller, turned and surveyed the room in which he was to spend the night. He saw with pleasure the four-poster bed, itself as large as a tiny room; the heavy oaken chairs and cupboards; the tall, twisting candlesticks, their candles burnt halfway, no doubt, by a previous guest; the ceiling, that he could touch with the flat of his hand. He touched it.

In the misty morning he could see no hint of the forest, and down the shallow staircase he found the hall thick with the odour of broth. The Sasserachs were seated already at the breakfast table, like two children, eager to begin the day with their favourite food. Crispin Sasserach was lifting his spoon and pouting his lips, while Myrtle was stirring her ladle round the tureen, her eyes downcast; and Mr Bond sighed inaudibly as he saw again the woman's dark and lustrous hair. He noticed also the flawless condition of the Sasserach skin. There was not a blemish to be seen on their two faces, on their four hands. He attributed this perfection to the beneficial qualities of the broth, no less than to the upland air; and he began to discuss, in his plangent voice, the subject of health in general. In the middle of this discourse Crispin Sasserach remarked, excitedly, that he had a brother who kept an inn a day's journey along the edge of the forest.

"Oh," said Mr Bond, pricking up his ears, "so you have a brother, have you?"

"Certainly," whispered the innkeeper. "It is most convenient."

"Most convenient for what?"

"Why, for the inns. His name's Martin. We share our guests. We help each other. The proper brotherly spirit, b'God!"

Mr Bond stared angrily into his broth. "They share their guests... But what," he thought, "has that to do with me?" He said aloud: "Perhaps I'll meet him one day, Mr Sasserach."

"Today!" cried Crispin, whacking his spoon onto the table. "I'm taking you there today! But don't you worry," he added, seeing the look on the other's face, and flattering himself that he had read it aright; "you'll be coming back to us. Don't you worry! Day after tomorrow—day after that—one of these days! Ain't that right, Myr? Ain't that right?" he repeated, bouncing up and down in his chair like a big child.

"Quite right," answered Myrtle Sasserach to Mr Bond, whose eyes were fixed upon her with heavy attention.

A moment later the innkeeper was out of his chair, making for the hall, calling back to Myrtle to have his boots ready. In the midst of this bustle, Mr Bond bowed stiffly to Myrtle Sasserach, and found his way with dignity to the back garden, that now appeared wilder than he had supposed—a fenced-in plot of grass reaching above his knees and scattered with burdock, whose prickly heads clung to his clothes as he made for the gate in the fence at the foot of this wilderness. He blinked his eyes, and walked on the rough turf that lay between him and the forest. By this time the sun was shining in an unclouded sky; a fine day was at hand; and Mr Bond was sweeping his eye along the endless wall of forest when he heard the innkeeper's voice calling to him in the stillness. "Mr Bond! Mr Bond!" Turning reluctantly, and stepping carefully through the garden in order to avoid the burrs of the burdock, the traveller found Crispin Sasserach on the point of departure, in a great bustle, with a strong horse harnessed to a two-wheeled cart, and his wife putting up her face to be kissed.

"Yes, I'll go with you," cried Mr Bond, but the Sasserachs did not appear to hear him. He lingered for a moment in the porch, scowling at Myrtle's back, scowling at the large young horse that seemed to toss its head at him with almost human insolence, then he sighed, and, slinging his knapsack over his shoulder, sat himself beside the driver; the horse was uncommonly large, restless between the shafts, and in perfect fettle, and without a word from Crispin the animal began to plunge forward rapidly over the worn track.

For some time the two men drove in silence, on the second stage of Mr Bond's adventure above the valley. The traveller sat up stiffly, inflating his lungs methodically, glaring through his small eyes, and forcing back his shoulders. Presently he began to talk about the mountain air, and received no answer. On his right hand the wall of the forest extended as far as his eyes could see, while on his left hand ran the brink of the valley, a mile away, broken here and there by rowan trees.

The monotony of the landscape, and the continued silence of the innkeeper, soon began to pall on Mr Bond, who liked talking and was seldom at ease unless his eyes were busy picking out new things. Even the horse behaved with the soundless regularity of a machine; so that, besides the traveller, only the sky showed a struggle to make progress.

Clouds came from nowhere, shaped and broke, and at midday the sun in full swing was riding between white puffs of cloud, glistening by fits and starts on the moist coat of the horse. The forest beneath, and the stretch of coarse grass running to the valley, were constantly shining and darkening, yet Crispin Sasserach never opened his mouth, even to whisper, though sometimes between his teeth, he spat soundlessly over the edge of the cart. The landlord had brought with him a casserole of the broth; and during one of these sunny breaks he pulled up the horse, without a word, and poured the liquor into two pannikins, which he proceeded to heat patiently over a spirit stove.

In the failing light of the afternoon, when the horse was still making his top speed, when Crispin Sasserach was buzzing fitfully between his teeth, and sleep was flirting with the traveller, a shape appeared obscurely on the track ahead, and with it came the growing jingle of bells. Mr Bond sat up and stared. He had not expected to meet, in such a God-forsaken spot, another cart, or carriage. He saw at length, approaching him, a four-wheeled buggy, drawn by two sprightly horses in tandem. A thin-faced man in breeches and a bowler hat was driving it. The two drivers greeted each other solemnly, raised their whips, but never slackened speed.

"Well—who was that?" asked Mr Bond, after a pause.

"My brother Martin's manservant."

"Where is he going?" asked Mr Bond.

"To The Rest of the Traveller. With news."

"Indeed? What news?" persisted Mr Bond.

The landlord turned his head.

"News for my Myrtle," he whispered, winking at the traveller.

Mr Bond shrugged his shoulders. "What is the use of talking to such a boor?" he thought, and fell once more into his doze; the harvest-moon climbed up again, whitening the earth; while now and then the landlord spat towards the forest, and never spoke another word until he came to Martin Sasserach's.

Then Crispin leapt to life.

"Out with you!" he cried. "Pst! Mr Bond! Wake up! Get out at once! We've reached The Headless Man, sir!"

Mr Bond, staggered by so much energy, flopped to the ground. His head felt as large as the moon. He heard the horse panting softly, and saw the breath from its nostrils flickering upwards in the cold air;

while the white-faced Crispin Sasserach was leaping about under the moon, whistling between his teeth, and calling out enthusiastically: "Mar-tin! Mar-tin! Here he is!"

The sheer wall of forest echoed back the name. Indeed, the whole of the moonlight seemed to be filled with the name "Martin"; and Mr Bond had a fierce desire to see this Martin Sasserach whose sign was hanging high above the traveller's head. After repeated calls from Crispin, the landlord of The Headless Man appeared, and Mr Bond, expecting a very giant in physical stature, was shocked to see the small and bespectacled figure that had emerged from the house. Crispin Sasserach grew quick and calm in a moment. "Meet again," he whispered to Mr Bond, shutting his eyes, and stretching his small mouth as though in ecstasy; then he gave the traveller a push towards the approaching Martin, and a moment later he was in his cart, and the horse was springing its way back to The Rest of the Traveller.

Mr Bond stood where he was, listening to the dying sound of the horse, and watching the landlord of The Headless Man; and presently he was staring at two grey flickering eyes behind the landlord's glasses.

"Anyone arriving at my inn from my brother's is trebly welcome. He is welcome not only for Crispin's own sake and mine, but also for the sake of our brother Stephen." The voice was as quiet and as clear as the moonlight, and the speaker began to return to his inn with scarcely a pause between speech and movement. Mr Bond examined curiously the strongly-lighted hall that in shape and size was the very double of Crispin's. Oil-lamps, gracefully columned, gleamed almost as brightly from their fluted silver surfaces as from their opal-lighted heads; and there was Martin stooping up the very stairs, it seemed, that Mr Bond had walked at Crispin Sasserach's—a scanty man, this brother, throwing out monstrous shadows, turning once to peer back at his guest, and standing at last in a bright and airy bedroom, where, with courteous words from which his eyes, lost in thought and gently flickering, seemed to be far distant, he invited his guest to wash before dining.

Martin Sasserach fed Mr Bond delicately on that evening of his arrival, presenting him with small, cold dishes of various kinds and always exquisitely cooked and garnished; and these, together with the almost crystalline cleanliness of the room and of the table, seemed appropriate to the chemist-like appearance of the host. A bottle of wine was opened for Mr Bond, who, amongst his own people, was known to drink nothing headier than bottled cider. During dinner, the wine warmed up a brief moment of attention in Martin Sasserach. He peered with sudden interest at his guest. "The Headless Man? There is, in fact, a story connected with that name. If you can call it a story." He smiled briefly, tapping his finger, and a moment later was examining an ivory piece, elaborately carved, that held the bill of fare. "Lovely! Lovely! Isn't it?... In fact, there are many stories," he ended, as though the number of stories excused him from wasting his thought over the recital of merely one. Soon after dinner he retired, alluding distantly to work from which he never liked to be away long.

Mr Bond went to bed early that night, suffering from dyspepsia, and glowering at the absence of home comforts in his bright and efficient bedroom.

The birds awakened him to a brisk, autumnal morning. Breathing heavily, he told himself that he was always very fond of birds and trees and flowers; and soon he was walking sleepily in Martin Sasserach's garden. The trimness of the beds began to please him. He followed the right-angled paths with dignified obesity, his very bones were proud to be alive.

A green gate at the garden-foot attracted Mr Bond's attention; but, knowing that it would lead him on to the wild grass beyond, and thence to the forest, whose motionless crest could be seen all this while over the privet hedge, he chose to linger where he was, sniffing the clear scent of the flowers, and losing, with every breath and step, another whiff of Crispin's broth, to his intense delight.

Hunger drew him back into the house at last, and he began to pace the twilit rooms. Martin Sasserach, he saw, was very fond of ivory. He stooped and peered at the delicate things. Ivory objects of every description, perfectly carved: paper-knives, chess-men, salad-spoons; tiny busts and faces, often of grotesque appearance; and even delicate boxes, fretted from ivory.

The echo of his feet on the polished floors intensified the silence of The Headless Man; yet even this indoor hush was full of sound, when compared with the stillness of the scene beyond the uncurtained windows. The tufted grass was not yet lighted by the direct rays of the sun. The traveller stared towards the rowan trees that stood on the brink of the valley. Beyond them stretched a carpet of mist, raising the rest of the world to the height of the plateau; and Mr Bond, recalling the house and town that he had left behind him, began to wonder whether he was glad or sorry that his adventures had brought him to this lost region. "Cold enough for my cape," he shivered, fetching it from the hall, and hurrying out of the inn; the desire had seized him to walk on the tufted grass, to foot it as far as the trees; and he had indeed gone some distance on his journey, wrapped in his thoughts and antique Inverness cape, when the note of a gong came up behind him, like a thread waving on the air.

"Hark at that," he whispered, staring hard at the ragged line of rowan trees on which his heart was set; then he shrugged his shoulders, and turned back to The Headless Man, where his host was standing lost in thought at the breakfast-table that still held the crumbs of the night before.

"Ah, yes. Yes. It's you... You slept well?"

"Tolerably well," said Mr Bond.

"We breakfast rather early here. It makes a longer day. Stennet will be back later. He's gone to my brother Crispin's."

"With news?" said Mr Bond.

Martin Sasserach bowed courteously, though a trifle stiffly. He motioned his guest towards a chair at the table. Breakfast was cold and short and silent. Words were delicate things to rear in this crystalline atmosphere. Martin's skin sagged and was the colour of old ivory. Now and then he looked up at his guest, his grey eyes focused beyond mere externals; and it seemed as though they lodged themselves in Mr Bond's very bones. On one of these occasions the traveller made great play with his appetite. "It's all this upland air," he asserted, thumping his chest.

The sun began to rise above the plateau. Again the landlord vanished, murmuring his excuses; silence flooded The Headless Man, the garden purred in full blaze of the sun that now stood higher than the forest, and the gravelled paths crunched slowly beneath Mr Bond's feet. "News for Myrtle", he pondered, letting his thoughts stray back over his journey; and frequently he drifted through the house where all was still and spacious: dusty, museum-like rooms brimming with sunlight, while everywhere those ivory carvings caught his eye, possessing his sight as completely as the taste of Crispin's broth had lodged in his very lungs.

Lunch was yet another meal of cold food and silence, broken only by coffee that the landlord heated on a spirit stove at the end of the table, and by a question from the traveller, to which this thin-haired

Martin, delicately flicking certain greyish dust off the front of his coat and sleeve, replied that he had been a collector of carvings for years past, and was continually adding to his collection. His voice drew out in length and seemed, in fact, to trail him from the sunlit dining-room, back to his everlasting work... and now the afternoon itself began to drag and presently to settle down in the sun as though the whole of time were dozing.

"Here's my indigestion back again," sighed Mr Bond, mooning about. At home he would have rested in his bedroom, with its pink curtains and flowered wallpaper.

He crept into the garden and eyed the back of the house. Which of those windows in the trimly-creepered stone lit up the landlord and his work? He listened for the whirring of a lathe, the scraping of a knife... and wondered, startled, why he had expected to hear such things. He felt the forest behind his back, and turned, and saw it looming above the privet hedge. Impulsively, he started to cross the sunswept grass beyond the gate; but within a few yards of the forest his courage failed him again: he could not face the wall of trees: and with a cry he fled into the house, and seized his Inverness.

His eyes looked far beyond the rowans on the skyline as he plodded over the tufted grass. Already he could see himself down there below, counties and counties away, on the valley level, in the house of his neighbours the Allcards, drinking their coffee or tea and telling them of his adventures and especially of *this* adventure. It was not often that a man of his age and secure position in the world went off alone, in search of joy or trouble. He scanned the distant line of rowan trees, and nodded, harking back: "As far as it has gone. I'll tell them this adventure, as far as it ever went." And he would say to them: "The things I might have seen, if I had stayed! Yes, Allcard, I was very glad to climb down into the valley that day, I can tell you! I don't mind admitting I was a bit frightened!"

The tippet of his cape caressed his shoulders, like the hand of a friend.

Mr Bond was not yet halfway to the rowan trees when, looking back, he saw, against the darkness of the forest wall, a carriage rapidly approaching The Headless Man. At once there flashed into his memory the eyes of the manservant Stennet who went between the Sasserach inns.

He knew that Stennet's eyes were on him now. The sound of the horses' feet was coming up to him like a soft ball bouncing over the grass. Mr Bond shrugged his shoulders, and stroked his pendulous cheeks. Already he was on his way back to The Headless Man, conscious that two flying horses could have overtaken him long before he had reached the rowans. "But why," he thought, holding himself with dignity, "should I imagine that these people are expecting me to run away? And why that sudden panic in the garden? It's all that deathly quietness of the morning getting on my nerves."

The carriage had disappeared some time before he reached the inn, over whose tiled and weather-stained roof the redness of the evening was beginning to settle. And now the traveller was conscious of a welcome that seemed to run out and meet him at the very door. He found a log fire crackling in the dining-room, and Mr Bond, holding his hands to the blaze, felt suddenly at ease, and weary. He had intended to assert himself—to shout for Martin Sasserach—to demand that he be escorted down at once from the plateau... but now he wished for nothing better than to stand in front of the fire, waiting for Stennet to bring him tea.

A man began to sing in the heart of the house. Stennet? The fellow's eyes and hawk-like nose were suddenly visible in the fire. The singing voice grew louder... died at length discreetly into silence and the tread of footsteps in the hall... and again the traveller was listening to the flames as they roared in the chimney.

"Let me take your coat, sir," Stennet said.

Then Mr Bond whipped round, his cheeks shaking with anger.

Why did they want to force this hospitality upon him, making him feel like a prisoner? He glared at the large-checked riding-breeches, at the muscular shoulders, at the face that seemed to have grown the sharper through swift driving. He almost shouted: "Where's that bowler hat?"

Fear?... Perhaps... But if fear had clutched him for a moment, it had left him now. He knew that the voice had pleased him, a voice of deference breaking into the cold and irreverent silence of The Headless Man. The cape was already off his shoulders, hanging on Stennet's bent and respectful arm. And—God be praised!—the voice was announcing that tea would be ready soon. Mr Bond's spirits leapt with the word. He and Stennet stood there, confidentially plotting. "China? Yes, sir. We have China," Stennet said.

"And buttered toast," said Mr Bond, softly rubbing his chin. Some time after tea he was awakened from his doze by the hand of the manservant, who told him that a can of boiling water was waiting in his room.

Mr Bond felt that dinner would be a rich meal that night, and it was. He blushed as the dishes were put before him. Hare soup! How did they know his favourite soup? Through entrée, remove, and toast, his hands, soft and pink from washing, were busier than they had been for days. The chicken was braised to a turn. Oh, what mushrooms au gratin! The partridge brought tears to his eyes. The Saxony pudding caused him to turn again to Martin, in Stennet's praise.

The landlord bowed with distant courtesy. "A game of chess?" he suggested, when dinner was over. "My last opponent was a man like yourself, a traveller making a tour of the inns. We started a game. He is gone from us now. Perhaps you will take his place?" smiled Martin Sasserach, his precise voice dropping and seeming to transmit its flow of action to the thin hand poised above the board. "My move," he whispered, playing at once; he had thought it out for a week. But although Mr Bond tried to sink his thoughts into the problem before him, he could not take them off his after-dinner dyspepsia, and with apologies and groans he scraped back his chair. "I'm sorry for that," smiled Martin, and his eyes flickered over the board. "I'm very sorry. Another night... undoubtedly... with your kind help... another night..."

The prospect of another day at The Headless Man was at once disturbing and pleasant to Mr Bond as he went wheezing up to bed.

"Ah, Stennet! Do *you* ever suffer from dyspepsia?" he asked mournfully, seeing the man at the head of the staircase. Stennet snapped his fingers, and was off downstairs in a moment; and a minute later he was standing at the traveller's door, with a bowl of Crispin's famous broth. "Oh, that!" cried Mr Bond, staring down at the bowl. Then he remembered its fine effect on his indigestion at Crispin's; and when at last he pulled the sheets over his head, he fell asleep in comfort and did not wake until the morning.

At breakfast Martin Sasserach looked up from his plate.

"This afternoon," he murmured, "Stennet will be driving you to my brother Stephen's."

Mr Bond opened his eyes. "Another inn? Another of you Sasserachs?"

"Crispin—Martin—Stephen. Just the three of us. A perfect number... if you come to think of it."

The traveller strode into the garden. Asters glowed in the lustreless light of the morning. By ten o'clock the sun was shining again, and by midday a summer heat lay on the plateau, penetrating even into Mr Bond's room. The silence of the forest pulled him to the window, made him lift up his head and shut his eyes upon that monstrous mass of trees. Fear was trying to overpower him. He did not want to go to Stephen Sasserach's; but the hours were running past him quickly now, the stillness was gone from the inn.

At lunch, to which his host contributed a flow of gentle talk, the traveller felt rising within him an impatience to be off on the third stage of his journey, if such a stage must be. He jumped up from his chair without apology, and strode into the garden. The asters were now shining dimly in the strong sunlight. He opened the gate in the privet hedge, and walked onto the tufted grass that lay between it and the forest. As he did so, he heard the flap of a wing behind him and saw a pigeon flying from a window in the roof. The bird flew over his head and over the forest and out of sight; and for the first time he remembered seeing a pigeon taking a similar course when he was standing in the garden at Crispin's inn.

His thought were still following the pigeon over the boundless floor of tree-tops when he heard a voice calling to him in the silence. "Mr Bond! Mr Bond!" He walked at once to the gate and down the garden and into the house, put on his Inverness, and hitched his knapsack onto his shoulder; and in a short while he was perched beside Stennet in the flying buggy, staring at the ears of the two horses, and remembering that Martin, at the last moment, instead of bidding his guest goodbye, had gone back to his work.

Though he never lost his fear of Stennet, Mr Bond found Martin's man a good companion on a journey, always ready to speak when spoken to, and even able to arouse the traveller's curiosity, at times, in the monotonous landscape.

"See those rowans over there?" said Stennet, nodding to the left. "Those rowans belong to Mr Martin. He owns them halfway to Mr Crispin's place, and halfway to Mr Stephen's. And so it is with Mr Crispin and Mr Stephen in their turn."

"And what about the forest?"

"Same again," said Stennet, waving his hand towards the right. "It's round, you know. And they each own a third, like a huge slice of cake."

He clicked his tongue, and the horses pricked up their ears, though on either side of the dashboard the performance was no more than a formality, so swiftly was the buggy moving. "Very much quicker than Crispin's cart!" gasped the passenger, feeling the wind against his face; yet, when the evening of the autumn day was closing in, he looked about him with surprise.

He saw the moon rise up above the valley.

Later still, he asked for information regarding the names of the three inns, and Stennet laughed.

"The gentlemen are mighty proud of them, I can tell you! Romantic and a bit fearsome, that's what I call them. Poetical, too. They don't say The Traveller's Rest, but The Rest of the Traveller, mind you. That's poetical. I don't think it was Mr Crispin's idea. I think it was Mr Martin's—or Mrs Crispin's. They're the clever ones. The Headless Man is merely grim—a grim turn of mind Mr Martin has—and it means, of course, no more than it says—a man without a head. And then again," continued Stennet, whistling to his horses, whose backs were gleaming in the moonlight, "the inn you're going to now—The Traveller's Head—well, inns are called The King's Head sometimes, aren't they, in the King's honour?

Mr Stephen goes one better than that. He dedicates his inn to the traveller himself." By this time a spark of light had become visible in the distance, and Mr Bond fixed his eyes upon it. Once, for a moment, the spark went out, and he imagined that Stephen's head had passed in front of the living-room lamp. At this picture, anger seized him, and he wondered, amazed, why he was submitting so tamely to the commands—he could call them no less—of these oddly hospitable brothers. Fanned by his rage, the spark grew steadily bigger and brighter, until at last it had achieved the shape and size of a glowing window through which a man's face was grinning into the moonshine.

"Look here, what's all this?" cried Mr Bond, sliding to his feet.

"The Traveller's Head, sir," answered Stennet, pointing aloft.

They both stared up at the sign above their heads, then Mr Bond scanned the sprawling mass of the inn, and scowled at its surroundings. The night was still vibrant, without sound; the endless forest stood like a wall of blue-white dust; and the traveller was about to raise his voice in wrath against the brothers Sasserach, when a commotion burst from the porch of the inn, and onto the moon-drenched grass strode a tall and ungainly figure, swinging its arms, with a pack of creatures flopping and stumbling at its heels. "Here *is* Mr Stephen," Stennet whispered, watching the approach; the landlord of the Traveller's Head was smiling pleasantly, baring his intensely white teeth, and when he had reached the traveller he touched his forehead with a gesture that was at once respectful and over-bearing.

"Mr Bond, sir?" Mr Bond muttered and bowed, and stared down at the landlord's children—large-headed, large-bellied, primitive creatures flopping round their father and pulling the skirts of the Inverness cape.

Father and children gathered round the traveller, who, lost within this little crowd, soon found himself at the entrance of The Traveller's Head, through which his new host urged him by the arm while two of the children pushed between them and ran ahead clumsily into the depths of the hall. The place was ill-lighted and ill-ventilated; and although Mr Bond knew from experience exactly where the living-room would be situated, yet, after he had passed through its doorway, he found no further resemblance to those rooms in which he had spent two stages of a curious adventure. The oil-lamp, standing in the middle of the round centre table, was without a shade; a moth was plunging audibly at the blackened chimney, hurling swift shadows everywhere over the ceiling and figured wallpaper; while, with the return of the children, a harmonium had started fitfully to grunt and blow.

"Let me take your cloak, your cape, Mr Bond, sir," the landlord said, and spread it with surprising care on one of the vast sofas that looked the larger because of their broken springs and the stuffing that protruded through their soiled covers: but at once the children seized upon the cape and would have torn it to pieces had not Mr Bond snatched it from them—at this, they cowered away from the stranger, fixing him with their eyes.

Amidst this congestion of people and furniture, Stephen Sasserach smiled and moved continuously, a stooping giant whom none but Mr Bond obeyed. Here was the type of man whose appearance the traveller likened to that of the old-time executioner, the axe-man of the Middle Ages—harsh, loyal, simple, excessively domesticated, with a bulging forehead and untidy eyebrows and arms muscled ready for deeds. Stephen kept no order in his house. Noise was everywhere, yet little seemed to be done. The children called their father Steve, and put out their tongues at him. They themselves were unlovely things, and their inner natures seemed to ooze through their skins and form a surface from which the traveller recoiled. Three of their names were familiar to Mr Bond. Here were Crispin and Martin and Stephen over again, while Dorcas and Lydia were sisters whose only virtue was their mutual devotion.

The food at The Traveller's Head was homely and palatable, and Stephen, the father, cooked it and served it liberally on chipped plates. He sat in his soiled blue shirt, his knotted arms looking richly sunburnt against the blue. He was never inarticulate, and this surprised Mr Bond. On the contrary, he spoke rapidly and almost as if to himself, in a low rugged voice that was always a pleasure to hear. At moments he dropped into silence, his eyes shut, his eyebrows lowered, and his bulging forehead grew still more shiny with thought; on such occasions. Dorcas and Lydia would steal to the harmonium, while, backed by a wail from the instrument, Crispin the Younger and Martin the Younger would jump from the sofas onto the floor.

Rousing himself at last, Stephen the Elder thumped his fist on the table, and turned in his chair to shout at the children: "Get along with you, devils! Get out your board, and *practise*, you little devils!" Whereupon the children erected a huge board, punctured with holes; and each child began to hurl wooden balls through the holes and into the pockets behind them with astonishing accuracy, except for Dorcas and Lydia. And presently their father reminded them: "The moon is shining!" At once the children scuttled out of the room, and Mr Bond never saw them again.

The noise and the figured wallpaper, and the fat moth beating itself against the only source of light, had caused the traveller's head to grow heavy with sleep; and now it grew heavier still as he sat by the fire with Stephen after supper was over, listening to the talk of that strangely attractive man in the soiled blue shirt. "You fond of chicken, Mr Bond, sir?" Mr Bond nodded.

"Children and animals..." he muttered drowsily.

"One has to let them have their way," sighed Stephen Sasserach. The rugged voice came clearly and soothingly into Mr Bond's ears, until at last it shot up, vigorously, and ordered the guest to bed. Mr Bond pulled himself out of his chair, and smiled, and said goodnight, and the moth flew into his face. Where were the children, he wondered. Their voices could not be heard. Perhaps they had fallen asleep, suddenly, like animals. But Mr Bond found it difficult to imagine those eyes in bed, asleep.

Lying, some minutes later, in his own massive bed in this third of the Sasserach inns, with an extinguished candle on his bedside table, and gazing towards the open window from which he had drawn apart one of the heavy embroidered curtains, Mr Bond fancied that he could hear faint cries of triumph, and sounds of knocking coming from the direction of the forest. Starting up into complete wakefulness, he went to the window, and stared at the forest beyond the tufted grass. The sounds, he fancied, putting his hand to his ear, were as those given forth by the children during their game—but louder, as though the game were bigger. Perhaps strange animals were uttering them. Whatever their origin, they were coming from the depth of trees whose stillness was deepened by the light of the moon.

"Oh, God!" thought Mr Bond, "I'm sick to death of the moonlight!"—and with a sweep of the arm he closed the curtains, yet could not shut out the sounds of the forest, nor the sight of the frosted grass beneath the moon. Together, sound and sight filled him with foreboding, and his cheeks shook as he groped for the unlighted candle. He must fetch his Inverness from below, fetch it at once, and get away while there was time. He found his host still sitting by the lamp in the living-room. Stephen's fist, lying on the table, was closed; he opened it, and out flew the moth.

"He thinks he has got away," cried Stephen, looking up, and baring his teeth in a smile: "but he hasn't! He never will!"

"I've come for my Inverness," said Mr Bond.

It was lying on one of the massive sofas. The fire was out, and the air chilly, and the depth of the room lay in darkness. An idea crossed the mind of Mr Bond. He said, lifting up the cape: "I thought I'd like it on my bed." And he shivered to show how cold he was. From one of the folds the moth flew out, and whirled around the room like a mad thing.

"That's all right, Mr Bond, sir. That's all right." The man had fallen into a mood of abstraction; his forehead shone in the rays of the lamp; and the traveller left the room, holding himself with dignity in his gay dressing-gown, the Inverness hanging on his arm.

He was about to climb the staircase when a voice spoke softly in his ear, and wished him goodnight.

Stennet! What was the man doing here? Mr Bond lifted his candle and gazed in astonishment at the back of Martin's manservant. The figure passed into the shadows, and the soft and deliberate ticking of the grandfather clock in the hall deepened the silence and fear of the moments that followed.

Mr Bond ran to his room, locked himself in, and began to dress. His dyspepsia had seized him again. If only he were back at Crispin's! He parted the curtains, and peeped at the night. The shadow of the inn lay on the yard and the tufted grass beyond, and one of the chimneys, immensely distorted, extended as far as the forest. The forest-wall itself was solid with moonlight; from behind it there came no longer the sounds of the knocking, and the silence set Mr Bond trembling again.

"I shall escape at dawn," he whispered, "when the moon's gone down."

Feeling no longer sleepy, he took from his knapsack a volume of *Mungo Park*, and, fully dressed, settled himself in an easy chair, with the curtains drawn again across the window, and the candle burning close behind him. At intervals he looked up from his book, frowning, running his eye over the group of three pagodas, in pale red, endlessly repeated on the wallpaper. The restful picture made him drowsy, and presently he slept and snored and the candle burned on.

At midnight he was awakened by crashing blows on his door; the very candle seemed to be jumping with fear, and Mr Bond sprang up in alarm.

"Yes? Who's that?" he called out feebly.

"What in the name of God is *that*?" he whispered, as the blows grew louder.

"What are they up to now?" he asked aloud, with rising terror.

A splinter flew into the room, and he knew in a flash that the end of his journey had come. Was it Stephen or Stennet, Stephen or Stennet behind the door? The candle flickered as he blundered to and fro. He had no time to think no time to act. He stood and watched the corner of the axe-blade working in the crack in the panel. "Save me, save me," he whispered, wringing his hands. They fluttered towards his Inverness, and struggled to push themselves into the obstinate sleeves. "Oh, come on, come on," he whimpered, jerking his arms about, anger rising with terror. The whole room shuddered beneath the axe. He plunged at the candle and blew it out. In the darkness a ray of light shone through a crack in the door, and fell on the window curtain.

Mr Bond remembered the creeper clinging beneath his window and as soon as possible he was floundering, scrambling, slipping down to the house-shadowed garden below. Puffing out his cheeks, he hurried onward, while the thuds of the axe grew fainter in his ears. Brickbats lay in his path, a zinc tub wrenched at his cape and ripped it loudly, an iron hoop caught in his foot and he tottered forward with outstretched hands. And now, still running in the far-flung shadow of the house, he was on the tufted grass, whimpering a little, struggling against desire to look back over his shoulder, making for the forest that lay in the full beams of the moonlight. He tried to think, and could think of nothing but the size and safety of the shadow on which he was running. He reached the roof of the inn at last: plunged aside from his course of flight: and now he was running up the monstrous shadow of the chimney, thinking of nothing at all because the forest stood so near. Blindingly, a moon-filled avenue stretched before him: the chimney entered the chasm, and stopped: and it was as though Mr Bond were a puff of smoke blowing into the forest depths. His shadow, swinging its monstrously distorted garments, led him to an open space at the end of the avenue. The thick-set trees encircled it with silence deeper than any Mr Bond had known. Here, in this glade, hung silence within a silence. Yet, halting abruptly, and pressing the flat of his hands to his ribs in the pain of his sudden burst of breathing, Mr Bond had no ears for the silence, nor eyes for anything beyond the scene that faced him in the centre of the forest glade: a group of upright posts, or stakes, set in a concave semi-circle, throwing long shadows, and bearing on each summit a human skull. "The Traveller's Head, The Headless Man," he whispered, stricken with terror, whipping his back on the skulls; and there was Stephen Sasserach in silhouette, leaping up the avenue, brandishing his axe as though he were a demented woodcutter coming to cut down trees.

The traveller's mind continued to run swiftly through the names of the three inns. "The Traveller's Head," he thought, "The Headless

Man, The Rest of the Traveller." He remembered the carrier pigeons that had flown ahead of him from inn to inn; he remembered the dust on the front of Martin's coat...

He was staring at the figure in the soiled blue shirt. It had halted now, as still as a tree, on the verge of the moon-filled glade: but the whirling thoughts of Mr Bond were on the verge of light more blinding than this; they stopped, appalled: and the traveller fled beyond the skulls, fruitlessly searching for covert in the farthest wall of trees.

Then Stephen sprang in his wake, flinging up a cry that went knocking against the tree-trunks.

The echoes were echoed by Mr Bond, who, whipping round to face his enemy, was wriggling and jerking in his Inverness cape, slipping it off at last, and swinging it in his hands, for his blood was up. And now he was deep in mortal combat, wielding his Inverness as the gladiators used to wield their nets in the old arenas. Time and again the axe and the cape engaged each other; the one warding and hindering; the other catching and ripping, clumsily enough, as though in sport. Around the skulls the two men fought and panted, now in darkness, now in the full light pouring down the avenue. Their moon-cast shadows fought another fight together, wilder still than theirs. Then Stephen cried: "Enough of this!" and bared his teeth for the first time since the strife had started.

"B-but you're my friend!" bleated Mr Bond; and he stared at the shining thread of the axe.

"The best you ever had, sir, Mr Bond, sir!" answered Stephen Sasserach; and, stepping back, the landlord of The Traveller's Head cut off the traveller's head.

The thump of the head on the sticks and leaves and grass of the forest glade was the first sound in the new and peaceful life of Mr Bond, and he did not hear it; but to the brothers Sasserach it was a promise of life itself, a signal that all was ready now for them to apply their respective talents busily and happily in the immediate future.

Stephen took the head of Mr Bond, and with gentle though rather clumsy fingers pared it to a skull, grinning back at it with simple satisfaction when the deed was over, and after that he set it up as a fine mark for his brood of primitives, the game's endeavour being to see who could throw the ball into the eye-sockets; and to his brother Martin, landlord of The Headless Man, he sent the headless man, under the care of Stennet: and Martin, on a soft, autumnal day, reduced the headless body to a skeleton, with all its troubles gone, and through the days and nights he sat at work, with swift precision in his fingers, carving and turning, powdering his coat with dust, creating his figures and trinkets, his paper-knives and salad-spoons and fretted boxes and rare chess-men; and to his brother Crispin, landlord of The Rest of the Traveller, Martin sent the rest of the traveller, the soft and yielding parts, the scraps, the odds and ends, the miscellaneous pieces, all the internal lumber that had gone to fill the skin of the man from the Midlands and to help to render him in middle years a prey to dyspepsia. Crispin received the parcel with a pursing of his small mouth, and a call to Myrtle in his clear falsetto: "Stennet's here!"

She answered from the kitchen. "Thank you, Cris!" Her hands were soft and swollen as she scoured the tureen. The back of the inn was full of reflected sunlight, and her dark hair shone.

"It's too late in the season now," she said, when teatime came. "I don't suppose we'll have another one before the spring."

Yet she was wrong. That very evening, when the moon had risen from beyond the valley, Myrtle murmured: "There he comes," and continued to stir her ladle in the bowl.

Her husband strolled into the hall and wound the clock.

He took the lamp from its bracket on the wall.

He went to the door, and flung it open to the moonlight; holding the lamp above his head.

"Come in, come in," he said, to the stranger standing there. "She is cooking a *lovely* broth tonight!"

1943

BETWEEN SUNSET AND MOONRISE

R. H. Malden

The ghost stories of Richard Henry Malden (1879–1951) are collected in a single volume, *Nine Ghosts*, first published in 1943. Malden was a significant figure in the Church of England, becoming Dean of Wells Cathedral in 1933 and publishing widely on ecclesiastical matters. He was, for many years, a friend of M. R. James, having attended both Eton and King's College, Cambridge. Indeed, Malden is rarely mentioned without reference to the father of the English ghost story, and it is in this light that his fiction has often been judged. However, "Between Sunset and Moonrise" demonstrates that Malden was far more than a Jamesian imitator when it came to uncanny tales.

Much of the story's power is derived from its eerie fenland setting, where the churchman at the heart of the action has his parish. In the opening of the tale, our narrator tells us the place is not far from Cambridge: "I will call it Yaxholme, though that is not its name." Malden may have had in mind the Cambridgeshire villages of Yaxley and Holme, both near the Holme Fen nature reserve, which lays claim to the lowest land point in Great Britain. Holme Fen is a fragment of ancient fenland in an area that was largely drained for agriculture; however, work is well underway to rejuvenate the local wetlands as part of the ambitious Great Fen project. Several walking routes cross Holme Fen nature reserve, while the nearby Woodwalton Fen sports droves not dissimilar to those described by Malden's terrified vicar.

During the early part of last year it fell to me to act as executor for an old friend. We had not seen much of each other of late, as he had been living in the west of England, and my own time had been fully occupied elsewhere. The time of our intimacy had been when he was vicar of a large parish not very far from Cambridge. I will call it Yaxholme, though that is not its name.

The place had seemed to suit him thoroughly. He had been on the best of terms with his parishioners, and with the few gentry of the neighbourhood. The church demanded a custodian of antiquarian knowledge and artistic perception, and in these respects too my friend was particularly well qualified for his position. But a sudden nervous breakdown had compelled him to resign. The cause of it had always been a mystery to his friends, for he was barely middle-aged when it took place, and had been a man of robust health. His parish was neither particularly laborious nor harassing; and, as far as was known, he had no special private anxieties of any kind. But the collapse came with startling suddenness, and was so severe that, for a time, his reason seemed to be in danger. Two years of rest and travel enabled him to lead a normal life again, but he was never the man he had been. He never revisited his old parish, or any of his friends in the county; and seemed to be ill at ease if conversation turned upon the part of England in which it lay. It was perhaps not unnatural that he should dislike the place which had cost him so much. But his friends could not but regard as childish the length to which he carried his aversion.

He had had a distinguished career at the University, and had kept up his intellectual interests in later life. But, except for an occasional *succès d'estime* in a learned periodical, he had published nothing. I was not without hope of finding something completed among his papers which would secure for him a permanent place in the world of learning. But in this I was disappointed. His literary remains were copious, and a striking testimony to the vigour and range of his intellect. But they were very fragmentary. There was nothing which could be made fit for publication, except one document which I should have preferred to suppress. But he had left particular instructions in his will that it was to be published when he had been dead for a year. Accordingly I subjoin it exactly as it left his hand. It was dated two years after he had left Yaxholme, and nearly five before his death. For reasons which will be apparent to the reader I make no comment of any kind upon it.

The solicitude which my friends have displayed during my illness has placed me under obligations which I cannot hope to repay. But I feel that I owe it to them to explain the real cause of my breakdown. I have never spoken of it to anyone, for, had I done so, it would have been impossible to avoid questions which I should not wish to be able to answer. Though I have only just reached middle-age I am sure that I have not many more years to live. And I am therefore confident that most of my friends will survive me, and be able to hear my explanation after my death. Nothing but a lively sense of what I owe to them could have enabled me to undergo the pain of recalling the experience which I am now about to set down.

Yaxholme lies, as they will remember, upon the extreme edge of the Fen district. In shape it is a long oval, with a main line of railway cutting one end. The church and vicarage were close to the station, and round them lay a village containing nearly five-sixths of the entire population of the parish. On the other side of the line the Fen proper began, and stretched for many miles. Though it is now fertile corn land, much of it had been permanently under water within living memory, and would soon revert to its original condition if it were not for the pumping stations. In spite of these it is not unusual to see several hundred acres flooded in winter.

My own parish ran for nearly six miles, and I had therefore several scattered farms and cottages so far from the village that a visit to one of them took up the whole of a long afternoon. Most of them were not on any road, and could only be reached by means of droves. For the benefit of those who are not acquainted with the Fen I may explain that a drove is a very imperfect sketch of the idea of a road. It is bounded by hedges or dykes, so that the traveller cannot actually lose his way, but it offers no further assistance to his progress. The middle is simply a grass track, and as cattle have to be driven along it the mud is sometimes literally knee-deep in winter. In summer the light peaty soil rises in clouds of sable dust. In fact I seldom went down one without recalling Hesiod's unpatriotic description of his native village in Bœotia. "Bad in winter; intolerable in summer; good at no time."

At the far end of one of these lay a straggling group of half a dozen cottages, of which the most remote was inhabited by an old woman whom I will call Mrs Vries. In some ways she was the most interesting of all my parishioners, and she was certainly the most perplexing. She was not a native, but had come to live there some twenty years before, and it was hard to see what had tempted a stranger to so unattractive a spot. It was the last house in the parish: her nearest neighbour was a quarter of a mile away, and she was fully three miles from a hard road or a shop. The house itself was not at all a good one. It had been unoccupied, I was told, for some years before she came to it, and she had found it in a semi-ruinous condition. Yet she had not been driven to seek a very cheap dwelling by poverty, as she had a good supply of furniture of very good quality, and, apparently, as much money as she required. She never gave the slightest hint as to where she had come from, or what her previous history had been. As far as was known she never wrote or received any letters. She must have been between fifty and sixty when she came. Her appearance was striking, as she was tall and thin, with an aquiline nose, and a pair of very brilliant dark eyes, and a quantity of hair—snow-white by the time I knew her. At one time she must have been handsome; but she had grown rather forbidding, and I used to think that, a couple of centuries before, she might have had some difficulty in proving that she was not a witch. Though her neighbours, not unnaturally, fought rather shy of her, her conversation showed that she was a clever woman who had at some time received a good deal of education, and had lived in cultivated surroundings. I used to think that she must have been an upper servant—most probably lady's maid—in a good house, and, despite the ring on her finger, suspected that the "Mrs" was brevet rank.

One New Year's Eve I thought it my duty to visit her. I had not seen her for some months, and a few days of frost had made the drove more passable than it had been for several weeks. But, in spite of her interesting personality, I always found that it required a considerable moral effort to call at her cottage. She was always civil, and expressed herself pleased to see me. But I could never get rid of the idea that she regarded civility to me in the light of an insurance, which might be claimed elsewhere. I always told myself that such thoughts were unfounded and unworthy, but I could never repress them altogether, and whenever I left her cottage it was with a strong feeling that I had no desire to see her again. I used, however, to say to myself that that was really due to personal pique (because I could never discover that she had any religion, nor could I instil any into her), and that the fault was therefore more mine than hers.

On this particular afternoon the prospect of seeing her seemed more than usually distasteful, and my disinclination increased curiously as I made my way along the drove. So strong did it become that if any reasonable excuse for turning back had presented itself I am afraid I should have seized it. However, none did: so I held on, comforting myself with the thought that I should begin the New Year with a comfortable sense of having discharged the most unpleasant of my regular duties in a conscientious fashion.

When I reached the cottage I was a little surprised at having to knock three times, and by hearing the sound of bolts cautiously drawn back. Presently the door opened and Mrs Vries peered out. As soon as she saw who it was she made me very welcome as usual. But it was impossible not to feel that she had been more or less expecting some other visitor, whom she was not anxious to see. However, she volunteered no statement, and I thought it better to pretend to have noticed nothing unusual. On a table in the middle of the room lay a large book in which she had obviously been reading. I was surprised to see that it was a Bible, and that it lay open at the Book of Tobit. Seeing that I had noticed it Mrs Vries told me—with a little hesitation, I thought—that she had been reading the story of Sarah and the fiend Asmodeus. Then—the ice once broken—she plied me almost fiercely with questions. "To what cause did I attribute Sarah's obsession, in the first instance?" "Did the efficacy of Tobias' remedy depend upon the fact that it had been prescribed by an angel?" and much more to the same effect. Naturally my answers were rather vague, and her good manners could not conceal her disappointment. She sat silent for a minute or two, while I looked at her—not, I must confess, without some alarm, for her manner had been very strange—and then said abruptly, "Well, will you have a cup of tea with me?" I assented gladly, for it was nearly half-past four, and it would take me nearly an hour and a half to get home. She took some time over the preparations and during the meal talked with even more fluency than usual. I could not help thinking that she was trying to make it last as long as possible.

Finally, at about half-past five, I got up and said that I must go, as I had a good many odds and ends awaiting me at home. I held out my hand, and as she took it said, "You must let me wish you a very happy New Year." She stared at me for a moment, and then broke into a harsh laugh, and said, "If wishes were horses beggars might ride. Still, I thank you for your good will. Goodbye." About thirty yards from her house there was an elbow in the drove. When I reached it I looked back and saw that she was still standing in her doorway, with her figure sharply silhouetted against the red glow of the kitchen fire. For one instant the play of shadow made it look as if there were another, taller, figure behind her, but the illusion passed directly. I waved my hand to her and turned the corner.

It was a fine, still, starlight night. I reflected that the moon would be up before I reached home, and my walk would not be unpleasant. I had naturally been rather puzzled by Mrs Vries' behaviour, and decided that I must see her again before long, to ascertain whether, as seemed possible, her mind were giving way.

When I had passed the other cottages of the group I noticed that the stars were disappearing, and a thick white mist was rolling up.

This did not trouble me. The drove now ran straight until it joined the high-road, and there was no turn into it on either side. I had therefore no chance of losing my way, and anyone who lives in the Fens is accustomed to fogs. It soon grew very thick, and I was conscious of the slightly creepy feeling which a thick fog very commonly inspires. I had been thinking of a variety of things, in somewhat desultory fashion, when suddenly—almost as if it had been whispered into my ear—a passage from the Book of Wisdom came into my mind and refused to be dislodged. My nerves were good then, and I had often walked up a lonely drove in a fog before; but still just at that moment I should have preferred to have recalled almost anything else. For this was the extract with which my memory was pleased to present me. "For neither did the dark recesses that held them guard them from fears, but sounds rushing down rang around them; and phantoms appeared, cheerless with unsmiling faces. And no force of fire prevailed to give them light, neither were the brightest flames of the stars strong enough to illumine that gloomy night. And in terror they deemed the things which they saw to be worse than that sight on which they could not gaze. And they lay helpless, made the sport of magic art." (*Wisdom* xvii. 4–6).

Suddenly I heard a loud snort, as of a beast, apparently at my elbow. Naturally I jumped and stood still for a moment to avoid blundering into a stray cow, but there was nothing there. The next moment I heard what sounded exactly like a low chuckle. This was more disconcerting: but common sense soon came to my aid. I told myself that the cow must have been on the other side of the hedge and not really so close as it had seemed to be. What I had taken for a chuckle must have been the squelching of her feet in a soft place. But I must confess that I did not find this explanation as convincing as I could have wished.

I plodded on, but soon began to feel unaccountably tired. I say "unaccountably" because I was a good walker and often covered much more ground than I had done that day.

I slackened my pace, but, as I was not out of breath, that did not relieve me. I felt as if I were wading through water up to my middle, or through very deep soft snow, and at last was fairly compelled to stop. By this time I was thoroughly uneasy, wondering what could be the matter with me. But as I had still nearly two miles to go there was nothing for it but to push on as best I might.

When I started again I saw that the fog seemed to be beginning to clear, though I could not feel a breath of air. But instead of thinning in the ordinary way it merely rolled back a little on either hand, producing an effect which I had never seen before. Along the sides of the drove lay two solid banks of white, with a narrow passage clear between them. This passage seemed to stretch for an interminable distance, and at the far end I "perceived" a number of figures. I say advisedly "perceived," rather than "saw," for I do not know whether I saw them in the ordinary sense of the word or not. That is to say—I did not know then, and have never been able to determine since, whether it was still dark. I only know that my power of vision seemed to be independent of light or darkness. I perceived the figures, as one sees the creatures of a dream, or the mental pictures which sometimes come when one is neither quite asleep nor awake.

They were advancing rapidly in orderly fashion, almost like a body of troops. The scene recalled very vividly a picture of the Israelites marching across the Red Sea between two perpendicular walls of water, in a set of Bible pictures which I had had as a child. I suppose that I had not thought of that picture for more than thirty years, but now it leapt into my mind, and I found myself saying aloud, "Yes: of course it must have been exactly like that. How glad I am to have seen it."

I suppose it was the interest of making the comparison that kept me from feeling the surprise which would otherwise have been occasioned by meeting a large number of people marching down a lonely drove after dark on a raw December evening.

At first I should have said there were thirty or forty in the party, but when they had drawn a little nearer they seemed to be not more than ten or a dozen strong. A moment later I saw to my surprise that they were reduced to five or six. The advancing figures seemed to be melting into one another, something after the fashion of dissolving views. Their speed and stature increased as their numbers diminished, suggesting that the survivors had, in some horrible fashion, absorbed the personality of their companions. Now there appeared to be only three, then one solitary figure of gigantic stature rushing down the drove towards me at a fearful pace, without a sound. As he came the mist closed behind him, so that his dark figure was thrown up against a solid background of white: much as mountain climbers are said sometimes to see their own shadows upon a bank of cloud. On and on he came, until at last he towered above me and I saw his face. It has come to me once or twice since in troubled dreams, and may come again. But I am thankful that I have never had any clear picture of it in my waking moments. If I had I should be afraid for my reason. I know that the impression which it produced upon me was that of intense malignity long baffled, and now at last within reach of its desire. I believe I screamed aloud. Then after a pause, which seemed to last for hours, he broke over me like a wave. There was a rushing and a streaming all round me, and I struck out with my hands as if I were swimming. The sensation was not unlike that of rising from a deep dive: there was the same feeling of pressure and suffocation, but in this case coupled with the most intense physical loathing. The only comparison which I can suggest is that I felt as a man might feel if he were buried under a heap of worms or toads.

Suddenly I seemed to be clear, and fell forward on my face. I am not sure whether I fainted or not, but I must have lain there for some minutes. When I picked myself up I felt a light breeze upon my forehead and the mist was clearing away as quickly as it had come. I saw the rim of the moon above the horizon, and my mysterious fatigue had disappeared. I hurried forward as quickly as I could without venturing to look behind me. I only wanted to get out of that abominable drove on to the high-road, where there were lights and other human beings. For I knew that what I had seen was a creature of darkness and waste places, and that among my fellows I should be safe. When I reached home my housekeeper looked at me oddly. Of course my clothes were muddy and disarranged, but I suspect that there was something else unusual in my appearance. I merely said that I had had a fall coming up a drove in the dark, and was not feeling particularly well. I avoided the looking-glass when I went to my room to change.

Coming downstairs I heard through the open kitchen door some scraps of conversation—or rather of a monologue delivered by my housekeeper—to the effect that no one ought to be about the droves after dark as much as I was, and that it was a providence that things were no worse. Her own mother's uncle had—it appeared—been down just such another drove on just such another night, forty-two years ago come next Christmas Eve. "They brought 'im 'ome on a barrow with both 'is eyes drawed down, and every drop of blood in 'is body turned. But 'e never would speak to what 'e see, and wild cats couldn't ha' scratched it out of him."

An inaudible remark from one of the maids was met with a long sniff, and the statement: "Girls seem to think they know everything nowadays." I spent the next day in bed, as besides the shock which I had received I had caught a bad cold. When I got up on the second I was not surprised to hear that Mrs Vries had been found dead on the previous afternoon. I had hardly finished breakfast when I was told that the policeman, whose name was Winter, would be glad to see me.

It appeared that on New Year's morning a half-witted boy of seventeen, who lived at one of the other cottages down the drove, had come to him and said that Mrs Vries was dead, and that he must come and enter her house. He declined to explain how he had come by the information: so at first Mr Winter contented himself with pointing out that it was the first of January not of April. But the boy was so insistent that finally he went. When repeated knockings at Mrs Vries' cottage produced no result he had felt justified in forcing the back-door. She was sitting in a large wooden armchair quite dead. She was leaning forward a little and her hands were clasping the arms so tightly that it proved to be a matter of some difficulty to unloose her fingers. In front of her was another chair, so close that if anyone had been sitting in it his knees must have touched those of the dead woman. The seat cushions were flattened down as if it had been occupied recently by a solid personage. The tea-things had not been cleared away, but the kitchen was perfectly clean and tidy. There was no suspicion of foul play, as all the doors and windows were securely fastened on the inside. Winter added that her face made him feel "quite sickish like," and that the house smelt very bad for all that it was so clean.

A post-mortem examination of the body showed that her heart was in a very bad state, and enabled the coroner's jury to return a verdict of "Death from Natural Causes." But the doctor told me privately that she must have had a shock of some kind. "In fact," he said, "if anyone ever died of fright, she did. But goodness knows what can have frightened her in her own kitchen unless it was her own conscience. But that is more in your line than mine."

He added that he had found the examination of the body peculiarly trying: though he could not, or would not, say why.

As I was the last person who had seen her alive, I attended the inquest, but gave only formal evidence of an unimportant character. I did not mention that the second armchair had stood in a corner of the room during my visit, and that I had not occupied it.

The boy was of course called and asked how he knew she was dead. But nothing satisfactory could be got from him. He said that there was right houses and there was wrong houses—not to say persons—and that "they" had been after her for a long time. When asked whom he meant by "they" he declined to explain, merely adding as a general statement that he could see further into a milestone than what some people could, for all they thought themselves so clever. His own family deposed that he had been absolutely silent, contrary to his usual custom, from teatime on New Year's Eve to breakfast-time next day. Then he had suddenly announced that Mrs Vries was dead; and ran out of the house before they could say anything to him. Accordingly he was dismissed, with a warning to the effect that persons who were disrespectful to Constituted Authorities always came to a bad end.

It naturally fell to me to conduct the funeral, as I could have given no reason for refusing her Christian burial. The coffin was not particularly weighty, but as it was being lowered into the grave the ropes supporting it parted, and it fell several feet with a thud. The shock dislodged a quantity of soil from the sides of the cavity, so that the coffin was completely covered before I had had time to say "Earth to earth: Ashes to ashes: Dust to dust."

Afterwards the sexton spoke to me apologetically about the occurrence. "I'm fair put about, Sir, about them ropes," he said. "Nothing o' that sort ever 'appened afore in my time. They was pretty nigh new too, and I thought they'd a done us for years. But just look 'ere, Sir." Here he showed two extraordinarily ravelled ends. "I never see a rope part like that afore. Almost looks as if it 'ad been scratted through by a big cat or somethink."

That night I was taken ill. When I was better my doctor said that rest and change of scene were imperative. I knew that I could never go down a drove alone by night again, so tendered my resignation to my Bishop. I hope that I have still a few years of usefulness before me: but I know that I can never be as if I had not seen what I have seen. Whether I met with my adventure through any fault of my own I cannot tell. But of one thing I am sure. There are powers of darkness which walk abroad in waste places: and that man is happy who has never had to face them.

If anyone who reads this should ever have a similar experience and should feel tempted to try to investigate it further, I commend to him the counsel of Jesus-ben-Sira.

"My son, seek not things that are too hard for thee: and search not out things that are above thy strength."

1951

THE TRAINS

Robert Aickman

For many, Robert Aickman (1914–1981) is as significant a figure in the world of weird fiction as the likes of M. R. James and Arthur Machen. Aickman's "strange stories", as he termed them, are imbued with a level of psychological depth and character detail rare within the genre. "The Trains" is taken from his first collection of short stories, *We Are for the Dark*, which features three of his stories alongside three from Elizabeth Jane Howard.

In *Literary Hauntings*, Aickman's biographer, R. B. Russell, notes that the tale is based upon a story Aickman was told at Diggle railway station in Greater Manchester. It was said that between Standedge and Huddersfield there was a lone house from which someone, presumed by several train drivers to be a girl, waved to the engines from a high window. This continued for many years, and it was eventually revealed that the waving person was not a girl, but an old woman who, according to the teller, had lost her mind.

Standedge would have been of particular interest to Aickman as not only the location of three railway tunnels, but also the longest and highest canal tunnel in the UK. Passionate about saving Britain's canals, Aickman had co-founded the Inland Waterways Association in 1946. The wild, open landscape of Marsden Moor, near Standedge, certainly aligns with that encountered by hikers

Margaret and Mimi in Aickman's story. The National Trust has mapped a 10-mile "Standedge circuit walk" from Marsden train station, with details online.

On the moors, as early as this, the air no longer clung about her, impeding her movements, absorbing her energies. Now a warm breeze seemed to lift her up and bear her on: the absorption process was reversed; her bloodstream drew impulsion from the zephyrs. Her thoughts raced from her in all directions, unproductive but joyful. She remembered the railway posters. Was this ozone?

Not that she had at all disliked the big industrial city they had just left; unlike Mimi, who had loathed it. Mimi had wanted their walking tour to be each day from one Youth Hostel to another; but that was the one proposal Margaret had successfully resisted. Their itinerary lay in the Pennines, and Margaret had urged the case for sleeping in farmhouses and, on occasion, in conventional hotels. Mimi had suggested that the former were undependable and the latter both dreary and expensive; but suddenly her advocacy of Youth Hostels had filled her with shame, and she had capitulated. "But hotels look down on hikers," she had added. Margaret had not until then regarded them as hikers.

Apart from the controversy about the city, all had so far gone fairly well, particularly with the weather, as their progress entered its second week. The city Margaret had found new, interesting, unexpectedly beautiful and romantic: its well-proportioned stone mills and uncountable volcanic chimneys appeared perfectly to consort with the high free mountains always in the background. To Mimi the place was all that she went on holiday to avoid. If you had to have towns, she would choose the blurred amalgam of the Midlands and South, where town does not contrast with country but merges into it, neither town nor country being at any time so distinct as in the North. To Margaret this, to her, new way of life (of which she saw only the very topmost surface), seemed considerably less dreadful than she had expected. Mimi, to whom also it was new, saw it as the existence from which very probably her great-grandfather had fought and climbed, a degradation she was appalled to find still in existence and able to devour her. If there had to be industry, let the facts be swaddled in suburbs. The Free Trade Hotel (RAC and AA) had found single rooms for them; and Mimi had missed someone to talk to in bed.

They had descended to the town quite suddenly from the wildest moors, as one does in the North. Now equally suddenly it was as if there were no towns, but only small, long-toothed Neanderthals crouched behind rocks waiting to tear the two of them to pieces. Air roared past in incalculable bulk under the lucent sky, deeply blue but traversed by well-spaced masses of sharply edged white cloud, like the floats in a Mediterranean pageant. The misty, smoky, reeking air of the city had enchanted Margaret with its perpetually changing atmospheric effects, a meteorological drama unavailable in any other environment; but up here the air was certainly like itself. The path was hard to find across the heather, the only landmarks being contours and neither of them expert with a map; but they advanced in happy silence, all barriers between them blown down, even Margaret's heavy rucksack far from her mind. (Mimi took her own even heavier rucksack for granted at all times.)

"Surely that's a train?" said Margaret, when they had walked for two or three hours.

"Oh God," said Mimi, the escapist.

"The point is it'll give us our bearing." The vague rumbling was now lost in the noisy wind. "Let's look."

Mimi unstrapped the back pocket on Margaret's rucksack and took out the map. They stood holding it between them. Their orientation being governed by the wind, and beyond their power to correct mentally, they then laid the map on the ground, the top more or less to the north, and a grey stone on each corner.

"There's the line," said Margaret, following it across the map with her finger. "We must be somewhere about here."

"How do you know we're not above the tunnel?" enquired Mimi. "It's about four miles long."

"I don't think we're high enough. The tunnel's further on."

"Couldn't we strike this road?"

"Which way do you suggest?"

"Over the brow of the next hill, if you were right about that being a train. The road goes quite near the railway and the sound came from over there." Mimi pointed, the web of her rucksack, as she lay twisted on the ground, dragging uncomfortably in the shoulder strap of her shirt.

"I wish we had a canvas map. The wind's tearing this one to pieces."

Mimi replied amiably. "It's a bore, isn't it?" It was she who had been responsible for the map.

"I'm almost sure you're right," said Margaret, with all the confidence of the lost.

"Let's go," said Mimi. With difficulty they folded up the map, and Mimi returned it to Margaret's rucksack. The four grey stones continued to mark the corners of a now mysterious rectangle.

As it chanced, Mimi was right. When they had descended to the valley before them, and toiled to the next ridge, a double line of railway and a stone-walled road climbed the valley beyond. While they watched, a train began slowly to chug upwards from far to the left.

"The other one must have been going downhill," said Mimi.

They began the descent to the road. It was some time since there had been even a sheep path. The distance to the road was negligible as the crow flies, but it took them thirty-five minutes by Mimi's wrist-watch, and the crawling train passed before them almost as soon as they started.

"I wish we were crows," Mimi exclaimed.

Margaret said, "Yes," and smiled.

They noticed no traffic on the road, which, when reached, proved to be surfaced with hard, irregular granite chips, somewhat in need of re-laying and the attentions of a steamroller.

"Pretty grim," said Mimi after a quarter of an hour. "But I'm through with that heather." Both sides of the valley were packed with it.

"Hadn't we better try to find out exactly where we are?" suggested Margaret.

"Does it really matter?"

"There's lunch."

"That doesn't depend on where we are. So long as we're in the country it's all one, don't you think?"

"I think we'd better make sure."

"OK."

Mimi again got out the map. As they were anchoring it by the roadside, a train roared into being and swept down the gradient.

"What are you doing?" asked Margaret, struggling with a rather unsuitable stone.

"Waving, of course."

"Did anyone wave back?"

"Haven't you ever waved to the driver?"

"No. I don't think I have. I didn't know it was the driver you waved to. I thought it was the passengers." The map now seemed secure.

"Them too sometimes. But drivers always wave to girls."

"Only to girls?"

"Only to girls." Mimi couldn't remember when she hadn't known that. "Where are we?" They stared at the map, trying to drag out its mystery. Even now that they were on the road, with the railway plain before them crossing contour after contour, the problem seemed little simpler.

"I wish there was an instrument which said how high we were," remarked Mimi.

"Something else to carry."

Soon they were reduced to staring about them.

"Isn't that a house?" Mimi was again pointing the initiative.

"If it is, I think it must be 'Inn'." Margaret indicated it. "There's no other building on the map this side of the railway tunnel, unless we're much lower down the valley than we think."

"Maps don't show every small building."

"They seem to in country districts. I've been noticing. Each farm has a little dot. Even the cottage by the reservoir yesterday had its dot."

"Oh well, if it's a pub, we can eat in the bar. OK by me."

Again they left behind them four grey stones at the corners of nothing.

"Incidentally, the map only shows one house between the other end of the tunnel and Pudsley. A good eight miles, I should say."

"Let's hope it's one of your farms. I won't face a night in Pudsley. We're supposed to be on holiday. Remember?"

"I expect they'll put us up."

The building ahead of them proved long deserted. Or possibly not so long; it is difficult to tell with simple stone buildings in a wet climate. The windows were planked up; slates from the roof littered the weedy garden; the front door had been stove in.

"Trust the Army," said Mimi. "Hope tonight's quarters are more weatherproof. We'd better eat. It's a quarter past two."

"I don't think it's the Army. More like the agricultural depression." Margaret had learnt on her father's estate the significance of deserted farmhouses and neglected holdings.

"Look! There's the tunnel."

Margaret advanced a few steps up the road to join her. From the black portal the tunnel bored straight into the rock, with the road winding steeply above it.

"There's another building," said Margaret, following the discouraging ascent with her eyes. "What's more, I can see a sign outside it. I believe the map's wrong. Come on."

"Oh well," said Mimi.

Just as they were over the tunnel entrance another train sped downwards. They looked from above at the blind black roofs of the coaches, like the caterpillar at the fair with the cover down.

It was hard to say whether the map was wrong or not. The house above the tunnel, though apparently not shown, was certainly not an inn. It was almost the exact opposite: an unlicensed Guest House.

"Good for a cup of tea," said Mimi. "But we'd better eat outside."

A little further up the road was a small hillock. They ascended it, cast off their heavy rucksacks, loosened their belts a hole or two, and began to eat corned beef sandwiches. The Guest House lay below them, occupied to all appearances, but with no one visible.

"Not much traffic," said Margaret, dangling a squashed tomato.

"They all go by train."

The distant crowing of an engine whistle seemed to confirm her words.

The sharp-edged clouds, now slightly larger, were still being pushed across the sky; but by now the breeze seemed to have dropped and it was exceedingly hot. The two women were covered with sweat, and Mimi undid another button of her shirt.

"Aren't you glad I made you wear shorts?"

Margaret had to admit to herself she was glad. There had been some dissension between the two of them upon this point; Margaret, who had never worn shorts in her life before, feeling intensely embarrassed by Mimi's proposal, and Mimi unexpectedly announcing that she wouldn't come at all unless Margaret "dressed like everybody else". Margaret now realised that for once "everybody" was right. The freedom was delightful; and without it the weight of the rucksack would have been unendurable. Moreover, her entire present outfit had cost less than a guinea; and it mattered little what happened to it. That, she perceived, was the real freedom. Still, she was pleased that none of her family could see her.

"Very glad indeed," she replied. "I really am."

Mimi smiled warmly, too nice to triumph, although the matter was one about which Margaret's original attitude had roused strong feelings in her.

"Not the ideal food for this heat," said Margaret. "We'll come out in spots."

"Lucky to get corned beef. Another girl and I hiked from end to end of the Pilgrim's Way on plain bread and marge. It was Bank Holiday and we'd forgotten to lay anything in." Then, springing to her feet with her mouth full, she picked up her rucksack. "Let's try for a drink." She was off down the road before Margaret could rise or even speak. She was given to acting on such sudden small impulses, Margaret had noticed.

By the time Margaret had finished her final sandwich, Mimi had rung the Guest House bell and had been inside for some time. Before following, Margaret wiped the sweat from her face on to one of the large handkerchiefs Mimi had prudently enjoined; then from one of the breast pockets of her shirt produced a comb and mirror, rearranged her hair so far as was allowed by sweat and the small tight bun into which, with a view to efficiency on this holiday, she had woven it, and returned the articles to her shirt pocket, buttoning down the flap, but avoiding contact as far as possible with her sticky body. She approached the front door slowly, endeavouring to beget no further heat.

The bell, though provided with a modern pseudo-Italian pull, was of the authentic country-house pattern, operated by a wire. The door was almost immediately opened by a plain woman in a Marks and Spencer overall.

"Yes?"

"Could I possibly have something to drink? My friend's inside already."

"Come in. Tea or coffee? We're out of minerals."

"Could I have some coffee?"

"Coffee." The word was repeated in a short blank tone. One would have supposed she had to deal with sixty orders an hour. She disappeared.

"Well, shut the door and keep the heat out."

The speaker, a middle-aged man wearing dirty tennis shoes, was seated the other side of a round wooden table from Mimi, who was stirring a cup of tea. There was no one else in the room, which was congested with depressing café furniture, and decorated with cigarette advertisements hanging askew on the walls.

"You know what they say in New York?" He had the accent of a north-country businessman. His eyes never left Mimi's large breasts distending her damp khaki shirt. "I used to live in New York. Ten years altogether."

Mimi said nothing. It was her habit to let the men do the talking. Margaret sat down beside her, laying her rucksack on the floor.

"Hullo." His tone was cheekier than his intention.

"Hullo," said Margaret neutrally.

"Are you two friends?"

"Yes."

His gaze returned to the buxomer, nakeder Mimi.

"I was just telling your friend. You know what they say in New York?"

"No," said Margaret. "I don't think so. What do they say?"

"It isn't the heat. It's the humidity."

He seemed still to be addressing Margaret, while staring at Mimi. Giving them a moment to follow what he evidently regarded as a difficult and penetrating observation, he continued, "The damp, you know. The moisture in the atmosphere. The atmosphere's picking up moisture all the time. Sucking it out of the earth." He licked his lower lip. "This is nothing. Nothing to New York. I lived there for ten years. Beggars can't be choosers, you know."

A door opened from behind and the taciturn woman brought Margaret's coffee. The cup was discoloured round the edge, and the saucer, for some reason, bore a crimson smear.

"One shilling."

Startled, Margaret produced a half-crown from a pocket of her shorts. The woman went away.

"Nice place this," said the man. "You've got to pay for that these times."

Margaret lifted up her cup. The coffee was made from essence and stank.

"What did I say? How's that for a cup of coffee? I'd have one myself, if I hadn't had three already."

"Are you staying here?"

"I live here."

The woman returned with one and sixpence, then departed once more.

"There's no need for a gratuity."

"I see," said Margaret. "Is she the proprietress?"

"It's her own place."

"She seems silent." Immediately Margaret rather regretted this general conversational initiative.

"She's reason to be. It's no gold mine, you know. I'm the only regular. Pretty well the only customer by and large."

"Why's that? It's a lovely country, and there's not much competition from what we've seen."

"There's none. Believe me. And it's not a nice country. Believe me again."

"What's wrong with it?" This was Mimi, who had not spoken since Margaret had entered.

"Why nothing really, sister, nothing really. Not for a little girl like you." Margaret noticed that he was one of the many men who classify women into those you talk to and those with whom words merely impede the way. "I was just kidding. I wouldn't be here else. Now would I? Not living here."

"What's wrong with the place?"

Margaret was surprised by Mimi's tone. She recollected that she had no knowledge of what had passed between the two of them while she had been combing her hair on the little hill.

"You know what the locals say?"

"We haven't seen any locals," said Margaret.

"Just so. That's what I say. They don't come up here. This is the Quiet Valley."

"Oh really," cried Margaret, not fully mistress of her motives all the same. "You got that name out of some Western."

But he only replied with unusual brevity, "They call it the Quiet Valley."

"Not a good place to start in business!" said Margaret.

"Couldn't be worse. But she just didn't know. She sank all she had in this place. She was a stranger here, like you."

"What's wrong with the valley?" persisted Mimi, her manner, to Margaret's mind, a little too tense.

"Nothing so long as you stay, sister. Just nothing at all."

"Is there really a story?" asked Margaret. Almost convinced that the whole thing was a rather dull joke, she was illogically driven to enquire by Mimi's odd demeanour.

"No *story* that I've heard of. It's just the Quiet Valley and the locals don't come here."

"What about you? If it's so quiet why don't you move?"

"I like quiet. I'm not one to pick and choose. I was just telling you why there's a trade recession."

"It's perfectly true," said Margaret, "that there seems very little traffic." She noticed Mimi refasten the shirt button she had undone to cool herself. The man averted his eyes.

"They all take the railroad. They scuttle through shut up like steers in a wagon."

Mimi said nothing, but her expression had changed.

"There seem to be plenty of trains for them," said Margaret, smiling.

"It's the main line."

"One of the drivers waved to us. If what you say is true, I suppose he was glad to see us."

For the first time the man concentrated his unpleasing stare on Margaret.

"Now as to that—" His glance fell to the table and remained there a moment. "I was just wondering where you two reckon on spending the night."

"We usually find a farmhouse," said Margaret shortly.

"It's wild on the other side, you know. Wilder than here. There's only one house between the tunnel and near Pudsley."

"So we noticed on the map. Would they give us a bed? I suppose it's a farm?"

"It's Miss Roper's place. I've never met her myself. I don't go down the other side. But I dare say she'd help you. What you said just now—" Suddenly he laughed. "You know how engine drivers wave at girls, like you said?"

"Yes," said Margaret. To her apprehension it seemed that an obscene joke was coming.

"Well, every time a train passes Miss Roper's house, someone leans out of the bedroom window and waves to it. It's gone on for years. Every train, mark you. The house stands back from the line and the drivers couldn't see exactly who it was, but it was someone in white and they all thought it was a girl. So they waved back. Every train. But the joke is it's not a girl at all. It can't be. It's gone on too long. She can't have been a girl for the last twenty years or so. It's probably old Miss Roper herself. The drivers keep changing round so they don't catch on. They all think it's some girl, you see. So they all wave back. Every train." He was laughing as if it were the funniest of improprieties.

"If the drivers don't know, how do you?" asked Mimi.

"It's what the locals say. Never set eyes on Miss Roper myself. Probably a bit of line-shooting." He became suddenly very serious and redolent of quiet helpfulness. "There's a Ladies' Room upstairs if either of you would like it."

"Thank you," said Margaret. "I think we must be getting on." The back of her rucksack was soaked and clammy.

"Have a cigarette before you go?" He was extending a packet of some unknown brand. His hand shook like the hand of a drug addict.

"Thanks," said Mimi, very offhand. "Got a match?" He could hardly strike it, let alone light the cigarette. Looking at him Margaret was glad she did not smoke.

"I smoke like a camp fire," he said unnecessarily. "You have to in my life." Then, when they had opened the door, he added, "Watch the weather."

"We will," said Margaret conventionally, though the heat had again smothered them. And once more they were toiling upwards beneath their heavy packs.

They said nothing at all for several minutes. Then Mimi said, "Blasted fool."

"Men are usually rather horrible," replied Margaret.

"You get used to *that*," said Mimi.

"I wonder if this really is called the Quiet Valley?"

"I don't care what it's called. It's a bad valley all right."

Margaret looked at her. Mimi was staring defiantly ahead as she strode forward. "You mean because there are no people?"

"I mean because I know it's bad. You can't explain it."

Margaret was inexpert with intuitions, bred out of them perhaps. The baking, endless road was certainly becoming to her unpleasant in the extreme. Moreover, the foul coffee had given her indigestion, and the looseness of her belt made it impossible to loosen it further.

"If you hadn't heard that train, we'd never have been here."

"If I hadn't heard it, we'd quite simply have been lost. The path on the map just gave out. That's apt to happen when you merely choose paths instead of making for definite places."

In her vexation Margaret raked over another underlying dissimilarity in their approaches to life, one already several times exposed. Then reflecting that Mimi had been perfectly willing to wend from point to point provided that the points were Youth Hostels, Margaret added, "Sorry Mimi. It's the heat."

A certain persistent fundamental disharmony between them led Mimi to reply none too amicably, "What exactly do you suggest we *are* going to do?"

Had Margaret been Mimi there would have been a row: but, being Margaret, she said, "I think perhaps we'd better take another look at the map."

This time she unslung her rucksack and got out the map herself. Mimi stood sulkily sweating and doing nothing either to help or to remove the sweat. Looking at her, Margaret suddenly said, "I wonder what's become of the breeze we had this morning?" Then, Mimi still saying nothing, she sat down and looked at the map. "We could go over into the next valley. There are several quite large villages."

"Up there?" Mimi indicated the rocky slope rising steeply above them.

"The tunnel runs through where the mountains are highest. If we go on a bit, we'll reach the other end and it may be less of a climb. What do you say?"

Mimi took a loose cigarette from a pocket of her shirt. "Not much else to do, is there?" Her attitude was exceedingly irritating. Margaret perceived the unwisdom of strong Indian tea in the middle of the day. "I hope we make it," added Mimi with empty cynicism. As she struck a match, in the very instant a gust of wind not only blew it out but wrenched the map from Margaret's hands. It was as if the striking of the match had conjured up the means to its immediate extinction.

Margaret, recovering, closed the map; and they looked behind them. "Oh hell," said Margaret. "I dislike the weather in the Quiet Valley." A solid bank of the dark grey cloud had formed in their rear and was perceptibly closing down upon them like a huge hood.

"I hope we make it," repeated Mimi, her cynicism now less empty. They left their third set of grey stones demarcating emptiness.

Before long they were over the ridge at the top of the valley. The prospect ahead entirely confirmed the sentiments of the man at the Guest House. The scene could hardly have been bleaker or less inviting. But as it was much cooler, and the way for the first time in several hours comfortably downhill, they marched forward with once-more tightened belts, keeping strictly in step, blown forward by a rising wind. The recurring tension between them was now dissipated by efficient exertion under physically pleasant conditions; by the renewed sense of objective. They conversed steadily and amiably, the distraction winging their feet. Margaret felt the contrast between the optimism apparently implicit in the weather when they had set out, and the doom implicit in it now; but she felt it not unagreeably, drew from it a pleasing sense of tragedy and fitness. That was how she felt until well after it had actually begun to rain.

The first slow drops flung on the back of her knees and neck by the following wind were sweetly sensuous. She could have thrown herself upon the grass and let the rain slowly engulf her entire skin until there was no dry inch. Then she said, "We mustn't get rheumatic fever in these sweaty clothes."

Mimi had stopped and unslung her rucksack. Mimi's rucksack was the heavier because its contents included a robust stormproof raincoat; Margaret's the less heavy because she possessed only a light town mackintosh. Mimi encased herself, adjusted her rucksack beneath the shoulder straps of the raincoat, tied a sou'wester tightly beneath her chin, and strode forward, strapped and buttoned up to the ears, as if cyclones were all in a day's work. After a quarter of an hour, Margaret felt rain beginning to trickle down her body from the loose neck of her mackintosh, to infiltrate through the fabric in expanding blots, and to be finding its way most disagreeably into the interior of the attached hood. After half an hour she was saturated.

By that time they had reached the far end of the tunnel and stood looking down into a deep, narrow cutting which descended the valley as far as the gusts of rain permitted them to see. Being blasted through rock, the cutting had unscalably steep sides.

"That's that," said Margaret a little shakily. "We'll have to stick to the Quiet Valley."

"It looks all right the other side," said Mimi, "if only we could get over." Despite her warm garb, she too seemed wan and shivery. On their side of the railway, and beyond the road that had brought them, was a sea of soaking knee-high heather; but across the cutting the ground rose in a fairly gentle slope, merely tufted with vegetation.

"There's no sign of a bridge."

"I could use a cup of tea. Do you know it's twenty-five past six?"

As they stood uncertain, the sound of an ascending train reached them against the wind, which, blowing strongly from the opposite direction, kept the smoke within the walls of the cutting. So high was the adverse gale that it was only a minute between their first hearing the slowly climbing train and its coming level with them. Steam roared from the exhaust. The fireman was stoking demoniacally. As the engine passed to windward of the two women far above, and the noise from the exhaust crashed upon their senses, the driver suddenly looked up and waved with an apparent gaiety inappropriate to the horrible weather. Then he reached for the whistle lever and, as the train entered the tunnel, for forty seconds doubled the already unbearable uproar. It was a long tunnel.

The train was not of a kind Margaret was used to (she knew little of railways); it was composed neither of passenger coaches nor of small clattering trucks, but of long windowless vans, giving no hint of their contents. A nimbus of warm oily air enveloped her, almost immediately to be blown away, leaving her again shivering.

Mimi had not waved back.

They resumed their way. Margaret's rucksack, though it weighed like the old man of the sea, kept a large stretch of her back almost dry.

"Do the drivers always wave first?" asked Margaret for something to say.

"Of course. If you were to wave first, they probably wouldn't notice you. There's something wrong with girls who wave first anyway."

"I wonder what's wrong with Miss Roper?"

"We'll be seeing."

"I suppose so. She doesn't sound much of a night's prospect."

"How far's Pudsley?"

"Eight miles."

"Very well then."

Previously it had been Mimi who had seemed so strongly to dislike the valley. It was odd that, as it appeared, she should envisage so calmly the slightly sinister Miss Roper. Odd but practical. Margaret divined that her own consistency of thought and feeling might not tend the more to well-being than Mimi's weathercock moods.

"Where exactly does Miss Roper hang out, do you suppose?" enquired Mimi. "That's the first point."

The only visible work of man, other than the rough road, was the long gash that marked the railway cutting to their left.

"The map hasn't proved too accurate," said Margaret.

"Hadn't we better look all the same? I'm really thinking of you, dear. You must be like a wet rag. Of you and a cup of tea."

The wind was very much more than it had so far at any time been, but they could find no anchoring stones. Walls had long since ceased to line the road, and there appeared to be no stones larger than pebbles. While they were poking under clumps of heather, a train descended, whistling continuously.

In the end they had to give up. The paper map, on being partly opened, immediately rent across. The downpour would have converted it into discoloured pulp in a few moments. They were both so tired and hungry, and Margaret, by general temperament the more determined, so wet, that they had no heart in the struggle. Mimi stuffed the already sodden lump back into Margaret's rucksack.

"We'd better get on with it, even if we have to traipse all the way to Pudsley," she said, re-tying a shoelace and then tightening her raincoat collar strap. "Else we'll have you in hospital." She marched forward intrepid.

But in the end, the road, which had long been deteriorating unnoticed, ended in a gate, beyond which was simply a rough field. They had reached a level low enough for primitive cultivation once to have been possible. Soaked and wretched though she was, Margaret looked back to the ridge, and saw that the distance to it was very much less than she had supposed. They leaned on the gate and stared ahead. Stone walls had reappeared, cutting up the land into monotonously similar untended plots. There were still no trees. The railway had now left the cutting and could presumably be crossed; but the women did not make the attempt, as visible before them through the flying deluge was a black house. It stood about six fields away: no joke to reach.

"Why's it so black?" asked Margaret.

"Pudsley. Those chimneys you're so fond of."

"The prevailing wind's in the other direction. It's behind us."

"Wish I had my climbing boots," said Mimi, as they waded into the long grass. "Or Wellingtons." The grass soaked the double hem of Margaret's mackintosh, which she found a new torture. Two trains passed each other, grinding up and charging down. Both appeared to be normal passenger trains, long and packed. Every single window was closed. This produced an odd effect, as of objects in a bottle; until one realised that it was, of course, a consequence of the weather.

By the time they had stumbled across the soaking fields, and surmounted the high craggy walls between, it was almost completely dark. The house was a square, gaol-like stone box, three storeys high, built about 1860, and standing among large but unluxuriant cypresses, the first trees below the valley ridge. The blackness of the building was no effect of the light, but the consequence of inlaid soot.

"It's right on top of the railway," cried Mimi. Struggling through the murk, they had not noticed that.

There was a huge front door, grim with grime.

"What a hope!" said Mimi, as she hauled on the bell handle.

"It's a curious bell," said Margaret, examining the mechanism and valiant to the soaking, shivering end. "It's like the handles you see in signal boxes."

The door was opened by a figure illumined only by an oil lamp standing on a wall bracket behind.

"What is it?" The not uneducated voice had a curious throat undertone.

"My friend and I are on a walking tour," said Margaret, who, as the initiator of the farmhouses project, always took charge on these occasions. "We got badly lost on the moors. We hoped to reach Pudsley," she continued, seeing that this was no farmhouse, open to a direct self-invitation. "But what with getting lost and the rain, we're in rather a mess. Particularly me. I wonder if you could possibly help us? I know it's outrageous, but we *are* in distress."

"Of course," said another voice from the background. "Come in and get warm. Come in quickly and Beech will shut the door." This slight inverted echo of the words of the man at the Guest House stirred unpleasing associations in Margaret's brain.

The weak light disclosed Beech to be a tall muscular figure in a servant's black suit. The face, beneath a mass of black hair, cut like a musician's, seemed smooth and pale. The second speaker was a handsome well-built man, possibly in the late forties, and also wearing a black suit and tie, which suggested mourning. He regarded the odd figures of the two women without any suggestion of the unusual, as they lowered their dripping rucksacks to the tiled floor, unfastened their outer clothes running with water, and stood before him, two dim khaki figures, in shirts and shorts. Margaret felt not only ghastly wet but as if she were naked.

"Let me introduce myself," said the master of the house. "I am Wendley Roper. I shall expect you both to dine with me and stay the night. Tomorrow will put an entirely different face on things." A slight lordliness of manner, by no means unattractive to Margaret, suggested that he mingled little with modern men.

Margaret introduced Mimi and herself; then said, "We heard higher up the valley that a Miss Roper lived here."

"My aunt. She died very recently. You see." He indicated his clothes.

"I am so sorry," said Margaret conventionally.

"It was deeply distressing. I refer to the manner of her death." He offered the shivering women no details, but continued, "Now Beech will take you to your room. The Rafters Room, Beech. I fear I have no other available, as the whole first floor and much else is taken up by my grandfather's collection. I trust you will have no objection to occupying the same room? It is a primitive one, I regret to say. There is only one bed at present, but I shall have another moved up."

They assured him they had no objection.

"What about clothes? My aunt's would scarcely serve." Then, unexpectedly, he added, "And Beech is too big and tall for either of you."

"It's quite all right," said Margaret. "Our rucksacks are watertight and we've both got a change."

"Good," said Wendley Roper seriously. "Beech will conduct you, and dinner will be served when you've changed. There'll be some hot water sent up."

"You are being most extraordinarily kind to us," said Margaret.

"We should take the chances life brings us," said Wendley Roper.

Beech lit a second oil lamp which had been standing on a large tallboy, and, with the women carrying their rucksacks, imperfectly illuminated the way upstairs. On the first-floor landing there were several large doors, such as admit to the bedrooms of a railway hotel, but no furniture was to be seen anywhere, nor were the staircase or either landing carpeted. At the top of the house Beech admitted them to a room the door of which required unlocking. He did not stand aside to let them enter first, but went straight in and drew heavy curtains before the windows, having set down the light on the floor. The women joined him. This time there was a heavy brown carpet, but the primitiveness of the room was indisputable. Beyond the carpet and matching curtains, the furnishings consisted solely of a bedstead. It was a naked iron bedstead, crude and ugly.

"I'll bring you hot water, as Mr Roper said. Then a basin and towels and some chairs and so forth."

"Thank you," said Margaret. Beech retired, closing the door.

"Wonder if the door locks?" Mimi crossed the room. "Not it. The key's on Beech's chain. I don't fancy Beech."

"Can't be helped." Margaret had already discarded her clothes, and was drying her body on a small towel removed from her rucksack.

"I'm not wet through, like you, but God it's cold for the time of year." Mimi's alternative outfit consisted of a dark grey polo-necked sweater and a pair of lighter flannel trousers. Soon she had donned it, first putting on a brassière and knickers to mark renewed contact with society. "Bit of a pigsty, isn't it?" she continued. "But I suppose we must give thanks."

"I rather liked our host. At least he didn't shilly-shally about taking us in." Margaret was towelling systematically.

"Got a nice voice too." Mimi decided that she would be warmer with her sweater inside her trousers, and made the alteration. "Unlike Beech. Beech talks like plum jam. Where, by the way, are the rafters?"

The room, which was much longer than it was wide, and contained windows only in each end wall, a great distance apart, was ceiled with orthodox, though cracked and dirty, plaster.

"I expect they're just above us."

"Up there?" Mimi indicated a trap-door in a corner of the ceiling.

Margaret had not previously noticed it. But before she could speak, the room was filled with a sudden rumbling crescendo, which made the massive floorboards vibrate and the light bed leap up and down upon them. Even the big black stones of the walls seemed slightly to jostle.

"The trains!"

Dashing to a window, Mimi dragged back the curtains, and lifting the sash, waved, her mood suddenly one of excitement, as the uproar swept down towards Pudsley.

Then she cried, "Margaret! The window's barred."

But Margaret's attention was elsewhere. During the din the door had opened, and Beech, a large old-fashioned can steaming in one hand, a large old-fashioned wash-basin dangling from the other, was in the room, and she absurdly naked.

"I beg your pardon," he was saying. "I don't think you heard me knock."

"Get out," said Mimi, flaming, her soul fired by an immemorial tabu.

"It's perfectly all right," intervened Margaret, grasping the small wet towel.

"I'll fetch you some towels."

He was gone again. He seemed totally undisturbed.

"He couldn't help it," said Margaret. "It was the train."

Mimi lowered the window and re-drew the thick curtains. "I've an idea," she said.

"Oh! What? About Beech?"

"I'll tell you later. I'm going to wait at the door."

Soon Beech returned with two large and welcome bath towels and a huge, improbable new cake of expensive scented soap. Margaret had filled the rose-encircled basin with glorious hot water; but before washing, Mimi stood by the door to receive two simple wooden bedroom chairs, a large wooden towel-horse and a capacious chamber-pot, before Beech descended to assist with dinner.

"I'll set you up another bed and bring along some bedding later," he said, as his tall shape descended the tenebrous stair, now lit at intervals by oil lamps flickering on brackets.

Mimi rolled up the sleeves of her sweater and immersed her rather fat arms to the elbows. Margaret was drawing on a girdle. Her spare clothes consisted in another shirt, similar to the one the rain had soaked, but stiff and unworn, a cream-coloured linen skirt of fashionable length, and a tie which matched the skirt. She also had two pairs of expensive stockings, and a spare pair of shoes of lighter weight than Mimi's. Soon she was dressed, had knotted her tie, and was easing the stockings up what she felt must be starkly weather-roughed legs. She felt wonderfully dry, warm, and well. Her underclothes felt delightful. She felt that, after all, things might have turned out worse.

While Margaret was dressing, Mimi had been scrubbing her hands and forearms, then submitting her short hair to a vigorous, protracted grooming with a small bristly hairbrush. She was too busy to speak. She concentrated upon her simple toilet with an absorption Margaret would not have brought to dressing for her first dinner in evening clothes with a man.

With one stocking attached to its suspender, the other blurring her ankle, Margaret leaned back comfortably and asked, "What was your idea?"

Mimi returned brush and comb to her rucksack. "I think it's obvious. Old Ma Roper was mad."

Margaret's warm world waned a little. "You mean the window bars? This might have been a nursery."

"Not only. You remember what he said? 'The manner of her death was deeply distressing.' And that's not all."

"What else?"

"Don't you remember? Her waving to the trains?"

"I don't think that means she was mad. She might merely have been lonely."

"Long time to be lonely. Let's go down if you're ready."

Beech was waiting for them in the gloomy hall. "This way, please."

He opened a huge door and they entered the dining room.

Very large plates, dishes, and cutlery covered the far end of a heavy-looking wooden table, at the head of which sat their host, with a place laid on either side of him. The room was lit by two sizzling oil lamps, vast and of antiquated pattern, which hung from heavy circular plaster mouldings in the discoloured ceiling. The marble and iron fireplace was in massive keeping with the almost immovable waiting-room chairs. On the dark-green lincrusta of the walls engravings hung behind glass so dirty that in the weak green light it was difficult to make out the subjects. A plain round clock clicked like a revolving turnstile from above the fireplace. As the women appeared, it jerked from 2:26 to 2:27. By habit Mimi looked at her watch. The time was just after eight o'clock.

"Immediately you entered the house, the rain stopped," said Wendley Roper by way of greeting.

"Then we'd better be on our way after dinner," said Mimi.

"Most certainly not. I meant only that if you'd arrived a few minutes later, I might have lost the pleasure of your company. Will you sit here?" He was drawing back the heavy chair for Mimi to sit on his right. Beech performed the like office for Margaret. "I should have been utterly disconsolate. You both look remarkably attractive."

Beech disappeared and returned with a tureen so capacious that neither of the women would have cared to lift it. Roper ladled out soup into the huge plates. As he did so, a train roared past outside.

"I suppose the railway came after the house had been here some time?" asked Margaret, feeling that some reference to the matter seemed called for.

"By no means," answered Roper. "The man who built the railway built the house. He was my grandfather, Joseph Roper, generally known as Wide Joe. Wide Joe liked trains."

"There's not much else for company," remarked Mimi, engulfing the hot soup.

"This was one of the last main line railways to be built," continued Roper. "Everyone said it was impossible, but they were keen all the same, partly because land in this valley was very cheap, as it still is. But my grandfather was an engineering genius, and in the end he did it. The engravings in this room show the different stages of the work."

"I suppose he regarded it as his masterpiece and wanted to live next to it when he retired?" politely enquired Margaret.

"Not when he retired. As a matter of fact, he never did retire. He built this house right at the beginning of the work and lived here until the end. The railway took twenty years to build."

"I don't know much about railway building, but that's surely a very long time?"

"There were difficulties. Difficulties of a kind my grandfather had never expected. The cost of them ruined the company, which had to amalgamate in consequence. They nearly drove my grandfather mad." Margaret could not stop herself from glancing at Mimi. "Everything conspired together against him. Things happened which he had not looked for."

Beech reappeared and, removing the soup, substituted a pile of sausages contained in a rampart of mashed potato. As he manoeuvred the hot and heavy dish, Margaret noticed a large, dull coal-black ring on the third finger of his left hand.

"Primitive fare," apologised Roper. "All you can get nowadays."

None the less, the two women found it unbelievably welcome.

"I do see now what you might call railway influences about the house," said Margaret.

"My grandfather lived in the days when a railway engineer was responsible for every detail of design. Not only of the tunnels and bridges, but the locomotives and carriages, the stations and signals, even the posters and tickets. He had sole responsibility for everything. An educated man could never have stood the strain. Wide Joe educated himself."

At intervals through dinner, passing trains rattled the heavy table and heavy objects upon it.

"Now tell me about yourselves," said Wendley Roper, as if he had just concluded the narrative of his own life. "But first have another sausage each. There's only stewed fruit ahead." They accepted.

"We're civil servants," said Mimi. "That's what brought us together. I come from London, and Margaret comes from Devonshire. My father is a hairdresser and Margaret's father is a Lord. Now you know all about us."

"An entirely bankrupt Lord, I regret to say," added Margaret quietly.

"I gather more Lords are bankrupt in these times," said Roper sympathetically.

"And many hairdressers," said Mimi.

"Everyone but civil servants, in fact?" said Roper.

"That's why we're civil servants," replied Mimi, eviscerating her last sausage from its inedible skin. "Though you don't seem altogether bankrupt," she added. Food was increasing her vitality.

He made no reply. Beech had entered with a big glass bowl, deeply but unbeautifully cut, filled with stewed damsons.

"The local fruit," said Roper despondently.

But they even ate stewed damsons.

"I am absolutely delighted to have you here," he remarked when he had served them. "I see almost no one. Least of all attractive women."

His tones were so direct and sincere that Margaret immediately felt pleased. Having, until this year she took a job, lived all her life against a background of desperate and, as she thought, undeserved money troubles, and in a remote country district, she had had little to do with men. Even such a simple compliment from a good-looking and well-spoken man still meant disproportionately much to her. She observed that Mimi seemed to notice nothing whatever.

"I don't know what would have become of us without you," said Margaret.

"Food for the crows," said Mimi.

Suddenly the conversation loosened up, becoming comparatively cordial, intimate, and general. Roper disclosed himself as intelligent, well-informed, and a good listener to those less intelligent and well-informed, at least when they were young women. Mimi's conversation became much steadier and more pointed than usual. Margaret found herself saying less and less, while enjoying herself more.

"Beech will bring us coffee in the drawing room," said Roper, "if drawing room's the right expression."

They moved across the hall to another bleak apartment, this time walled with official-looking books, long series of volumes bound in dark-blue cloth or in stout, rough-edged paper. Again there were two complicated but not very efficient lamps hissing and spurting from the coffered ceiling. The furniture consisted in old-fashioned leather-covered armchairs and sofas; and, before the window at the end of the room, a huge desk, bearing high heaps of varied documents, disused and dusty. About the room in glass cases were scale models of long-extinct locomotives and bygone devices for ensuring safety on the railways. Above the red marble mantel was a vast print of a railway accident, freely coloured by hand.

"You do keep things as the old man left them," said Mimi.

"It is a house of the dead," said Roper. "My aunt, you know. She would never have anything touched."

Beech brought coffee: not very good and served in over-large cups; but pleasantly warm. Margaret still found the house cold. She hoped she was not ill after the soaking and strain of the day. She continued, however, to listen to Mimi and Roper chatting together in surprising sympathy; every now and then made an observation of her own; and, thinking things over, wondered that on the whole they had turned out so well. It was Margaret who poured out the coffee.

What were Mimi and Roper talking about? He was asking her in great detail about their dull office routine; she was enquiring with improbable enthusiasm into early railway history. Neither could have had much genuine interest in either subject. It was all very unreal, but comfortable and pleasing. Roper, many aspects of whose position seemed to Margaret to invite curiosity, said nothing of himself. Every now and then a train passed.

"A pension at sixty doesn't make up for being a number all your life. A cipher. You want to get off the rails every now and then."

"You only get on to a branch line, a dead end," said Roper with what seemed real despondency. "It's difficult to leave the rails altogether and still keep going at all."

"Have you ever tried? What *do* you do?" It was seldom so long before Mimi asked that. She despised inaction in men.

"I used to work in the railway company's office. All the Ropers were in the railway business, as you will have gathered. I was the only one to get out of it in time."

"In time for what?"

"In time for anything. My father was the company's Chief Commercial Manager. Trying to meet the slump killed him. Things aren't what they used to be with railways, you know. My grandfather was run over just outside that window." He pointed across the dusty desk at the end of the room.

"What a perfectly appalling thing!" said Margaret. "How did it happen?"

"He never had any luck after he took on this job. You know how two perfectly harmless substances when blended can make something deadly? Building the railway through this valley was just like that for my grandfather. A lot of things happened… One thing the valley goes in for is sudden storms. On a certain night when one of these storms got up, my grandfather thought he heard a tree fall. You noticed the trees round the house? The original idea was that they'd provide shelter. My grandfather thought this tree might have fallen across the line. He was so concerned that he forgot the time-table, though normally he carried every train movement in his head. You can guess what happened. The noise of the approaching train was drowned by the wind. Or so they decided at the inquest."

When a comparative stranger tells such a story, it is always difficult to know what to say, and there is a tendency to fill the gap with some unimportant question. "And was the tree across the line?" asked Margaret.

"Not it. No tree had fallen. The old man had got it wrong."

"Then surely they were rather lax at the inquest?"

"Wide Joe had always been expected to meet a bad end, and the jury were all local men. He was pretty generally disliked. He made his daughter break off her engagement with a railwayman at Pudsley depot. Marrying into the lower deck, and all that. But it turned out he was a bit wrong. The man got into Parliament and ended by doing rather better for himself than my grandfather had done by sticking to the railway. By then, of course, it was too late. And my grandfather was dead in any case."

"That was your aunt?" enquired Mimi.

"Being my father's sister, yes," said Roper. "Now let us change the subject. Tell me about the gay world of London."

"We never come across it," said Mimi. "It's just one damn thing after another for us girls."

The moment seemed opportune for Margaret to get her pullover, as she still felt cold. She departed upstairs. In some ways she would have been glad to go to bed, after the exhausting day; but she felt also an unexplained reluctance, less than half-conscious, to leave Mimi and Roper chatting so intimately alone together. Then, ascending the dim staircase with its enormous ugly polished banisters in dark wood, she received a shock which drove sleep temporarily from her.

The incident was small and perfectly reasonable; it was doubtless the dead crepuscularity of the house which made it seem frightening to Margaret. When she reached the first-floor landing she saw a figure which seemed hastily to be drawing back from her and then to retreat through one of the big panelled doors. The impression of furtiveness might well have resulted solely from the exceedingly poor lighting. But as to the opening and shutting of the door, Margaret's ears left her in no doubt. And upon another point their evidence confirmed the much less dependable testimony of her eyes: the withdrawing feet tapped; the half-visible figure was undoubtedly a woman's. She appeared to be wearing a dark coat and skirt, which left her lighter legs more clearly discernible.

Stamping on absurd fears, quite beyond definition, Margaret ascended the second flight and entered the bedroom. After all, it was quite probable that Beech did not do all the work of the house: most likely that Roper's staff should consist of a married couple. Margaret sat upon one of the hard chairs Beech had brought, and faced her fear more specifically. It took shape before the eyes of her mind: a faceless waxwork labelled "Miss Roper", mad, dead, horribly returned. The costume of the figure Margaret had seen was not that of the tragic Victorian in Wendley Roper's narrative: but then Miss Roper had died only recently, and might have kept up with the times in this respect, as more and more old ladies do. That would be less likely, however, if she had really been mad, as Mimi had suggested, and as the tale of the broken engagement would certainly require had it been told by one of the period's many novelists.

The room Margaret was in had seen it all. Suddenly, as this fact returned to memory, the grimy dingy papered walls seemed simultaneously to jerk towards her, the whole rather long and narrow attic to contract upon her threateningly. Though enormously larger, the room suddenly struck Margaret as having the proportions of a railway compartment, a resemblance much increased by the odd arrangement of the windows, one at each end. Old-fashioned railway carriage windows were commonly barred, Margaret was just old enough to have noticed. This recollection brought rather more comfort than was strictly reasonable. Relaxing a little, Margaret found that she had been seated motionless. Her muscles were stiff and she could hear her heart and pulses, whether or not proceeding at the normal rate it was hard to say. Some time must have passed while she had sat in what amounted to a trance of fear. But their only watch was on Mimi's wrist, her own having been stolen while she washed in the Ladies' Lavatory of an expensive restaurant to which her father had taken her for her birthday. Above all, she was colder than ever. She extracted the pullover from her rucksack and put it on. It was V-necked and long-sleeved. The warmth of its elegant, closely woven black wool was cheering. Before once more descending, Margaret adjusted the lamp which had been left in the bedroom. Then she recalled Roper's remark that the whole first floor of the house was occupied by his grandfather's collection; which for some reason did not make the actions of the woman she had seen seem more reassuring. But a minute later she crossed the first-floor landing firmly, though certainly without making any investigation; and reached the door of the preposterous "drawing room" without (she was quite surprised to realise) any particular incident.

Immediately she entered, however, it was obvious that the atmosphere in the room had very much altered since she had left. Her fears were cut off like the change of scene in a film, to be replaced by a confused emotion as strong and undefined as the very different sensations which had accompanied the short period between her glimpsing the woman on the stairs and reaching the chair in her bedroom. Not only were Mimi and Roper now seated together on the vast leather-covered sofa before the empty fireplace, but Margaret even felt that they had vulgarly drawn further away from each other upon hearing her return.

"Hullo," said Mimi cheekily. "You've been a long time."

For a moment Margaret felt like giving the situation a twist in her direction (as she felt it would be), by relating some of the reason for her long absence; but, in view of the mystery about Miss Roper, managed to abstain. Could it be that Miss Roper was not dead at all? she suddenly wondered.

"Mind your own business," she replied in Mimi's own key.

"I hope you found your way," said Roper politely.

"Perfectly, thank you."

There was a short silence.

"I fear Beech has gone to bed, or I'd offer you both some further refreshments. I have no other servant."

After the initial drag of blood from her stomach, Margaret took a really hard pull on her resolution.

"Do you live alone here with Beech?"

"Quite alone. That's why it's so pleasant to have you two with me. I've been telling Mimi that normally I have only my books." It was the first time Margaret had heard him use the Christian name.

"He leads the life of a recluse," said Mimi. "Research, you know. Dog's life, if you ask me. Worse than ours."

"What do you research into?" asked Margaret.

"Can't you guess, dear?" Mimi had become very much at her ease.

"Railways, I'm afraid. Railway history." Roper was smiling a scholar's smile, tired and deprecating, but at the same time uniquely arrogant. "If you're a Roper you can't get it quite out of the blood. I've been showing Mimi this." He held out a book with a dark-green jacket.

"*Early Fishplates*," read Margaret, "by Howard Bullhead." The print appeared closely packed and extremely technical. The book was decorated with occasional arid little diagrams.

"What has this to do with railways?"

"Fishplates," cried Mimi, "are what hold the rails down."

"Well, not quite that," said Roper, "but something like it."

"Who's Mr Bullhead?"

"Bullhead is a rather technical railway joke. I'm the real author. I prefer to use a pseudonym."

"The whole book's one long mad thrill," said Mimi. "Wendley's going to sell the film rights."

"I can't get it altogether out of my blood," said Roper again. "The family motto might be the same as Bismarck's: Blood and Iron."

"Do you *want* to get it out?" asked Margaret. "I'm sure it's a fascinating book."

But Mimi had leapt to her feet. "What about a cup of tea? What do you say *I* make it?"

Roper hesitated for a moment. Margaret thought that disinclination to accede conflicted with desire to please Mimi.

"I'll help." Normally tea at night was so little Margaret's habit that Mimi stared at her.

"That would be very nice indeed," said Roper at last. Desire to please Mimi had doubtless prevailed, though indeed it was hard to see what else he could say. "I'll show you the kitchen. It's really very nice of you." He hesitated another moment. Then they both followed him from the room.

Before the kettle had boiled in the square cold kitchen, Margaret's mind was in another conflict. Roper no longer seemed altogether so cultivated and charming as towards the end of dinner; there were now recurrent glimpses in him of showiness and even silliness. The maddening thing was, however, that Margaret could no longer be unaware that she found him attractive. Some impulse, of which her experience was small and her opinion adverse, was loose in her brain, like the spot of light in a column of mercury. Upon other matters her mind was perfectly clear; so that she felt like two people, one thinking, one willing. Possibly even there was a third person, who was feeling; who was feeling very tired indeed.

Mimi, sometimes so quick to tire, seemed utterly unflagging. She darted about the strange domesticities, turning taps, assembling crocks, prattling about the gas cooker: "Your gas doesn't smell. I call that service."

"The smell is *added* to coal gas as a safety precaution," said Roper.

"Why don't they choose a nice smell, then?"

"What would you suggest?"

"I don't mean Chanel, but new-mown hay or lovely roses."

"The Gas Board don't want all their customers in love with easeful death."

"What's your favourite method of committing suicide?"

Though this was one of Mimi's most customary topics, Margaret wished that she had chosen another. But Roper merely replied, "Old age, I think." He seemed fascinated by her. Neither he nor Margaret was doing anything to help with the preparations. In the end Mimi began positively to sing and the empty interchange of remarks came to an end.

As Mimi was filling the teapot, Roper unexpectedly departed.

"Do you like him?" asked Margaret.

"He's all right. Wonder if there's anything to eat with it." Mimi began to peer into vast clanging bread bins.

"Have you found out anything more about him?"

"Not a thing."

"Don't you think it's all rather queer?"

"Takes all sorts to make a world, dear."

"It seems to take an odd sort to make a railway. You yourself suggested—" But Roper returned.

"I thought we might end this delightful evening in my den; my study, you know. It's much warmer and cosier. I don't usually show it to visitors. I like to keep somewhere quite private. For work, you know. But you are no ordinary visitors. I've just looked in and there's even a fire burning." This last slightly odd remark was not to

Margaret made less odd by the way it was spoken; as if the speaker had prepared in advance a triviality too slight to sustain preparation convincingly. "Do come along. Let me carry the tray."

"I've been looking for something to eat," said Mimi. "Do you think Beech has laid by any buns or anything?"

"There's some cake in my den," said Roper, like the hero of a good book for boys.

This time the door was open and the room flooding the hall with cheerful light.

It was entirely different from any other room they had entered in that house: and not in the least like a den, or even like a study. The lamps were modern, efficient, adequate, and decorative. The furniture was soft and comfortable. The railway blight (as Margaret regarded it) seemed totally absent. As Roper had said, there was an excellent fire in a modern grate surrounded by unexciting but not disagreeable Dutch tiles. This seemed the true drawing room of the house.

"What a lovely lounge!" cried Mimi. "Looks like a woman in the house at last. Why couldn't we come in here before?" Her rapidly increasing command of the situation seemed to Margaret almost strident.

"I thought the occasion called for more formality."

"Dog in the manger, if you ask me." Mimi fell upon a sofa, extending her trousered legs. "Pour out, Margaret, will you?"

Margaret, conscious that whereas Mimi ought to be appearing in a bad light, yet in fact it was she, Margaret, who, however unjustly, was doing so, repeated with the tea the office she had already performed with the coffee. Roper, who had placed the tray on a small table next to an armchair in which Margaret proceeded to seat herself beside the fire, carried one of the big full cups to Mimi. He poured her milk with protective intimacy and seemed to find one of her obvious jokes about the quantity of sugar she required intoxicatingly funny. He moved rather well, Margaret thought. Mimi, moreover, had been right about his voice. His remarks, however, though almost never about himself, seemed mostly, in the light of that fact, remarkably self-centred. It would be dreadful to have to listen to them all one's life.

Suddenly he was bearing cake. Neither of the women saw where it came from but, when it appeared, both found they still had appetites. It tasted of vanilla and was choked with candied peel.

In the kitchen Margaret had noticed that despite the late hour the traffic on the railway had seemed to be positively increasing; but in the present small room the noise was much muffled, the line being on the other side of the house. None the less, frequent trains were still to be heard.

"Why are there so many trains? It must be nearly midnight."

"Long past, dear," interjected Mimi, the time-keeper. The fact seemed to give her a particular happiness.

"I see you're not used to living by a railway," said Roper. "Many classes of traffic are kept off the tracks during ordinary travelling hours. What you hear going by now are the loads you don't see when the stations are open. A railway is like an iceberg, you know: very little of its working is visible to the casual onlooker."

"Not visible, perhaps. But certainly audible."

"The noise does not disturb you?"

"No, of course not. But does it really go on day and night?"

"Certainly. Day and night. At least on important main lines, such as this is."

"I suppose you've long ceased to notice it?"

"I notice when it's not there. If a single train is missing from its time, I become quite upset. Even if it happens when I'm asleep."

"But surely only the passenger trains have time-tables?"

"My dear Margaret, every single train is in a time-table. Every local goods, every light engine movement. Only not, of course, in the time-table you buy for sixpence at the Enquiry Office. Only a small fraction of all the train movements are in that. Even the man behind the counter knows virtually nothing of the rest."

"Only Wendley knows the whole works," said Mimi from the sofa.

The others were sitting one at each side of the fire in front of which she lay and had been talking along the length of her body. Margaret had realised that this was the first time Roper had used her Christian name. It seemed hours ago that he had called Mimi by hers. Suddenly, looking at Mimi sprawling in her trousers and tight high-necked sweater, Margaret saw the point, clearer than in any book: Mimi was physically attractive; she herself in all probability was not. And nothing else in all life, in all the world, really counted. Nothing, nothing. Being cleverer; on the whole (as she thought) kinder; being more refined; the daughter of a Lord: such things were the dust beneath Mimi's chariot wheels, items in the list of life's innumerable unwantable impedimenta. Margaret stuck out her legs unbecomingly.

"Can I have another cup of tea?" said Mimi. Her small round head was certainly engaging.

"There you are," said Margaret. "Now will you both forgive me if I go to bed? I think I could do with some sleep after my soaking."

"I'm a beast," cried Mimi, warmly sympathetic. "Is there anything I can do? What about a hot water bottle, Wendley? Margaret is always as helpless as a butterfly. I have to look after her." She was certainly rather sweet too.

"Not a hot water bottle, please," replied Margaret. "They're not in season yet. I'll be all right, Mimi. See you later. Good night."

Between sympathy and the desire to get her out of the room, Margaret thought on her way upstairs, Mimi had absolutely no conflict whatever; she merely took her emotions in turn, getting the most out of all of them, and no doubt giving the most also.

This time there was no vague figure which crept back from the stairs: or possibly it was that Margaret's thoughts attended a different will-o'-the-wisp. Immediately she entered the bedroom, she noticed that the promised second bed had arrived, as lean and frugal as the first. In the long room the two beds had been set far apart. Margaret was unable to be sure whether the second bed had or had not been there when she had last entered the room.

Her mind still darting and plunging about the scene downstairs, she selected the bed which stood furthest from the door. At that moment Mimi seemed to her in no particular need of consideration. Margaret dashed off her clothes in the clammy atmosphere, dropping the garments with unwonted carelessness upon one of the two dark, thin-legged chairs; then, as a train pounded past, rattling the small barred windows at each end of the room and causing the curtains to shake apart, letting in the infernal glare outside, she climbed into her pyjamas and into the small, tight bed. She now realised for the first time that there were no sheets, but only clinging blankets. To put out the single oil lamp was more than her courage or the cold permitted. She buttoned her jacket to the top and wished it had long sleeves. It had been only an absurd dignity, a preposterous aggression, which had led her to reject a hot water bottle.

She was quite unable to sleep. Her mind had set up a devil's dance which would not subside for hours at the best. The bed was the first really uncomfortable one in which Margaret had ever slept:

it was so narrow that blankets of normal size could be and were tucked in so far that they overlapped beneath the occupant, interlocking to bind her in; so narrow also that the cheap hard springs of the wire framework gave not at all beneath the would-be sleeper's weight; and the mattress was inadequate to blur a diamond pattern of hard metallic ridges. Although she liked by day to wear garments fitting closely at the throat, Margaret found that the same sensation in bed, however much necessitated by the temperature, amounted to suffocation. Nor had she ever been able, since first she could remember, to sleep with a light in the room. Above all, there were the trains: not so much the periodical thunder rollings, she found, as the apparently lengthening intervals of waiting for them. Downstairs the trains had seemed to become more and more frequent; here they seemed to become slowly sparser. It was probably, Margaret reflected, a consequence of the slowness with which time is said to pass for those seeking sleep. Or perhaps Wendley Roper would have an answer in terms of graphicstatics or inner family knowledge. The ultimate effect was as if the train service were something subjective in Margaret's head, like the large defined shapes which obstruct the vision of the sufferer from migraine. "No sleep like this," said Margaret to herself, articulating with a clarity which made the words seem spoken by another.

She forced herself from the rigid blankets, felt-like though far from warm, opened the neck of her pyjama jacket, and extinguished the light, which died on the lightest breath. What on earth was Mimi doing? she wondered with schoolgirl irritation.

Immediately she had groped into the pitch-dark bed, a train which seemed of an entirely new construction went past. This time there was no blasting of steam and thundering or grinding of wheels: only a single sustained rather high-pitched rattling; metallic, inhuman, hollow. The new train appeared to be descending the bank, but Margaret for the first time could not be sure. The sound frightened Margaret badly. "It's a hospital train," her mother had said to her long ago on an occasion of which Margaret had forgotten all details except that they were horrible. "It's full of wounded soldiers."

In a paroxysm of terror, as this agony of her childhood blasted through her adult life, Margaret must have passed into sleep, or at least unconsciousness. For the next event could only have been a dream of hallucination. The room seemed to be filling with colourless light. Though even now this light was extremely dim, the process of its first appearance and increase seemed to have been going on for a very long time. As she realised this, another part of Margaret's mind remembered that it could none the less have been only a matter of minutes. She struggled to make consistent the consciousness of the nearly endless with the consciousness of the precisely brief. The light seemed, moreover, the exact visual counterpart of the noise she had heard made by the new train. Then Margaret became aware of something very horrible indeed: it began with the upturned dead face of an old woman, colourless with the exact colourlessness of the colourless light; and it ended with the old woman's crumpled shape occultly made visible hanging above the trap-door in the corner of Margaret's compartment-shaped room. Up in the attic old Miss Roper had hanged herself, her grey hair so twisted and meshed as itself to suggest the suffocating agent.

Margaret's hands went in terror to her own bare throat. Then the door of the room opened, and someone stood inside it bearing a light.

"I don't think you heard me knock."

As when she and Mimi had arrived she had noticed in Roper's first words the echo of the man at the Guest House, so now was another echo—of Beech's cool apology for that bedroom contretemps which had so fired Mimi's wrath. To Margaret it was as if a nightmare had reached that not uncommon point at which the sufferer, though not yet awake, not yet out of the dream, yet becomes aware that a dream it is. Then all was deep nightmare once more, as Margaret recalled the shadow woman on the stairs, and perceived that the same woman was now in the room with her.

Margaret broke down. Still clutching her throat, she cried repeatedly in a shrill but not loud voice. "Go away. Go away. Go away. Go away." It was again like her childhood.

The strange woman approached and, setting down the lamp, began to shake her by the shoulders. At once Margaret seemed to know that, whoever else she was, she was not the dead Miss Roper; and that was all which seemed to matter. She stopped wauling like a terror-struck child: then saw that the hand still on one of her shoulders wore a dull coal-black ring; and, looking up, that the face above her and the thick black hair were Beech's, as had been that indifferently apologetic voice. Nightmare stormed forward yet again; but this time only for an adult speck of time. For Margaret seemed now to have no doubt whatever that Beech was indeed a woman.

"Where's your friend?"

"I left her downstairs. I came up to bed early."

"Early?"

"What's the time? I have no watch."

"It's half past three."

The equivocal situation returned to life in Margaret's mind in every detail, as when stage lights are turned on simultaneously.

"What business is it of yours? Who are you?"

"Who do you think I am?"

"I thought you were the manservant."

"I looked after old Miss Roper. Until she died."

"Did that mean you had to dress like a man?" The woman now appeared to be wearing a dark grey coat and skirt and a white blouse.

"Wendley could hardly live alone in the house with a woman he wasn't married to. Someone he had no intention of marrying."

"Why haven't you left, then?"

"After what happened to Miss Roper?"

"What did you do to Miss Roper?" Margaret spoke very low but quite steadily. All feeling was dead in her, save, far below the surface, a flickering jealousy of Mimi, a death-wish sympathy with the murdering stranger beside her. So that Margaret was able to add, steadily as before, "Miss Roper was mad, wasn't she?"

"Certainly not. Why do you say that?"

"Her father preventing her marrying. The bars on the windows."

"You can be crossed in love without going mad, you know. And madhouse windows are not the only ones with bars." The large white hand with the black ring on the engagement finger had continued all this time to rest on Margaret's shoulder. Now with a sharp movement it was withdrawn.

"So this was simply a prison? Why? What had Miss Roper done?"

"Something to do with the railway. Some secret she had from the old man and wouldn't tell Wendley. I never asked for details. I was in love. You know what that means as well as I do."

"What sort of secret? And why did it have to be a secret?"

"I don't know what sort of secret. I don't care now. She wanted to keep it secret from Wendley because she knew what he would do with it. She spent all her time trying to tell other people."

"That's why..." Margaret was about to say "that's why she waved", then stopped herself. "*What* would Wendley have done with it?"

"Your friend should have some idea of that by this time." This unexpected remark was delivered in a tone of deepest venom.

"What do you mean? Where is Mimi?" Then a sudden hysteria swept over her. "I'm going to find Mimi." She struggled out of the crib-like bed, bruising herself badly on the ironwork. The trains seemed to have long ceased and everything was horribly quiet in the Quiet Valley.

The woman, approaching the cheap little bedroom chair on which Margaret's clothes lay tumbled where she had dropped them, picked up Margaret's tie, and held it between her two hands twelve inches or so apart.

In the negligible light of one oil lamp there began a slow chase down the long narrow room.

"You're not on his side really," cried Margaret, everything gone. "You know what's happening downstairs."

The woman made no answer, but slightly decreased the distance between her hands. Margaret perceived how foolish had been her error in deliberately selecting the bed furthest from the door. None the less, a certain amount of evasion, as in a childhood game of "Touch", was possible before she found herself being forced near the end wall, being corralled almost beneath the trap-door in the ceiling above. If only she could have reached the other door, the door of the room! Much would then have been possible.

As they arrived at the corner beneath the trap, Margaret's heel struck Mimi's open rucksack, dropped there by its casual owner, hitherto forgotten or unnoticed by Margaret, and concealed by the dim light. Margaret stooped.

Three seconds later her adversary was lying back downwards on the floor, bleeding darkly and excessively in the gloom, Mimi's robust camping knife through her rather thick white throat. "Comes from Sweden, dear," Mimi had said. "Not allowed to sell them here."

It did not take Margaret long, plunging into the pockets in the dead woman's jacket, to find Beech's bunch of keys. This was fortunate, as the scream of the murdered woman, breaking into the course of events below, was followed by running footsteps on the murky stairs. The agile Mimi burst into the room crying, "Lock it. For God's sake lock it"; and Margaret had raced the length of the Rafters Room and locked it before Wendley Roper, heavy and unused to exercise, had arrived at the landing outside. The large key turned in the expensive, efficient lock with a grinding snap he could not have mistaken. The railway hotel door was enormously thick, a beautiful piece of joinery. Margaret waited, her body drooping forward, for Roper to begin his onslaught. But it was a job for an axe, and nothing whatever happened; neither blows on the door, nor a voice, nor even retreating footsteps.

Mimi, ignorant that the room had a third occupant, was seated on the side of her bed with her hands distending her trousers' pockets. She was panting slightly, but her hair was habitually cut too short ever to show much disorder. Margaret had previously thought her manner strident; it was now beyond bearing. She began to blow out a stream of curses, particularly horrible in the presence of the dead woman.

"Mimi, my dear," said Margaret gently. "What are we going to do?" Still in her pyjamas, she was shivering spasmodically.

Mimi, keeping her hands in her pockets, looked round at her. "Catch the first departure for Hell, I should say."

Though she was not weeping, there was something unbearably desolate about her. Margaret wanted to comfort her: Mimi's experiences had been unimaginably worse even than her own. She put her cold arms round Mimi's stiff hard body; then tried to drag Mimi's hands from her pockets in order to take them in her own. Mimi, though offering no help, did not strongly resist. As Margaret dragged at her wrists, one of her own hands round each, a queer little trickle fell to the floor on each side of her. Mimi's pockets were tightly stuffed with railway tickets.

Dropping Mimi's wrists, Margaret picked up one of the tickets and read it by the light of the strange woman's lamp: "Diamond Jubilee Special. Pudsley to Hassell-wicket. Third Class. Excursion 2s. 11d. God Save Our Queen." Mimi's fists were clenched round variegated little bundles of pasteboard rectangles.

It was impossible to tell her about the dead woman.

"I'm going to dress. Then we'll get out." Margaret began to drag on the clothes she had worn for dinner. She buttoned the collar of her shirt, warm and welcome about her neck. She looked for her tie, and could just see it in one hand of the dead woman as she lay compact on the floor at the end of the room behind Mimi's back.

"I'll pack our rucksacks." Fully dressed, Margaret felt more valiant and less vulnerable. She groped at the feet of the corpse for Mimi's rucksack and assembled the scattered contents. But, though feeling the omission to be folly, she did not go back for Mimi's knife. In the end, she had packed both rucksacks and was carefully fastening the straps. Mimi had apparently emptied her pockets of tickets, leaving four small heaps on the dark carpet, one from each fist, one from each pocket; and was now sitting silent and apparently relaxed, but making no effort to help Margaret.

"Are you ready? We must plan."

Mimi gazed up at her. Then she said quietly, "There's nowhere for us to go now." With the slightest of gestures she appeared to indicate the four heaps of tickets.

No argument that Margaret used would induce Mimi to make the least effort. She just sat on the bed saying that they were prisoners and there was nothing they could do.

Feeling that Mimi's reason might have been affected, though of this there was no sign, Margaret began to contemplate the dreadful extremity of trying to escape alone. But apart from the additional perils to body and spirit (there was no knowing that Roper was not standing outside the door), she felt that it would be impossible for her to leave Mimi alone to what might befall. She set down her rucksack on the floor beside Mimi's. When filled, she always found it heavy to hold for long.

"Very well. We'll wait till it's light. It should be quite soon."

Mimi said nothing. Looking at her, Margaret saw that for the first time she was weeping. Margaret once more put her arms round her now soft body, and the two women tenderly kissed. They came from very different environments and it was the first time they had ever done so.

The desperate idea entered Margaret's mind that help might be obtained. Surely there must be visitors to the house of some kind sometimes; and neither she nor Mimi was a powerless old woman. Margaret's eyes unintendingly went to the knife in the victim's throat.

For a long time the two women sat close together saying little.

Margaret had not for hours given a thought to the railway outside. Since that strange and dreamlike new train, nothing had passed. Then, from the very far distance, came the airy ghost of an engine whistle: utterly impersonal at that hour and place, but, to Margaret, filled with promise.

She rose and drew back the curtains from one of the queer barred windows.

"Look! It's dawn."

A girdle of light was slowly edging over the horizon, offering a fine day to come, unusual in such mountainous country. Margaret, aflame for action, looked quickly about the room. She herself was wearing colours unlikely to stand out in the yet faint light. Mimi's grey was hardly more helpful. There was only one thing to be done. Leaping across the room, Margaret ripped a large piece of material from the dead woman's white blouse patched with blood. Then as in the growing radiance Mimi turned and for the first time saw the body, Margaret, throwing up the narrow window, waved confidently to the workmen's train which was approaching.

ALSO AVAILABLE

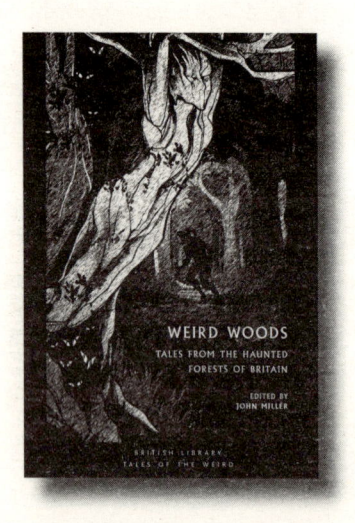

But foliage surrounded him, branches blocked the way; the trees stood close and still; and the sun dipped that moment behind a great black cloud. The entire wood turned dark and silent. It watched him.

Woods play a crucial and recurring role in horror, fantasy, the gothic and the weird. They are places in which strange things happen, where it is easy to lose your way. Supernatural creatures thrive in the thickets. Trees reach into underworlds of pagan myth and magic. Forests are full of ghosts.

Lining the path through this realm of folklore and fear are twelve stories from across Britain, telling tales of whispering voices and maddening sights from deep in the Yorkshire Dales to the ancient hills of Gwent and the eerie quiet of the forests of Dartmoor. Immerse yourself in this collection of classic tales celebrating the enduring power of our natural spaces to enthral and terrorise our senses.

ALSO AVAILABLE

There was no sleep for him that night; he fancied he had seen the stone—which, as you know, was a couple of fields away— as large as life, as if it were on watch outside his window.

The standing stones, stone circles, dolmens and burial sites of the British Isles still resonate with mystery of their primeval origins, enthralling our collective consciousness to this day. Rising up in the field of weird fiction, ancient stones and the rituals and dark forces they once witnessed have inspired a wicked branch of the genre by writers devoted to their eerie potential.

Gathered in tribute to these relics of a lost age—and their pagan legacy of blood—are fifteen stories of haunted henges, Druidic vengeance and solid rock alive with bloodlust, by authors including Algernon Blackwood, Lisa Tuttle, Arthur Machen and Nigel Kneale.

For more Tales of the Weird titles
visit the British Library Shop (shop.bl.uk)

We welcome any suggestions, corrections or feedback you may have, and will
aim to respond to all items addressed to the following:

The Editor (Tales of the Weird), British Library Publishing,
The British Library, 96 Euston Road, London NW1 2DB

We also welcome enquiries through our X (Twitter) account, @BL_Publishing.